A Fair Pretender

A Fair Pretender

Janet Woods

ROBERT HALE · LONDON

© Janet Woods 2004
First published in Great Britain 2004

ISBN 0 7090 7540 5

Robert Hale Limited
Clerkenwell House
Clerkenwell Green
London EC1R 0HT

2 4 6 8 10 9 7 5 3 1

Typeset in 11/13.5 pt Sabon by
Derek Doyle & Associates in Liverpool.
Printed in Great Britain by
St Edmundsbury Press, Bury St Edmunds, Suffolk.
Bound by Woolnough Bookbinding Limited

For my granddaughter.
Beth Anne Larsen,
with love

The author is happy to receive feedback from readers.
She can be contacted via her website:
http://members.iinet.net.au/~woods
or write to:
P.O. Box 2099
Kardinya 6163
Western Australia

1

From now on I must respond only to being called Evelyn Adams.

So thought Graine Seaton as she straightened the skirt of her travelling gown. Her gloved fingers plucked at a lace handkerchief, which now bore the elaborately entwined and inexpertly embroidered initials of her late mistress in the corner.

Evelyn Adams's estate had already been sold, her wealth transferred and the nuptial agreements exchanged – and since Evelyn had drowned *en route* from the West Indies when their ship had foundered, Graine had seized the opportunity to better her own lot in life by assuming her identity and marrying the English gentleman in her place.

But could she pull the deception off?

Of course she could. She and Evelyn were similar in appearance, if not in size, with Evelyn being a good head taller and larger boned. Related as they were through their mutual father, their similarities were understandable, though Graine's hair and eyes were tawnier shades of brown.

Not that Evelyn had known they were sisters. How could she when Graine's mother had stated in her letter that Seth Adams denied he'd fathered a child on the wrong side of the blanket? All the parties concerned had died long before the convent nuns had secured her the position of companion to Evelyn.

Graine had not known of the connection herself then, for the sisters of the convent she'd grown up in hadn't seen fit to inform her. She only discovered the identity of her father in a letter left for her in her mother's few personal effects, and those had been handed to her long after she'd been hired.

The coincidence had hardly mattered to Graine. She'd been orphaned for too long to miss any ties with which close family might furnish her. She enjoyed her job as Evelyn's companion, and had grown to love her over the four years she'd been with her.

Her half-sister had been in the care of the ageing male guardian who was also the manager of *South Winds*, the Adams's sugar plantation. Evelyn had not been quick-witted or beautiful, but she was generous natured and pleasant. She'd been pleased to have the company of a girl six years her junior and had overlooked Graine's ineptitude, treating her more like the younger half-sister she was, than a hired companion.

'Be damned if I'd have agreed to wed John Lamartine sight unseen,' Graine had said to her.

To which Evelyn had shrugged. 'I'm twenty-six years old and the only offer I've had was from a sea captain with a reputation for cruelty and licentiousness. John Lamartine comes with impeccable references from an earl and an archbishop. Better to marry him than stay here as an old maid and grow sugar cane.' She shuddered. 'England will be such fun. I'll be able to go to balls and such and will try and find a suitable husband for you.'

'I refuse to marry anyone I do not love just to provide him with children,' Graine said, which ironically, was something that would now come to pass.

Evelyn's eyes had softened with longing. 'Most women have to. I should like a child or two to love. For whosoever fathered them, the bond would be that of mother and child and they'd be close to my heart.'

And Evelyn would have made the best of mothers. Graine hoped she hadn't suffered too much as the sea had taken her life. Confined to the cabin with sea-sickness, she must have been trapped there when the ship had foundered. Graine had been on deck, enjoying the buffeting wind and the slap and crack of the sails when the huge wave had borne down on them. Washed overboard, she'd thought the crushing weight of the water would prevent her from ever seeing the sky again. But it hadn't. The sea had spat her to the surface like a cork from a bottle. The ship was half submerged on its side some distance away, floating in a tangle of sails, spars and ropes. Then she lost sight of it.

Clinging to some debris, she floated for several hours before being picked up by some of the crew in the ship's boat. Somehow, they'd made it back to the nearest port, where she'd been looked after by the ship's agent for a month before being placed aboard another ship.

The crew had mistakenly called her Miss Adams, and it was that which had given her the idea of taking Evelyn's place.

But England had turned out to be colder than she'd expected, and the skies were as grey and heavy as convent oatmeal. Rain hissed and slanted against the carriage roof with unrelenting fury. She was tempted to turn around and go back home. But to what? At least she would have a roof over her head and food in her belly, here.

She just hoped John Lamartine was not as cold-hearted as she'd heard the English were, and that he treated her with kindness rather than the condescension they were known for in this cold land.

She went flying as the carriage hit a pothole and lurched to an abrupt halt, canting them sideways. The driver gave a curse as he hurtled from his seat to crash upon the ground, where he cried out in agony. The horses squealed and fretted.

Graine was out of the carriage in an instant, to gently soothe the matched pair of greys. Up to her calves in oozing mud, she led them out of the muddy pothole and away from the driver, who was in danger of being trampled on. Luckily, the carriage wheel had not sprung.

She turned to slosh her way back through the mud, to administer aid to the driver. He was dazed. Blood trickled from a cut on his head, his arm hung awkwardly and his head was pulled to one side. His collar bone was broken, an injury she was familiar with after helping the nuns work in the charity hospital. Helping him to the carriage, she fashioned a sling from her scarf to support his injury and staunched the blood flowing from his head with her handkerchief.

'How much further is it to Rushford House, Tom?' she asked him.

'A mile or so around the bend, miss.' Although shaking with shock, he looked concerned. 'It's not long until dusk. As soon as I feel better I'll try and go for help.'

'You'll do no such thing,' Graine said gently, as Tom collapsed into the corner of the cushions, ashen faced. Tucking a rug around him she climbed up on the driver's seat and picked up the reins.

'Now listen to me,' she said to the muscular grey rears and swishing tails, and was gratified when two pairs of ears on the far end of the horses swivelled towards her. 'I've only ever driven a horse and wagon before, and that was an old nag who couldn't have run if a pack of wolves were after him. I'm relying on the pair of you to convey us home slowly. I will tell your master of your good behaviour and, no doubt, there will be a nice warm stable, a rub down and a feed as a reward. Do you understand?'

One of the horses snickered, the other stamped its foot on the ground. Graine took it as a sign of assent. 'Right, let us now proceed.' Flicking the reins she clicked her tongue as she'd heard their usual driver do.

'Good girls,' she said, smiling with relief when they slowly began to move forward. The rain was coming down in torrents now. It slanted from the greys' backs to hit the ground beneath them. There, it turned into instant mud and splashed upwards again to cake them all in slime. With the rain came dusk, until finally she could hardly see. Frozen to the marrow she mulled over events as her temper began to fray at the edges.

What sort of man was John Lamartine? The least he could have done was be there to greet her when she'd stepped ashore in Poole. She imagined him sitting in a warm, comfortable room, sipping port, his legs propped up on a stool in front of a fireplace and with a huge fire roaring up the chimney. He'd probably consumed a huge dinner of roast beef surrounded by roast vegetables and dripping with juice. At least, that's what Evelyn had told her the English ate. Graine felt very empty herself, her stomach rattling with hunger.

After what seemed an age of gingerly encouraging the horses forward, over to her right Graine spied a light shining through the watery darkness. Rushford, at last! She guided the horses into a wide carriageway. Not that they needed guiding, she realized. With the scent of home in their nostrils they'd suddenly picked up speed.

'Whoa!' she yelled in alarm, pulling on the reins. The beasts took no notice. Graine hung on like grim death, fighting their forward momentum as they lengthened their stride. The house loomed closer and closer. Frantically, she applied all her strength to the reins and yelled, 'Stop, you stupid beasts. You promised to get me here safely.'

Suddenly, dim figures appeared. One stood in front of the horses, arms outstretched, shouting, 'Whoa there, nags! Whoa!' Another leaped nimbly astride one of the mares and applied some strength to the reins. The carriage and pair came to a shuddering stop.

'What in hell's name is going on here?' somebody roared from the porch. Footsteps crunched across gravel. When one of the servants held a lantern aloft, there came a curse. 'Good God! You look like a drowned rat. Where's Tom?'

'In the carriage,' she said, her teeth beginning to chatter. 'The carriage hit a pothole, he was thrown, and is badly injured.'

'You drove the horses by yourself?' The man shook his head. 'You little fool. You could have killed yourself, or worse still, killed my horses. Look at them, they're all lathered up.'

A growl gathered momentum inside her. 'They're not the only ones lathered up. I'm exceedingly angered by your incivility. I'm incensed! In fact, I'm *seething* with fury.'

Surprise filled his eyes. 'Are you, by God? Now there's a thing.'

He barked out orders to the men around him, sending them scurrying in all directions. Tom was gently lifted out and carried away. A great hairy dog came to stand by the man's side, his tail lashing back and forth. The man absently fondled its head, gazed up at her again and began to laugh. 'Well, are you going to sit up there seething with fury all night? The groom wants to stable the horses.'

The arrogant, cold-hearted, mealy-mannered ogre! Not one word of thanks for bringing his horse and carriage home. Not one word of enquiry for her own welfare, either. Was this what Evelyn had drowned for? Her memory deserved better.

'If you think I'm going to wed you, you're very much mistaken,' she spat out. 'You're not worth a penny of the money you cost me. In fact, both you and your horses need to learn some manners.'

So saying, she launched herself from the seat. If she'd been expecting assistance she was disappointed. He chose that moment to take a casual step backwards. She landed awkwardly, tripped over her skirt and sprawled face down on the gravel, her nose a scant few inches away from the toes of his boots. Rain pounded relentlessly down on her back. The dog came to slurp a tongue over her face.

'Get off, you slobbering beast,' she yelled and, glaring up at the man looming over her, said, 'Kindly feed your dog, sir. He seems to be hungry.'

He hunched down in front of her, hardly able to contain his laughter. 'I hope you're feeling better now.'

'You're despicable.' She struggled on to her knees and did the only thing possible under the circumstances. She burst into tears and scolded, 'Isn't being shipwrecked and losing everything I own enough for you? Isn't it enough that your beastly horses wouldn't do what they were told and this damned England of yours is a grey and freezing bog? Couldn't you, at least, have come to fetch me yourself? The only person who seems intent on welcoming me is your smelly dog.'

The dog licked her face in sympathy, then sat and pressed his pungent rain-soaked body against hers. At least he cared about her. She put her arms around him in a comforting hug.

The man's expression didn't accommodate much in the way of compassion. 'John understood the ship was to dock in London. That's where he is at the moment, in the capital. There he will remain, until spring.'

'Didn't he get a message from the East India Company that the ship had foundered off Barbados? I was put aboard another vessel that docked at Poole.'

'So I was given to understand this morning, and that was only by chance. Unfortunately, my favourite mare was having difficulty dropping her foal, so I couldn't leave her. I'll send a message to John to let him know that you're safe, as soon as the weather clears.'

She suddenly realized what he was saying. 'You mean you're not John Lamartine?'

'I'm Saville Lamartine, The Earl of Sedgley. John is my cousin. So, you're not obliged to wed me, after all, though I'm certain I could have provided you with good value for every penny you spent. And as for manners . . .' His hand described an arc through the rain. 'This is Rushford, my home. I bid you welcome to it. Is that mannerly enough?'

She swallowed a niggle of disappointment at the announcement, but refused to succumb to his charm. 'Damn it, my knees are skinned, sir,' she said accusingly.

He didn't turn a hair at her unladylike retort. 'How was I to know you were about to leap from the driver's seat like a flea-bitten monkey from a rock?' He sighed and held out a hand. 'Here, let's stop this bickering and get out of this confounded rain. You're soaked through and you must be hungry.'

Pulled upright, she was swung up into his arms. He strode off with her towards the house, the dog racing on ahead. She couldn't see her host's face properly, but there was an impression of strength about him, for he carried her easily and without effort.

'I'm quite capable of walking,' she fumed.

A soft chuckle warmed her ear. 'No doubt you are, but not until your knees have been looked at. I cannot have you suffering further damage whilst you're my guest. John is most particular about things. He would never forgive me if I handed over his bride in a less than perfect condition. Still, what can you expect from a man of the cloth.'

'He's a church cleric?' she said, aghast at the thought when she'd spent most of her life in the company of nuns.

'Pious, pernickety and pompous, that's John. You'll be expected to pray a lot, but I imagine you'd be used to that, sore knees or not.'

Her eyes sharpened; his remained bland.

'John mentioned you prayed on a daily basis.'

Relief came in a hot, shameful rush, as she was reminded of her dishonesty. Instantly, Graine prayed he'd never discover she was deceiving them.

Not that she relied much on prayer, having learned in the past that it rarely produced results. Though now she thought of it, Evelyn had prayed for a husband and received an offer the very next day. But when all was said and done, that hardly counted when John Lamartine had been after her fortune. Poor, lonely Evelyn had really wanted to be loved for herself – as did she.

She mumbled something banal to her host. 'Yes, of course.'

'He has his good points,' Saville said cheerfully as he kicked the door open. 'He's honest, and he respects his mother, even though . . .' He chuckled. 'But then, it would not be gentlemanly of me to pass judgement on somebody you have yet to meet.'

Her ears pricked. 'Even though, what? You cannot leave it at that,' she prompted, after he deposited her on the cushions of the hall settle and knelt before her.

The dog shook himself free of water and sat attentively beside his master. His coat was dark and roughly spiked. So was his master's hair. A pair of guileless blue eyes gazed through dark lashes to meet hers in a delicious confrontation. His mouth was a curve of dubiety. 'Oh, nothing. I expect you'll be able to manage the old termagant. God knows, you're strong-minded enough. Given time, Aunt Harriet will relinquish her position as head of the household, I expect, even though she chose you herself from likely candidates.'

She stared at him. 'John Lamartine allowed his mother to choose his wife?'

'Oh don't sound so ruffled. There were only two other candidates, neither of which reached Harriet's main requisite for her son.'

'Which was?'

The side of his mouth twitched. 'Harriet has ambitions of John becoming a bishop, so his wife must be lacking of strong opinion and have a biddable nature.'

Disbelieving, she stared at him.

'I suspect you're neither,' he said gloomily.

'You're right.' Graine let out an exasperated sigh. 'I will soon rout that notion from her head.'

He chuckled. 'Don't ask John to take your part. He's been dominated by my Aunt Harriet all his life, and old habits die hard.' His smile warmed her. 'Pull your skirt up so I can inspect the damage to your knees.'

'Certainly not. I'm capable of tending to them myself.' In truth,

14

she'd greatly exaggerated the damage and knew they were hardly touched at all. She'd be surprised if the skin had even been broken. Her teeth began to chatter and a shudder racked her body.

His expression became one of concern. 'We must make you comfortable before you catch cold, Miss Evelyn Adams.'

Who was the *we* he referred to, his wife? Was Saville Lamartine a married man? He looked to be under thirty years of age. A man in his prime, in fact. Yes, he was bound to be married, she decided.

He shouted for servants. Soon, Graine was borne to an upstairs chamber by two maids where a fire burned cheerfully in the grate. Stripped of her muddy clothes she was bathed and cosseted. Dry clothes were found. She was enveloped in a voluminous garment of flannel, which was perfumed with lavender. Her hair was damp dried into ringlets and curls. Steam rose from it as she sat by the fire, eating a bowl of thick chicken broth.

Later, feeling relaxed and clean, she lay in a four-poster bed watching the candle flame flicker in the draught caused by the maid bustling back and forth as she lifted garments from storage boxes to inspect and sort. She set some aside for repair.

Graine contemplated her future. She had not expected to feel such guilt over her impersonation, even though Evelyn's demise was not her fault. Poor, dear Evelyn. So good and so kind. She'd deserved much better. A tear slid down her cheek for her sister, hastily wiped away when there was a rap at the door.

Saville Lamartine called out. 'May I enter?'

Graine nodded to the maid, who opened the door to allow the earl entry. He'd changed into dry breeches and hose. His shirt was open at the neck, and over it he wore an embroidered waistcoat. His long legs carried him to the bed, where he sat and scrutinized her face.

Her cheeks heated under that intense gaze. 'Why are you looking at me, thus?'

'Now the mud has been washed off you appear younger than I'd been led to expect.'

'I expect the candlelight flatters me.'

'Your hair has sunlight threaded through it.'

Graine's hands went to her cheeks. 'Now, you're being too personal, sir.'

'It was a statement of fact, not an inappropriate compliment, though I must admit it was more on the poetic side than is usual with me.' He grinned at the thought. 'I've come to make sure you're comfortable and have everything you need.' He turned to the companion. 'Jessie, have you found something for Miss Adams to wear in the morning?'

'Yes, sir. Lady Charlotte left several garments behind when she departed for Kent.'

So, the earl *was* married. 'You've been very kind. I hope your wife won't mind me borrowing her clothes.'

'The clothes belong to my sister.' There was something mocking about his smile, as if he knew her remark was more than casual query. He wasn't going to satisfy her curiosity, however, leaving the specifics of the query hanging in the air. 'You shall have your own clothes before too long.'

'But I have no money with which to pay for them.'

'John will settle things up from your dowry, no doubt.'

How careless of her to forget already. She must pay more attention to her role, else this man would soon expose her lie. He was no fool. 'Oh, yes, of course.'

There was an awkward silence for a moment, broken when the dog pattered across the floor. Placing his head on the bed, he stared at her. The whole of his body wagged with his tail and his rough eyebrows operated independently, going up and down with each movement of his eyes.

She laughed and fondled the rough head. 'What's his name?'

'Rebel.'

'He doesn't look very rebellious, to me.'

'Looks can be deceiving.' Saville rose. 'The carriage driver has asked me to convey his thanks to you. I've strapped his shoulder and the bone will mend before too long.' He took her scarf from his waistcoat pocket and dangled it from his finger. 'He asked me to return this.'

When she held out her hand for it he chuckled and returned it to his pocket. 'It's covered in mud. I'll have it laundered before I return it. Now we have you clean, and looking more the lady, we must try and keep you that way. Good night, Miss Adams. Sweet dreams.'

He strode off, leaving behind him the lingering aroma of soap. Rebel went to follow after his master, then changed his mind, came back and hauled himself on to the bed. He curled up on the end with a dog deflating sigh of bliss.

'Reb. *I trust you haven't made yourself comfortable on Miss Adams's bed*!' Coming from somewhere in the corridor, the statement was followed by a sharp whistle.

The animal's eyebrows waggled, he gave a grumbling sigh, then unfolded himself on to the floor and trotted off reluctantly after his master.

Graine giggled.

Sleep came not long after. It was a novelty to be in a bed that didn't move beneath her, to be surrounded by walls which didn't creak, crack or strain with every movement. It was wonderful that the air was so dry and warm when the inhospitable wind hurled rain against the windows.

'I know you'd understand why I've done this, dearest Evelyn,' she said sleepily, 'but I do wish you'd picked a less worthy man for a mate. Someone like Saville Lamartine would have suited me so much better.'

2

Saville found it hard to sleep. Sprawled on a chair in front of the fire he gazed into the glowing embers and growled, 'Damn the girl.'

He hadn't expected someone quite so spirited, so exquisite, or so wealthy, to have remained unattached for so long. And what of her guardian's taste for feminine attributes to have described her so negatively? Theodore Chambers must either have been blind, or a misogynist by nature. *Plain, awkward, a dull conversationalist but virtuous and obedient.* He'd made Evelyn sound like a cart horse.

Why, he was quite taken by her. She was delicious, a delectable morsel, a provocation of desirable femininity. And she was promised to his cousin, a worthy fellow, but the very epitome of establishment. Saville told himself, John would crush the light from her. And if he didn't, Aunt Harriet would.

'And to think I arranged the deal for John after I turned down a match with her,' he fumed. 'I should have gone to Antigua and inspected the little baggage first-hand. No, I must write to John and tell him she's unsuitable for him, after all.'

But perhaps he should consider his options first. It wouldn't be fair to Evelyn to withdraw her expectations of a decent marriage and family, especially since he'd pushed John into the deal in the first place. And he must remember his cousin needed the dowry whilst he didn't, which was why John had agreed to the scheme in the first place.

Saville grinned as he recalled her muddy appearance. She'd been caked in slime from head to toe, her eyes gleaming through it like angry little wasps. Her temper tantrum had made him laugh, until he'd begun to realize what she'd been through, and how close to collapse she'd been. A plucky little thing, too, bringing the carriage in when she was too slight to handle such horses. Or foolhardy! She certainly didn't fit into his expectations of Miss Evelyn Adams.

He frowned. But he was thinking of her too much when he should be sleeping. Snuffing the candle, he dropped his robe to the floor and strolled naked across to his bed.

Soon he began to toss and turn. He scowled when it became obvious why – he shouldn't be thinking of Miss Evelyn Adams at all, especially when she had such a disastrous effect on his physical comfort!

When dawn came he was not sure whether he'd slept or not. He opened one eye and stared out of the window. The sky was a solid sheet of pewter threatening more rain – or even snow. 'To hell with it,' he said and, turning over, went back to sleep.

Although Graine was up at the crack of dawn, the maid assigned to her was earlier. Already, the energetic Jessie had stirred life into the embers of the fire and added fuel. She was an expert with the needle and thread, it seemed. Lying over the back of the chair was a gown of pale-green taffeta and a velvet over-bodice the colour of moss.

'Miss Charlotte never did take to this gown, said it was too plain,' Jessie chatted, pulling a warm flannel chemise over her head. 'It will suit your colouring real fine. I've put some tucks into the waist to make it a better fit.' Stockings were pulled up her legs and tied with ribbons. Her feet were slipped into brocade slippers with tiny heels. Jessie gazed dubiously at them. 'They might be too big. I reckon we'll have to tie ribbons around them to keep them on.'

Soon, a hairbrush was drawing sparks from her hair, Jessie's nimble fingers fashioned it into a fat braid, drawing the sides up into a lace-trimmed round cap decorated with frills. The maid looked her over with approval in her eyes.

'There, that be a right pretty turn out, miss. I'll fetch you a shawl. You're going to feel the cold after the heat of them there foreign parts, and the fires won't be stoked up downstairs as yet.

You'll soon get used to the cold, especially when you marry Reverend John Lamartine. A real pinch penny, he be. But there, he be nice enough in his own way, and I daresay he can't afford to burn fires in all the rooms. They only be lit at night and then only in the drawing-room. A body would, like as not, freeze to death at this time of year in his home. Best you stay here this winter.'

Graine's eyes filled with dismay. The more she heard of John Lamartine, the less attractive he became. She managed a smile for the woman in the mirror. 'You've made me look lovely, Jessie.'

'There's some that has looks and some that ain't, and I would-n't be so bold as to tell you which you be. You're not what we was expecting, and that be a fact.' The woman placed her fists on her hips. ' "Jessie", says the master, just before he sent auld Tom to fetch you from the boat. "Miss Evelyn Adams be a homely spinster lady, a bit past her prime and set in her ways. You make sure you treat her like a princess and make her feel good about herself".' Jessie cackled. 'He was fair mazed when he set eyes on you, I reckon . . . fair mazed.'

And fair mazed Saville Lamartine still seemed to be, for Graine learned he was still abed. Rebel was awake though, and came hurtling down the staircase after her, his nails skittering on the wooden floors as he greeted her with a variety of yelps. He twisted and turned, nose to tail and back again, in his eagerness for a pat on the back.

She obliged him for a few moments. 'Now you can show me where to go,' she told him, and followed after him through a maze of corridors, where he stopped to scratch on the door.

It was opened by a stout woman, whose mouth dropped open at the sight of Graine. 'Glory be,' she whispered and, hastily drop-ping a curtsy, stood aside to let her into what proved to be the kitchen.

'My pardon,' Graine said, for she could see the woman was quite flustered and put out by her sudden appearance. 'I didn't know quite where to go so I followed Rebel.'

'Come for his treat, he has.' The cook tipped some left-over scraps into a bowl and Rebel snatched them up in quick time before giving a satisfied belch. The cook gazed silently at her for a few moments, then said hesitantly, 'Can I get you anything, miss?

20

It's a bit early for breakfast, though it should be ready in an hour or so in the dining hall.'

'I should like some chocolate if you have any, Mrs um. . . . ?' Her glance took in the blackened iron kettle, which swung gently back and forth on a hook over the fire. The spout exhaled steam in little spurts.

' 'Tis Aggie Harris, her who's married to Tom Harris, who fetched you from Poole in the carriage. I was just going to have one myself.'

'How is your husband?'

Aggie gave a beam of a smile. 'All the better for you being there, miss. The master said you do have a good head on your shoulders. Instead of having the vapours like most women of his acquaintance, you did some right good doctoring. My man Tom'll mend in the shake of a lamb's tail if he behaves hisself and keeps still.'

Graine took a seat on the bench pulled up at the scrubbed wooden table. Seating himself beside her, Rebel placed his great head in her lap and stared adoringly up at her.

Aggie laughed when she set a steaming glass of chocolate before her. 'That there Rebel doesn't usually take to strangers, and only minds the master's orders. It looks as if he's moon-struck, right enough.'

Aggie seated herself opposite and slurped her chocolate down, smacking her lips with satisfaction when she finished. She didn't talk as much as the chattering Jessie, but thought to advise Graine when she announced her intention of becoming acquainted with the garden.

' 'Tis cold out, but dry underfoot if you stay to the paths. Looks like it might snow before too long. Mind you wear a cloak for warmth, there's one hanging in the porch.'

Graine made her way back to the hall where she wrapped herself in a voluminous black cloak. Rebel pawed at the door and gazed back at her, his expression telling her to hurry up.

The cold air was a never experienced wonder. Her breath was exhaled in a cloud of vapour. It was a novelty, but an uncomfortable one. She followed a winding path, ending up on a cliff top. Ahead of her, a grey sea stretched to a sky so equally grey she couldn't distinguish where the one ended and the other began.

She'd come further than she'd intended. Behind her, Rushford House was a looming silhouette against the sky. It was a pretty place, comfortably sized and built from light coloured stone which was encroached upon by ivy in places. The windows appeared long and narrow from where she stood, a gentle arching at the apex giving them elegance. The trees had a winter grace. Displayed in an ironwork of patterned darkness, they etched stark against the sky. It shone, that sky, exuding a faint pearl-essence.

She started back, Rebel making investigative and noisy forays into the undergrowth, or burying his great head up to the shoulders in a rabbit hole. He was a funny sight with his bushy rear exposed and his tail whipping back and forth with excitement. She imagined the rabbits' surprise when his snout and eyes appeared in their cosy little burrows, and laughed.

The sound carried in the cold air like the clear tone of a bell. Saville, almost fully clothed now, wandered to the window with his body servant in pursuit. He smiled broadly when he saw her and, raising his arms for his jacket to be slipped over his arms, said absently, 'Now there's a sight a man would never tire of looking at.'

'Yes, m'lord,' the servant said, grinning to himself.

Graine was nearing the house when something brushed delicately against her cheek. Gazing upwards she saw the white flakes swirling about and grinned. Snow! She'd heard of it, of course, and had learned from reading that a snowflake was little more than water frozen into ice crystals. She hadn't realized snow was so light and pretty though, and now she could experience it for herself. Extending her tongue she collected one on the tip and drew it into her mouth. It melted in an instant.

Rebel was jumping up in the air, barking and twisting to catch the flakes in his mouth. Spreading her arms, Graine whirled and leaped about in it too, laughing. If only Evelyn was here to experience this. How she would have delighted in it.

From his chamber window, Saville watched them, a smile on his face. She looked like an excited child. Then she noticed him at the window. Coming to a sudden stop, she drew the cloak around her and hurried towards the house, the dog at her heels.

Hurrying downstairs, Saville intercepted her in the hall.

Snowflakes were melting in her hair. She shrugged, her smile uncertain. 'I've never seen snow before. It's pretty.'

'If it's prolonged and heavy we'll be marooned at Rushford for weeks.'

'I shan't mind that; it's beautiful here.'

He grinned. 'Yesterday you described it as a grey, wet bog.'

'It *was* yesterday. Yesterday, I was tired and I indulged in a childish temper tantrum. Quite rightly, you set me firmly in my place. There, I have admitted it.' The amusement in his eyes was hard to hide, and she gave a delightfully soft giggle that made the hair on his nape prickle. 'May I remind you that you paid me back by allowing me to fall flat on my face?'

'Quite unintentional. How are your knees this morning?'

'Perfectly well, thank you.' She allowed him to take the cloak, which he handed to a hovering servant. His glance touched on the green gown and his eyes widened a trifle. 'Charlotte said green was too hard a colour to wear, but you look exquisite in it.'

Her cheeks flamed, but she didn't draw attention to it by shielding it with her hands. 'You're embarrassing me, sir.'

'Ah, you are not used to receiving compliments, I see. There must be something the matter with men in the West Indies to let a jewel of your ilk slip through their fingers.'

'Please remember I'm promised to your cousin,' she almost pleaded, which was something Saville found hard to do, since the depths of her eyes cupped a liquid amber warmth and her mouth had an irresistible softness to it. All he had to do was lean forward a little to steal a kiss.

As if sensing his intention, Rebel pushed between them. The damned dog has fallen instantly in love with her, too, Saville thought wryly.

She took a step back, looking almost as rueful as he felt.

'I will despatch a message to my sister, asking her to return and act as your chaperon.' In the meantime he must learn to control himself. His expression became a fraction less personal as he held out an arm to her. 'You do well to remind me of my place, Miss Adams. Allow me to escort you into breakfast. You must be hungry after your exercise.'

Graine *was* hungry. She ate a small bowl of oatmeal followed by a coddled egg and a slice of ham. Afterwards she spread a slice of bread with creamy butter and honey. Picking up the last crumb from her plate with her finger she looked up to find Saville gazing at her with a smile on his face.

'The cold weather has made me hungry,' she said unnecessarily.

'Aggie likes to see justice done to her cooking, and Mr Jackson here, who always serves the breakfast and evening meal in the dining hall, will no doubt report back to her.'

Indeed, the old servant called Mr Jackson was beaming at them both in approval.

'Thank Aggie for me,' she said. 'I can't remember the last time I ate such a good meal.'

When Mr Jackson's smile grew even wider, it occurred to Graine that all the servants working in this house seemed happy. Her glance came back to Saville Lamartine, handsomely attired in black breeches and jacket, and with a pearl grey waistcoat buttoned over an immaculate shirt and stock.

He rose a little higher in her estimation. When Graine had worked for Theodore Chambers, the man who'd been Evelyn's guardian, he'd been an absolute tyrant. The man had kept her working from dawn to midnight, and treated her with disdain when she was not in company with Evelyn, going so far as to cuff her on occasion. The only reason Graine hadn't walked out, was because of her relationship with, and her love for her half-sister. She'd never told Evelyn of her ill-treatment at his hands.

Saville's chair scraped over the floor as he stood up. 'You'll have to excuse me, Miss Adams. You need a wardrobe, and I should start out for town before the snow becomes heavier, otherwise I might not be able to get back.'

'You need not brave this cold weather on my account. Jessie has found several garments, which will serve me for the time being.'

'I have seen them, and they will not serve. Although Jessie is clever with her needle, most of my sister's discarded clothing is too large to accommodate you in comfort. I cannot have you running around my home looking like a ragamuffin. Jessie has given me a list of your minimum needs. I will take a horse and cart to accommodate the parcels, and will be back in no time at all.'

Ten minutes later she watched him leave, a sturdy horse

strapped between the shafts of a light, covered cart. A tricorn kept the snow from his head and his cloak was wrapped warmly around him.

Graine watched as Rebel went bounding down the drive after him to jump up on the back of the cart. Saville's head turned towards the dog and he pointed towards the house. Rebel looked in the opposite direction and yawned. She grinned when Saville shrugged and flicked at the reins.

The snow thickened during the afternoon, the flakes becoming heavier and more prolific. Soon, Graine couldn't discern where the carriageway became lawn. The tree limbs grew blankets of white fluff along their lengths. Soon, there was an unblemished white landscape in a white vortex of snow. The scene enchanted her.

Now and again, servants went to stare worriedly out of windows, until one assumed a permanent watch from a window on the stairs. One braved the snow to tramp down the carriageway, lifting each step up high and leaving deep footprints behind him. He tramped back again, shaking his head.

It was almost dark when Saville returned, leading the horse and cart by the reins. Rebel stood on a covered mound of parcels, barking instructions to him as he practically dragged the vehicle through the snow.

Two of the stable hands rushed to take responsibility for the vehicle, others shooed Saville indoors and began to unload the parcels. Graine heaved a sigh of relief at his safe return, and went in search of him.

She found him in the drawing-room, his back to the fire, his hands cupped round a brandy. It was a comfortable room, furnished with deep chairs covered in tapestry or blue velvet. A large Aubusson rug, intricately designed in reds and blues, stretched across a floor of polished wood. The walls were panelled at the bottom, and covered with watered taffeta at the top. Window hangings of pale-blue velvet were tied back with gold tassels. A French clock ticked loudly on the mantle, its pendulum swinging a stately measure back and forth.

Rebel was lying almost on the embers of the fire, steam rising from his coat.

Graine stated the obvious almost accusingly. 'You look frozen.'

'Were you worried about me?' he said, trying to smile through his chattering teeth.

'Of course not. I assumed you were intelligent enough to know what you were doing.'

'Thank you.'

'Your servants were, though. And they know you better than I.'

'They're paid to worry about me,' he said lightly, 'and you're not a servant, are you?'

Graine stared at him, wide-eyed and slightly dry mouthed. Had he discovered her deception?

She trod carefully. 'Everyone is a servant to something, whether it be land, family, or by hiring out of one's labour.'

'Then you think people are equal in status, that the difference lies only in wealth, or the obtaining of that wealth?'

'I didn't say that exactly. Status is a state of mind. Why should a lady's maid be classed as inferior, when her mistress doesn't have the same skill to attend to her own toilette? Why should a man's bastard be considered inferior to a child of his marriage? And why should an aristocrat who cheats, lies and gambles and is unfaithful to his wife, be considered superior to a faithful, honest man, who earns his bread by the strength of his back and the sweat of his brow?'

'Enough,' he protested, half laughing. 'You display too much passion and opinion for a woman of quality.'

Graine felt like stamping her foot. Her years with the nuns, who'd been far from submissive in either mind or practicality, had given her a less than conventional approach to life. 'Have I indeed? Who gave men the right to decide that a female must have no opinion or passion?'

'My dear, Miss Adams, do calm down. I'm not disagreeing with the thrust of your argument. However, men make the laws and govern the land. Until that changes it would be wiser if such opinions were not aired, especially in front of John. The hierarchy of the Church of England does not favour such liberal views.'

The blue of his eyes had sharpened to a mercurial brightness. It seemed he had a mark she must not overstep, a mark she was fast approaching. She allowed her temper to cool then, framed an insubstantial apology. 'I'm sorry if I offended you.'

He swallowed the remains of his brandy and chuckled 'You're not sorry, at all. You delight in the cut and thrust of argument. I enjoyed the encounter. It warmed me.'

'But John Lamartine would not approve.'

Saville shrugged and turned to Rebel, saying casually, 'Move away from the fire, Reb. Your coat is beginning to scorch.'

Rebel sighed, lumbered to his feet, turned around thrice, then subsided to the floor and offered his other side to the flames.

Graine giggled. 'He certainly has a mind of his own.'

'He seems to have formed a strong attachment to you, Miss Adams. Be careful he doesn't lead you astray.'

'I promise I'll not attempt to stick my head down rabbit holes or scratch behind my ear with my foot.'

Saville laughed when Rebel lifted his head and gave her a brief, but superior look.

A servant entered to light the candles in the sconces and draw the hangings across the window. When he'd finished, he gently coughed to draw his master's attention. 'Jessie has unpacked Miss Adams's parcels, m'lord.'

'Thank you. She shall come directly to inspect them. Inform Cook that my guest will be dining with me tonight, and tell Jeffries I'll be changing for dinner shortly.' His eyes gleamed when he smiled at her. 'I will see you at eight, Miss Adams.'

By that, Graine took it she was being dismissed. But much as she enjoyed his company she was also eager to see what his purchases consisted of. Without thinking she bobbed him a curtsy. 'Yes, my lord.'

A pained look appeared on his features as he protested, 'My dear Miss Adams, I thought we'd agreed you were not a servant.'

Shame filled her. The placement of her hands over the tell-tale display of heat on her cheeks was involuntary. She turned away from him in consternation, heading rapidly for the door.

Now what in the devil brought that about? Saville thought when the door closed behind her.

He moved away from the fire and poured himself another brandy. His rear was nicely toasted now, his toes were beginning to lose their numb feeling. Throwing himself in a chair he draped a leg inelegantly over one of the arms and watched the firelight lick at the golden fluid in his glass. The colour reminded him of Evelyn's eyes.

The girl had such fire in her. How could he have been so wrong about someone? The one letter he'd received from her was badly written in a childish hand, and had given no indication of such intelligence and wit. He knew it by heart, every awkward phrase and misspelt word. From it he'd formed an opinion of a likeable, trusting woman with a big heart.

Dear Lord Lamartine.
My gardiun and uncle, Mister Theodore Chambers, has recently departed this world. As negoshiashuns were concluded to the satisfaction of all partys, and the plantashun has now been sold and my dowry transferred. I shall be leaving for England at the date previously arranged, and told to you by my unfortunately demised relative in his last letter.
I will be accompanied on the sea journey by a young woman who acts as my personal companion. Her name is Graine. She will remayne in my employ until her situashun is made clear to all concerned at a later date. I wish her to remayne under my protection after my marriage, whilst I teach her some graces, because sometimes she speaks too bluntly and forceful.
Though she be not much use at sewing and fashuning hair and such, Graine is a dear little lovable girl, if a bit pertly inclined, on account of being brought up with nuns in a convent orphanage, who couldn't make her pious enuff to join the order however much they tried, because she was too lively a girl who didn't enjoy praying on her knees so much. But who can blame her for that?
Please convey my felicitashuns to my betrothed, John Lamartine.
I have the honour to remain your faithfull servant.
Evelyn Adams (Miss)

Saville grinned widely. At first her remarks about her compan-

28

ion had made him laugh, then the affection contained in them endeared her to him. He was sorry the orphan girl had drowned, because he'd been looking forward to observing her antics for himself.

He usually prided himself on being a good judge of character, but Evelyn had surprised him in the flesh. She would not make a suitable wife for John, and he knew his cousin to be an honourable man who would not back out of the union without good excuse now.

Still, Evelyn Adams struck him as being a girl with a mind of her own, and she must make her own decision when she met John face to face. He intended to counsel her to that end.

Upstairs in her chamber, Graine's eyes were feasting on several gowns of various colours. There were skirts, bodices, and two riding outfits, though she hardly knew one end of a horse from the other so knew she wouldn't need them. There were boxes of shoes, two pairs of boots fashioned from soft leather, silk hose, ribbons, hats and furbelows. Chemises of the softest material were heaped on the bed. She reddened when she picked one up and it drifted through her finger.

'Surely he didn't purchase these himself.'

Jessie cackled with laughter. 'And why not, pray? At his age the master would know his way around a woman.'

Graine asked the question she hadn't dared directly ask Saville Lamartine himself. 'Does he have a wife, then?'

'Not him. He said he won't marry until he meets his true love, though I don't know how he expects to meet a sweetheart of suitable birth, not when he lives here in the depths of Dorset.'

Isolated as Rushford was, it wasn't as remote as Jessie made it sound. Her giggle earned her a suspicious look.

'He rarely goes to London now, even though he keeps a house and staff there, not unless there's a bill of particular interest being debated in the House to interest him, that is. The master says there's plenty to do here, what with running the estate and his duties as a magistrate.'

A tremor of unease ran through Graine, though she could not see how anyone could find out about her lie. To distract herself, she picked up a cornflower-blue gown with a delicate tracing of embroidery on the bodice and hem. She held it against her body. 'This is so pretty.'

'I thought you'd like that one. See, it has a little velvet jacket with laces at the front. You should wear it to dinner. Blue is the master's favourite colour.'

3

Saville watched Evelyn Adams throughout dinner. The fact that she'd become an enigma to him was bothersome.

Her age for a start. Even in the cold light of day she did not appear to be twenty-six years old. Her skin was smooth with hardly a blemish, if one ignored the tiny scar just visible in her hair-line. She certainly did not act twenty-six either. There was a certain naïveté about her, a lack of full control over her emotions which suggested a girl emerging from her youth.

Her appetite was good, but without greed. She ate small portions of everything offered. Finally, she put her spoon down and heaved a sigh of relief. 'I have hardly room for it all and can eat no more.'

'You were not obliged to eat everything in the first place.'

There was a little twist of puzzlement in the eyes which met his. 'But it's a sin to waste food when others are starving.'

'How can it be wasted when the servants will eat what we do not, and the dog will eat what they do not, and the pigs will eat what he does not?'

'Oh!' She looked deliciously perplexed for a moment, then she smiled. 'I'm truly impressed by the way you treat your servants.'

'How were yours treated in Antigua?'

Her eyes clouded over as she remembered her own treatment. 'They were treated a little better than the plantation slaves, but not much.' Theodore Chambers had made them work from dawn until midnight and he'd seemed to resent her presence in the house.

Saville decided not to pursue the subject. Slavery was an unpleasant conversation to introduce to the dinner-table, one which stirred great passions. 'You were lucky to have foundered near Barbados rather than in the middle of the North Atlantic.'

An expression of great sadness appeared on her face. Tears glistened on the surface of her eyes. 'I was lucky, yes, but others were not. So many lives were lost, including that of my beloved . . . uh . . . companion. I cannot bear to think of her lost in the depths of that great ocean whilst I'm still alive.'

He pushed his chair back held out his hand to assist her up. 'It was not my intent to upset you so. Come, we will go to the drawing-room and you will sip a small glass of brandy. We shall talk of gayer things whilst you recover from your sadness. That blue gown looks well on you, Miss Adams.'

'I must thank you for your kindness and compliment you on your good taste.'

She slanted him a sideways look from under her lashes, which although he knew to be entirely without guile, was unconsciously provocative, all the same.

'Must you call me Miss Adams in such a stuffy manner?'

His heart unexpectedly lifted and he found himself grinning foolishly at her. 'Unless I'm given permission to do otherwise, yes.'

'You have it. And I shall address you as Saville, with or without your permission. It's a splendid name which suits you well. You do not mind?'

He chuckled. 'You've already stated your intent in a quite determined manner. You are my guest and I'm yours to command.'

'Which is easy to say, but I'm sure you would not be so gallant if your resolve ran in the opposite direction to mine,' she said, tossing her gilded head as she laughed. 'You do not strike me as a man who would jump easily to the dictates of a woman.'

He laughed at her sally. 'It would depend on the circumstances, of course.' And Saville reflected that this delicious Eve might be able to furnish him with a thousand such circumstances, as he handed her a brandy and water.

She sipped it slowly, regarding him over the glass as, calling on his obligations as host, Saville attempted to entertain her with snippets of gossip from his last visit to London, or the parties and balls he'd attended. The information was out of date, but she wouldn't be aware of that.

After a while, she murmured, 'All those balls and assemblies sounds to be an indolent way to spend one's life. Tell me about yourself. Are your visits to the capital city merely a pursuit of pleasure, or do you have a profession to occupy your time, like your worthy cousin John Lamartine?'

Sensing sarcasm, he gazed sharply at her. Leaning into the corner of the chair with her eyes closed, his guest had slipped her feet from her shoes and had tucked her legs up under her skirt. He experienced a moment of chagrin that he'd bored her into such a relaxed state, then noticing the empty glass in her hand, he grinned and rose to pluck it from her fingers.

She opened her eyes to reveal the honeyed depths of them, then smiling lazily up at him, murmured, 'Forgive me, Saville. I'm unaccustomed to drinking spirituous liquor and it has relaxed me too much, I fear.'

She had never seemed so luscious to him. 'You're still fatigued from the journey.'

But Eve had drifted into sleep now. Her breast rose and fell evenly with each breath as he sat and watched her, content to gaze upon her beauty. The fact that he'd fallen instantly in love with her was deeply disturbing to him.

Saville was twenty-eight years old. Although a romantic at heart, he considered himself the possessor of sound logic and reason, not a man easily led by a pretty face or a coquettish smile. He'd made his conquests in the past, and still did on occasion, though not on his own doorstep, and always with women who did not expect more than he was prepared to give in return. He was careful, and discreet regarding matters of the flesh.

Saville knew he was considered a good catch. He had played the game, surveying the worthy maids thrown on to the marriage market each season with a union in mind. He'd been half-hearted about it, and even though desirous of having a wife and producing heirs, something had held him back from making an offer, however suitable the candidate had seemed to be.

Deep down, he'd always harboured expectations of falling in love. Now it had happened, striking him down without warning, swiftly and surely. But it should not have happened with this girl. He'd spent the last two years haggling with her guardian on another's behalf. His beautiful Eve had been carefully selected for John, a man too proud and particular for his own poor living.

The whole issue was now in doubt. Her eyelids began to flutter. She was dreaming, and began to whimper, her head moving from side to side. He crossed to her side and carefully lifted her. She quieted when he gently shushed her. A perfect armful, was Eve, her head fell against his shoulder and her breath stroked deliciously against his ear like a downy feather.

Up the stairs he went, his feet treading as surely as those of a cat, though he had no light to guide him. Her chamber door was slightly ajar, revealing the flickering light of a candle. Jessie was moving about inside, humming softly to herself.

Smitten, Saville gazed down at his beautiful burden. He was stuck like a fly in the honey pot and had been from the moment his hound had licked her face free of mud. He chuckled, remembering her indignance when she'd taken him to task, and his own incredulous reaction.

Looking around him to make sure he wasn't observed, he inclined his head and, seeking out her mouth with his, stole a lingering kiss. Her lips were soft and moist, tasting deliciously of brandy. In her sleep there came the hint of a yielding response. Dear Lord, what was he doing to himself, to her? Only a rogue would take advantage of such a situation. So, he would be a rogue. Darling Eve, forgive me. I will make you love me, he thought, and kissed her again to make sure the forgiving was worth the crime.

Kicking open the door he smiled when Jessie looked up, and he laid his offering gently on the bed. 'She has fallen asleep,' he whispered unnecessarily.

'Aye,' said Jessie, giving him a withering look. 'And if you asks me the dog isn't the only creature moon-struck in this house.'

'I didn't ask you, Jessie.'

'You didn't have to. I've knowed you since you was in the cradle, and 'tis written all over your face.' She gazed down at Evelyn and smiled. 'Can't say I blames you. She be a rare piece of goods, I say, and not too fancy in her ways. Best grab her up quick before your cousin sees her.'

Saville grinned sheepishly to himself as he backed away, only too aware of the dilemma he'd placed himself in. 'It's not that simple.'

The look she gave him was withering. 'Sure it is. You've allus known how to catch yourself a woman when you wanted one.'

Face pressed against the window, the next morning Graine gave an exclamation of delight. This England of Saville's was a marvel. The landscape was a stretch of quiet, white expanse from one end to the other. Like a parcel layered in sparkling white paper, there was an anticipation about it, as if one day it would be unwrapped to reveal a surprise to her.

'I wager a ha'porth to a strawmote it will be cleared by morning,' Jessie muttered, and Graine, who didn't know a halfpenny from a piece of straw, could only agree with her.

The sky was almost clear now. The sun was a pale yellow light through the drifting haze which curtained the sky.

Jessie began to lay out her clothes, something Graine had often done for Evelyn, though not half as expertly. Not that Evelyn had cared. 'After all, I have nobody to encourage any vanity I might possess,' she'd been inclined to say.

Here, was a day gown prettier than even Evelyn could have imagined. Of rose pink damask, it was matched with a plum coloured jacket edged in fur. With a flannel chemise under for warmth, Graine felt special in it as Jessie brushed the tangles from her curls. Deftly, her hair was drawn into pink ribbons and secured into a frilled cap atop her head. The rest was left to curl softly about her shoulders.

Saville was standing in the hallway when Graine descended. His eyes wandered over her from head to toe and he looked bemused when she smiled widely at him. 'I must apologize for my behaviour last night. I had not intended to fall asleep.'

He pretended to frown. 'Then my conversation must have bored you. I will endeavour to be more entertaining.'

'You need not go to such great effort to try and please me, for I'm used to a simple life and simple pleasures.'

'May I ask what those pleasures are?'

'At home I mostly used to read, or write a little poetry.' Her mind scrambled to think of how Evelyn had passed the time. But they'd not had the same interests or skills, and Graine couldn't suddenly learn to embroider expertly. It was a relief to tell him the truth. 'Sometimes, I'd walk and admire the flowers, or if Mr Chambers was absent, we would find a secluded cove and swim in the shallows.'

'We?'

'My . . . companion,' she said carefully.

Although Evelyn had been reserved on the surface, when her guardian had been absent and the repressive atmosphere had lifted, she'd relaxed completely. Sometimes, they'd been like two unrestrained children together. Evelyn had been unable to swim, but had waded in with her chemise belling out around her, laughing and splashing about in a most undignified manner.

His eyebrow raised a trifle at her reply. 'The latter pursuit is considered an unsuitable one for ladies here to indulge in.'

'Had I not been able to swim, I would be dead,' she pointed out, and shuddered as she remembered the water closing over her and the pull of the currents.

The expression in his eyes became slightly more compassionate. 'Quite so, but no doubt you would find the water here too cold after the tropics. What other interests have you?'

'I'm well tutored in Latin, mathematics, history, geographical studies and the arts. Had I been a man, I daresay I would have become a physician or a scientist instead of becoming a wife to a stranger.'

His brows knitted together in a slightly perplexed manner, then a smile played around his mouth, as if he was trying to humour her. 'You're welcome to use my library for study, if that will please you. It's fairly extensive. I'll order a fire to be lit and maintained there for your convenience.'

His servant fixed a black cloak around his shoulders, which made him look rather mysterious and dashing, she thought. 'It's early to be going out.'

'I have some business to attend to. One of my estate workers has suffered an accident and the new doctor is not yet in residence.'

'Perhaps I could help. I've worked amongst the sick and injured in a hospital.'

'Handing out comforting words and very little else, no doubt.'

She stiffened and met his glance square on. 'You're wrong in reaching such a conclusion, I was brought up to possess a great deal more practicality than that.'

The indulgent chuckle he gave was at odds with the astute steadiness of his gaze. 'You seem to be a woman of many talents, Eve. A paragon of industriousness.'

She coloured. 'My intention was not to brag, and your ironic tone of voice is insulting. It's unworthy of you to mock me, as if my accomplishments are unnatural or of no value.' She walked away from him, her cheeks burning, her head held high.

'Come back, Evelyn,' he said with a sigh.

In her anger, Graine forgot she was supposed to be Evelyn and kept on walking.

'Damn it. Don't ignore me!' he roared.

Already at the dining-room door, she turned and scowled at him. 'I will not be spoken to like that.' In an instant she was inside, closing the door behind her with a definite thud and locking it. Leaning an ear against the panel, she allowed her heartbeat to subside to normal. At least he hadn't come after her. She gave a sigh of relief, then turned to find him standing right behind her.

Giving a yelp of surprise she stared at him, wide-eyed.

'You should have checked there was no other door into this room.' His arms came out on either side of her, trapping her against the door. 'There are two things you need to know: first, I am the master of this house, and will not be ignored or disobeyed in front of my servants.'

The reprimand was probably deserved, but no less wounding for it.

'Second. I was not belittling any accomplishments you might possess. The fact is, you, are completely different to what I was led to expect by your guardian. You puzzle me.'

'I'm sorry,' she spluttered.

'I'm not.' His lips turned up in a rueful smile, 'Who are you, Evelyn Adams?'

Her heart thumped in alarm.

'No, don't tell me,' he said, when she gave a small gasp. 'You are a changeling, emerging from the sea in the guise of a goddess. You are Aphrodite. You are the moon in the form of a female and I can only worship at your feet.'

'Than you are a bigger fool than I first thought,' she said a little caustically.

'Aye, I think I am, and you seem to have learned nothing from my caution, which left you with so crestfallen a face that I regretted my bullying ways immediately.' He brushed his mouth against hers, as light as the wings of a butterfly. 'My apologies for shouting at you, my darling Eve, though I cannot guarantee not doing so again when you provoke me so. I'm too arrogant at times, and you were right to chastise me on this occasion.'

'You are certainly bold,' she said, and not knowing whether to be annoyed or not, her laugh contained a strange, breathless quality.

There was a moment of charged intensity when their eyes clung each to the other, Then he was gone, leaving her weak at the knees and trembling.

She placed her hand against her mouth, as if keeping the sensation of the kiss intact. But it had been and gone in an instant. How insubstantial a thing it had been, a tiny taste, a tease, a crumb. But a crumb of something tasty created a desire for a bigger crumb, a bite, a slice, then the whole cake.

One tended to become more than satiated by pleasure, she'd been warned. First a small taste of sweetness, then a little more. Then when it was withdrawn the cravings started, so one would do almost anything to regain the sensation.

Of course, the nuns had been warning about the narcotics drawn from plants, and used by slaves to produce hallucinations to make their lives a little more bearable but it could apply equally to love. Saville was older, more experienced. Was this some test to make sure she was a suitable wife for John Lamartine?

She must beware of him, and of the deliciously vagrant sensations inside her. They were surely the sinful ones, of which she'd been warned on several occasions, for they'd been caused by a man engaging her eyes in an immodest manner, and then stealing a kiss from her mouth. Still, she couldn't feel guilty about that when she'd enjoyed it so much. She would simply prevent him doing it again.

She ate a substantial and solitary breakfast, then sought directions to the library from Mr Jackson, who had waited on her in regal style.

'The fire has not yet been lit,' he said apologetically.

'You need not light it on my account. I shall select a book to read and take it up to my chamber. From now on I shall be the quietest guest you have ever had, and will cause you no trouble at all.'

But Mr Jackson made sure his master's orders were carried out, and Graine was glad of its warmth, for selecting a book proved easier said than done when the whole room was lined with shelves, each filled with books.

Here was a book of heraldry, beautifully illustrated. There, an illuminated Bible, decorated with paintings of saints. There was a book containing drawings of flowers, with details of their separate parts listed. It was so heavy she could hardly lift it.

She took a leather-bound book from a shelf, placed it on a reading stand and opened it at a random page. A sonnet by William Shakespeare fell under her gaze.

> *That time of year thou mayst in me behold*
> *When yellow leaves, or none, or few, do hang*
> *Upon those boughs which shake against the cold –*

The door creaked open and Rebel gazed at her, eyebrows signalling, There was a pleased expression on his face, as if he'd been searching for her all morning and just been rewarded for his diligence.

She said, 'Pray, sir, do come and take a seat, for I'm performing a recitation of poetry and am in need of an audience.'

Rebel slid through the door and rolled over on his back with his legs in the air.

'I hope I do not always have that effect on my audience,' she said drily, 'for I'll not be able to complete my performance for laughing. Now, where had I got to. Ah yes—

> *Bare ruin'd choirs, where late the sweet birds sang.*
> *In me, thou see'st the twilight of such day*
> *As after sunset fadeth in the west*

Which by and by black night doth take away—

Tears filled her eyes. 'I will skip the next few lines, Rebel. It is too sad, and crying makes me look like a fright. I will end up with—'

Saville's deep voice interjected:

*'This thou perciev'st, which makes thy love more strong
To love that well which thou must leave ere long.'*

The door swung open to reveal him standing there. His face was grave. 'If you possess the doctoring skills you hinted at, I have need of you, now. My estate worker has sliced deeply into his thigh, the wound is gaping open and the blood cannot be staunched, except with a tourniquet.'

'I see,' she said calmly. 'The edges of the wound will need stitching together then. We will need a needle and some strong thread, and something to clean the wound with. Some brandy perhaps.'

'I thought it would save time if I brought him back with me. Jessie is fetching the medicinal chest.'

'I hope the lad can stand pain. If not, someone will need to hold him down.'

'I'll attend to it myself.'

His name was Clem, and he was lying on the kitchen table. Hardly more than a lad, his skin was pale and his eyes displayed the fright he felt. Swathed in a large apron Jessie had thought to tie around her, Graine smiled reassuringly at him. 'I'm going to stitch the edges of the wound together. Then you must rest until it heals.'

'Will it hurt?'

'Of course it will hurt,' Jessie said, 'but 'tis better than bleeding to death, ain't it? I don't know how you grew up to be such a gawkhammer, Clem Hastings.'

Graine smiled at the lad as she tucked her sleeves back from her wrists, all the time trying to recall the method of tying knots in flesh wounds. 'You must try to be brave. I've done this lots of times before.' *But only on a piece of meat*, for she'd not been allowed to do otherwise.

She took a deep breath and nodded to Saville, who placed his hands on the patient's knees to stop him jerking. All went smoothly, mainly because Clem fainted as soon as the needle pierced his skin.

She worked without hurry, her concentration absolute. When she finished she swabbed the gore from the patient's leg. Gradually, she loosened the tourniquet Saville had applied. When she was sure the bleeding was under control and her stitching was going to hold, she coated the wound with honey to aid healing, then bound it with clean strips of rags.

Clem woke to find himself still alive, and smiled gratefully at the girl who'd brought about this miracle. He was thinking how kind and pretty she was, and not at all grand, like the gentry was supposed to be.

'You mustn't use the leg until I have taken the stitches out in about two weeks' time,' Graine told him. 'The dressings must be changed every day until it is healed, so infection doesn't set in. An infusion of willow bark can be swallowed for the pain.'

'I can see to that, for it ain't work a lady should be doing.' Jessie said. 'He can stay in the servants' quarters for a few days. Now, remember your manners and say thank you to the master and Miss Adams, you ungrateful wretch. Your ma will be right shamed by you, else.'

Clem Hastings turned bright red and spluttered the appropriate words before he was borne away by a couple of servants. A bowl of water, soap and cloth was brought for Graine to wash and dry her hands, her apron was removed and she was inspected for stains. Jessie fussed around her proprietorially, straightening this and smoothing that, patting her hair into place.

At last she escaped from Jessie's clutches, assisted by Saville's hand tucked under her elbow. He was laughing as he bore her away. 'The servants have taken an uncommon liking to you.'

'I'm pleased.'

He brought them to a halt and turned to face her. His eyes searched her face and he half smiled as he took her hands in his. 'I feel the need to apologize. I was unforgivably rude when first you offered your services. Will you forgive me?'

'Of course.'

His expression became self-mocking. 'You're not going to use this moment of abasement to take me to task, then?'

'Why should I? It's not an easy thing to recognize a lapse in one's behaviour, then apologize for it. I accept that the apology was sincerely offered and we shall dwell no more on it.'

'You are a rare female, indeed.'

'Am I?' She was also a cheat and a liar. In the face of his honesty, she felt like the lowest of the low. She had placed herself in a fine trap. If she told Saville the truth now, he would lose credibility with his servants and would have no choice but to throw her out into the snow. There, she would die of hunger and cold. The alternative was a public trial and imprisonment. She must keep up this pretence, and she must wed the cold and stern John Lamartine. She would not feel so bad lying to a man who'd wanted Evelyn only for her fortune – a man she knew she'd never like as much as his cousin, who was now sheltering her under his roof.

But when all was said and done, who had more right to Evelyn's fortune than herself, a woman who shared her blood, if not her family name? Had Evelyn been able to predict the future, Graine knew her sister would have made provision for her in some way, for she was a charitable woman who would not have left her companion in need.

'Why so pensive?' Saville asked softly.

'I was thinking of someone.'

'Graine?'

He spoke her name so tenderly, like a caress. She gazed at him, thinking for a moment she'd been discovered.

'You wrote to me of your affection for her. The way you described her made me smile and I liked her straight away, without even seeing her.'

'Oh.' Graine looked into the blue of his eyes and swallowed. Why couldn't he see she was lying? Was she so good at it? It didn't feel so. 'What did I say about her? I forget.'

'You told me she was a lovable girl who was inexpertly trained and slightly pert. You indicated she was not pious enough to become a nun, and didn't like praying.'

Graine slowly expelled a breath. She didn't know whether to laugh or cry at Evelyn's assessment of her. She tried a smile, but still a tear rolled down her cheek. Saville scooped it up on his finger. 'I did not intend to make you sad. I'll send Jessie for your cloak and boots and I will take you to see my new foal. Perhaps you'd like to choose a name for her.'

The snow was slushy and wet underfoot, the air warmer than she'd expected, and the sky heavy. The stables smelled strongly, which Saville didn't seem to notice. It was a solid stone building with stalls on either side. Here were housed the two carriage horses, who now munched comfortably on mouthfuls of hay. They gazed at her incuriously, unaware they had nearly killed her in their effort to get back to that which was familiar to them.

Two plough horses loomed large over the rest of the inhabitants, their eyes soft brown, their tails flicking. There were a couple of geldings, both chestnuts, and a young, dark bay filly, who frisked her tail and turned soulful eyes her way. Graine fell in love with her straight away. In the next stall, a black mare nudged her foal to her teat. The mare snickered when they approached.

Saville spoke softly to the mare. The foal detached from its mother and turned to gaze at them. Her forelegs tapped a delicate dance on the ground. It was dark all over, velvety coated. 'She's beautiful, isn't she,' Saville whispered, a smile playing round his mouth.

'Yes, but so is this one,' she said, stroking the filly's soft muzzle.

'That's her sister, Ebony. They were sired by the same stallion.'

Just like Evelyn and herself. Her smile faded a little. 'She's beautiful. I love her.'

Saville turned to gaze at her, drawling, 'Yes . . . so do I.'

Disconcerted by the intense gaze, Graine's cheeks warmed. 'I'd better go back to the house,' she stammered. 'I'm not used to the cold.'

'You've not chosen a name for the foal yet.'

'Dancer, for she moves so delicately.'

His smile took her breath away. 'Dancer . . . yes, a good choice. Her sister Ebony will be my gift to you. She's nearly old enough to be trained for you to ride.'

'That's too generous a gift,' she protested, but weakly because she knew she'd never wanted to accept a gift so much. Her smile embraced the filly called Ebony. 'And I think I will need to be trained to ride her, for I'm inexperienced.'

He grinned at that, for he'd been assured she had a good seat on a horse. 'That's for me to decide. You only have to decide whether to accept my gift or not.'

'Of course I'll accept it. How could I not accept such a wonderful animal.' Her smile faded when she remembered why she was here. 'John Lamartine might not allow me to accept a gift of such magnitude.'

'Perhaps John will be given no say in the matter,' Saville said gently and, leaning forward, brushed his lips against her cheek.

4

He must stop giving in to the urge to kiss Eve's soft lips, Saville thought to himself a little later. In fact, he must stop thinking about her for at least one hour of the day, especially the next hour.

With difficulty, he dragged his mind back to the task at hand and, pulling on his boots, turned to Edmund Scanlon, his steward, and his father's steward before him. 'How many this time?'

'Seven, my lord. One of the women is with child.'

'How did they get here?'

'Josiah Harrison's fishing boat.'

Saville frowned. 'Risky at this time of year.'

'Not with Josiah at the tiller. He's an old sea dog who knows these waters like the back of his hand.'

Saville nodded. 'Josiah used to take me fishing as a child.'

Edmund's eyes centred on the past and a smile touched his mouth. 'He conspired with your father and Seth Adams to smuggle goods across the channel in their youth,' the older man said. 'Adventure-seeking rogues, the three of them. Most of the Lamartine men were, 'cepting your uncle, the bishop. Upright, he was, but with a mind of his own, I'll give him that. Nobody was going to lead him off the path of righteousness, and your cousin John takes after him.' Edmund slowly shook his head. 'Your great-grandfather took to the highway, as well as smuggling. It's said he only stole kisses from the ladies, but one or two of the merchant families bear a striking resemblance to the Lamartines.'

A grin licked at Saville's lips as his body servant placed a warm cloak about his shoulders. He'd heard all these tales before, but knew he would never tire of them, and offered the expected response. 'I must have proved to be a disappointment to my father, then.'

'Hardly, sir. He allus said you favoured your mother and would bring respectability to the family name. Had he lived to witness your courage, he would have been proud.'

Faintly surprised by the praise, Saville gazed at the man.

Edmund shrugged as he picked up a sack containing bread, boiled mutton, cheese and eggs. 'You've turned out to be more like him than he'd imagined. Only you're less reckless, and have a stronger instinct for self-preservation. Call it good sense if you like.'

'Thank you, Edmund.' Sometimes, Saville wished he could remember his mother, who'd perished in childbirth when he'd still been in his infancy. Vague memories of his father often snatched at him, especially here at Rushford. He'd been larger than life itself – a man who crackled with energy and possessed a deep, booming laugh.

Saville recalled worshipping the hero figure his father had represented. But although he'd felt loved in his presence, and proud to be worthy of his attention, he'd always felt diminished by him.

He couldn't remember his father dying, just of himself being put in a coach one day and conveyed to London to grow up with his cousin, John. His sister Charlotte, his senior by three years, was sent to be raised by their matriarchal grandmother. John's father had been a bishop, a heavy-handed man who'd used punishment as a preventative rather than a cure.

Over time, Saville had learned that his father had been shot to death by a Customs officer. His partner in crime, a man with the minor title of baronet and very little else, Seth Adams, had escaped to the West Indies with only the clothes he wore on his back. There, Evelyn's father had acquired the sugar plantation South Winds, on the turn of a card. He'd wed the sickly heiress to the neighbouring plantation and the pair had produced Evelyn. Seth had died in his prime, leaving behind a wealthy daughter and a consumptive wife who'd perished shortly afterwards.

When Saville had grown old enough to assume his rightful place, Josiah had contacted him. It had been he who'd suggested that the daughter of Seth Adams might make a suitable bride for one of the Lamartine cousins.

But not for himself. Saville possessed a natural repugnance for the way her wealth had been accumulated, even though he knew it was not her fault. Besides, he had no need to contract a marriage with a woman who had no breeding of note, sight unseen.

But Evelyn Adams had seemed a suitable match for John. Despite the differences in personality between John and himself, his cousin was a good and honest man. He was also Saville's heir, and more Lamartines needed to be produced, so the title and estate could continue safely into the future.

Now he'd fallen in love with the prospective bride himself. Although he found the situation ironic, it was also an unforeseen and unfortunate occurrence. The heavy sigh he gave brought a look of enquiry from his servant.

He shrugged and, dismissing the man, sent him back to his bed, for it was after midnight. He and Edmund went downstairs with hardly a sound, followed by Rebel who appeared from the direction of his guest's room. He had noticed the rug placed outside her door as she'd tried to make her doggy admirer and self-appointed guardian comfortable. Saville smiled to think Rebel guarded her so well. He'd sleep there himself if he was a dog.

It was numbingly cold outside. A bright moon sailed through a sky of ragged, silver-edged clouds. The earlier snowfall had melted away, as often happened with the first snow-fall. There was more to come. Saville could smell it in the air pushing at the cloud banks, which were massed along the line where sea and sky joined.

Beneath his feet, the ground was rimed with crunchy hoarfrost. Ahead, the lake was glazed with a thin layer of ice. In a few days the surface should be safe to walk on, if one stayed near to the edges.

They made their way across the grounds to a walled orchard. The trees, so fruitful in early autumn, were now grotesquely gnarled and twisted specimens. But the brown nubs of spring were held captive under the lichen embroidered bark, an indication of summer fecundity.

In the orchard garden stood a solid stone outbuilding used for storage. Its sturdy door was keyed open and it swung inward on oiled hinges at his touch.

An odour of apples greeted their nostrils as they passed storage racks, each individual fruit wrapped cosily in straw. Beyond the racks, a second door admitted entrance to an inner room, where drying herbs hung in bunches from hooks on the ceiling. Tools lined the walls.

Mice scattered in all directions when Saville pulled aside a bale of straw to reveal a trapdoor. Rebel snapped at them, but the number of squeaking grey bodies fleeing in all directions confused him, and all streaked safely into the rafters and racks.

Beneath the trapdoor, steps pitched steeply downwards into the darkness. Without hesitation Rebel headed down into the void. The two men followed, one after another, closing the trapdoor behind them.

At the bottom of the steps was a small chamber, twice the height of a man and four times his width. Here, the air was still and close, pressuring against the ears with the clamouring hush of bodily function and awareness. When one grew used to it, the occasional drip of water into a quiet pool intruded and the earth sighing as it shifted. Down here, one knew the earth was alive. Saville always said a short prayer that it would allow him safe passage.

Those unfamiliar with the network of caves and passages would have been confused and disorientated within a couple of minutes, for the tunnels twisted this way and that. But at some time in the distant past, someone had hammered spikes into the walls and slung a thick rope between them to form a crude handhold.

Stalactites hung in grotesque shapes, to explode into sparkling beauty as they were touched by the lantern glow. Short passages led into small chambers containing still, dark pools of water. They sloped gently, but ever downwards, cave after cave, one after another.

Saville and Edmund moved quickly. In a short while the air changed, becoming fresher as they neared the bottom, where they detected a faint lightening of the gloom up ahead. Saville gave a low whistle and Rebel came to his side.

The main, large chamber was a sheer and steep drop around the next bend. Descent could be achieved with the aid of a rope ladder, which could be pulled up afterwards if necessary. The level chamber could be overlooked through a series of spy holes, placed there by his adventurer forebears.

The sea never reached this far into the caves, not even during spring tides. It was a place of warmth and safety, the shore being half the distance of the passages they'd already negotiated from Rushford. Twisting passages branched off. Some led into small caves. Used for storage chambers in the past, now they stored human cargo and the goods necessary for their survival. A couple were conduits for trickling streams, which could suddenly flush water into the cavern when rainfall was heavy.

Through the spy holes Saville saw Josiah Harrison, his rascally, grey-bearded face illuminated by the light of several altar candles fixed to a sconce. Attempting to light a fire, some half-a-dozen dark-skinned and dejected looking people sat or slumped on boxes around him.

Rebel gave a low, grumbling growl as he picked up the strangers' scents. Saville muzzled his snout with his palm.

Josiah looked up from what he was doing and a grin split his chin from the rest of his weathered face. 'Come out, you young varmint. I may be old but I ain't deaf, not by a long chalk.'

Kicking the rope ladder over the side, the two men descended and indulged in an emotion charged moment or two of back-slapping.

Josiah had taken a risk. He must have slipped down the Bristol channel and around the coast in full view of the black-birders. Dubiously, Saville wondered if he'd be able to get back safely.

But Josiah Harrison had other plans. 'They're on to me, so this will be my last trip,' he stated. 'I've found mesself a widder-woman to wed, and we've bought ourselves a tavern overlooking the channel. It's called The Leaky Boat and you're welcome to drop in for an ale any time you're in Bristol.'

'What will you do with the *Nellie Jane*?'

'Weather will hold up for a day or two. I'll sail her back tomorrow, just as if I'd been out after a shoal. Then I'll set fire to her in sight of land and row myself back to shore in the dingy. *Nellie Jane* be weakened by worm, now, and would break up at the smell of a gale in the wind. Better she goes down dignified and with her secrets intact. Much better, especially since she's insured for more than she's worth.'

Saville grinned. 'Which, being a magistrate, is something I'd prefer not know about.'

'Aye, well.' Josiah gave a cackle of laughter. 'We've all got something to hide, I reckon. 'Sides, it's about time I got something for my sins, because be damned if I ever profited from them in the past. Nor did your pa, come to that.'

The fire crackled into flame, the smoke drifting up to the cavernous roof to disappear into fissures.

Saville spared a glance for the slaves, who had begun to talk amongst themselves. There were four men and two women, one of whom was heavily with child.

'We'll get this lot settled in, then you can come up to the house for the night. There's a lady I'd like you to meet on the morrow.'

'You've taken a wife,' Josiah grinned. 'Can't say I'm surprised. It was about time you found a lass to warm your bed, and fill that big, empty old house of your'n up with sprats.'

'It's Seth Adams's daughter.'

Josiah shook his head. 'You took Evelyn in, knowing her fortune was earned from the sweat of slavery? Why, you was adamant you wouldn't wed her when I first suggested it.'

'How her fortune was obtained isn't her fault.'

'All the same, I'm surprised. Seth Adams didn't give a damn for anyone's rights. He took what he wanted and discarded that which he didn't.'

'Including you,' Saville suggested wryly. 'He didn't give a damn about anyone except himself when it came to it.'

'True. And that included women. Seth was murdered about a year after he seduced Blanche Seaton, who was just out of school. He led her into a life of debauchery then discarded her. They think Blanche's brother did for him. Francis Seaton has the reputation of being a vicious bugger, especially where his slaves are concerned. I guess we'll never find out for sure if he killed him or not.'

Interested, Saville gazed at him. 'What happened to Blanche Seaton and the child?'

'Blanche took to the streets and died, choking on her own vomit in a back alley. The child he foisted on to her was disowned by the Seaton family and packed off to an orphanage.'

How sad, the situations sometimes forced on the innocents,

Saville thought. 'How do you know all this?'

Josiah shrugged. 'I was one of the executors of Seth's will. Conscience must have pricked him at the end, for he left his bastard a small legacy. Theo and I discussed it, then decided to use it to pay for her keep and education until she was old enough to join the order. To avoid complications, we thought it best to keep the child's existence a secret from Evelyn.'

'So, if Evelyn Adams had perished, there would have been another daughter to inherit?'

'I guess the girl would've been able to make a bid for Seth's fortune as long as she could've proved she was his natural daughter. But that's by the by now the pair of you are wed.'

Saville's lips tightened and he grunted, 'Miss Adams is my guest, not my wife. She's contracted to John.'

A puzzled look crossed Josiah's face. 'So what's she doing at Rushford?'

'Her ship foundered. The girl was put aboard another, which docked at Poole instead of London.'

Josiah nodded. 'As I recall, Evelyn did seem more like John's type. She would have been about ten years old the last time I set eyes on her. She was a plain, lonely child, badly educated and easy to overlook.'

Saville frowned. 'Both you and Theo Chambers were mistaken in your assessment of her. Evelyn has turned out to be lively and charming. As for her wit, there is nothing of the dullard in her that I can see. She is fair of face, a beauty, in fact.'

Josiah flicked him a look and grinned, as if he'd detected the admiration in his voice. Saville's shrug was one of studied nonchalance. 'At least, that is the way she struck me.'

'She be only a young'n when I met her. Could be she's blossomed since then,' he conceded. 'Theo was a miserable auld bugger, and too old and set in his bachelor ways to be her guardian. But he managed the estate well, was decent and scrupulously honest, and did his best for her. He had nowhere else to go and needed the wage.'

Josiah sighed and, turning away, called over one of the slaves to explain they could possibly be there for several weeks. He pointed out the chambers to be used for sleeping, then showed them the ones prone to flooding. He helped them with the distribution of utensils, bedding, warm clothes and dry food such as oats and barley flour. There was a good supply of driftwood, to provide fuel for the fire.

Saville added a firm warning that they should be careful not to be spotted, and to venture on the beach only at night when the tide was low. 'My steward or myself will call on you every day. I'll make arrangements for you to be conveyed to London as soon as possible. Or you can be shipped back home as soon as possible, if that's what you wish.'

Home was probably the same West African coast, where they would most likely fall prey to the same slave traders who grew fat by selling them into slavery in the first place. One of the slaves rolled his eyes in fear, thinking no doubt, of the stinking slave ships, on which hundreds of men were usually chained together for the duration of the voyage.

'Perhaps you'd prefer paid work in London. There are many homes with sympathetic masters who need house servants. They will pay a wage and treat you kindly.'

He grimaced as he examined the shackles hobbling a slave's ankles and nodded to Edmund, who handed him a mallet and chisel. It took but a few moment to break the chains.

The pregnant girl's eyes filled with tears when she found she could move unfettered. The men stood huddled together, tall and quiet, full of tension, their faces closed and secretive.

Saville thought the girl looked far too young to be a mother and addressed her directly. 'When is your infant due?'

The girl shrugged and hung her head.

The other female was a little older. Tall and defiant looking, with high, refined cheekbones and a proud look, her skin was the colour of honey and she spoke with the sing-song patois peculiar to West Indian slaves. 'Amy don't know. The ship's officers used her for sport on the journey.' She spat into the dust at Saville's feet. 'Crew took their turn at her just before we reached shore, then the captain sold her to a bawdy house. Amy don't talk much no more.'

'And you?'

She shrugged and said nothing, but her eyes burned with the shame and anger she felt, for her story would have been similar.

Her defiance was apparent in every gesture, in her voice and in the depths of her eyes. She would have been trouble, and as a result would have been badly treated. However, she'd learned to survive, and Saville would wager that under her coarse linen gown was a back scarred by the lash.

Saville glanced at Josiah, feeling just as angry as the woman appeared to be. 'What would you estimate the younger girl's age to be?'

'No more'n fourteen I shouldn't wonder,' Josiah murmured. 'One of William Younger's ships brought the pair of them here.'

Edmund would write down the runaways' stories. A time would come when their tales of hardship would reach the right ears, people who would bring the lucrative practice of trading in slave labour to a halt. The slave depositions would be preserved, and might be useful evidence in the future. Unfortunately, it would not be in his lifetime, but Saville liked to think his children or grandchildren might embrace the cause. If he ever had any he'd teach them compassion and respect for the unfortunate people in the world.

His lips were pursed as they retraced their steps back through the tunnels. He was thinking furiously. Amy was little more than a child herself. She couldn't have ended up in worse hands. William Younger was a notorious black-birder who sailed out of Bristol. The man had a son born in his image. Brought up to a life at sea, he'd been hardened to it. Both men had been up before him at the assizes for drunk and disorderly behaviour. So far, Saville had been lenient with them, but now he had a score to settle on Amy's behalf. Score it he would, however long it took him.

Seth Adams came into his mind, and the young girl he'd ruined. What had been her name. Blanche Seaton? He wondered if the unwanted child she'd given birth to was happy being a nun. He knew Josiah would have done what he'd thought best, but did the girl yearn for a life different to that which she'd been born into? Did she ever wonder who her parents were?

He shrugged. How would Evelyn react if she learned she had a sister in a religious order? Would she hasten back to Antigua to find her? But then, the girl had been brought up on a plantation, the success of which had been earned at the expense of others.

Conditioned to the hardships experienced by others on her behalf, he doubted if she would care about some half-sister, when the West Indies was awash with the bastards of slave owners.

He liked to think she would. He didn't want to believe his Eve was that hardened to the plight of others less fortunate than herself. A smile inched across his face when he realized he was thinking of her again. He'd determined to cast her from his mind for an hour – an hour which had obviously passed.

Alerted by the bark of the dog, Graine left the warmth of her bed to gaze out of the window. The night was bright with moonlight, brittle with ice. It glittered on bare bough and leaf, a reminder of the cold outside. Rebel was bounding about outside, in the way he did when he was seeking attention. His breath steamed with each bark.

Pulling the shawl around her shoulders, she was wondering how he'd managed to get himself locked out of the house, when three men on foot came into view. A gruff command and the dog was called to heel by the tallest of the three. Tail whipping back and forth, he thrust his nose into his master's hand to be fondled.

Two of the dark outlines she knew. The third was a stranger to her. They had come from the direction of the orchard, which lay beyond the trees. What had they been doing abroad at this time of night?

Not that it was any of her business, of course, but still, she was curious. She made no move to conceal herself. As the men came closer, Saville glanced up at her window. Bathed in moonlight as she was, he couldn't fail to see her and she saw no reason to hide from view. Although his face was in shadow, his eyes were a faint glitter as her own clung to them for the moment or two it took him to move out of her sight.

Scrambling back into bed she waited to hear Rebel come scrabbling up the corridor to take up his post outside her door. It was reassuring to know he was there. Not that he'd be much use if she needed help; he was much too friendly.

She smiled when she heard his claws patter-patter over the floorboards. There was a whine against the keyhole, a hopeful scratch at the door, then he subsided with a martyred-sounding grumble. She grinned and closed her eyes.

The next morning she said to Jessie, 'Your master keeps late hours.'

For some reason a chill entered the servant's voice. 'What master does or doesn't do be his concern, missy.'

Dismayed, Graine stared at her. 'Goodness, Jessie, there's no need to assume such affront. I wasn't prying, just making comment.'

'Sometimes it's best to keep comments like that to yourself, lest folks read something more into them.' Jessie went bustling about, taking clothes from the press, tut-tutting before busily shaking the creases out of them and folding them away again, all of which was quite unnecessary.

Graine's eyes narrowed. Jessie's reaction to an entirely innocent comment was interesting. Was there more to Saville's activities than first met the eye? Pulling on a soft pink jacket she began to lace it over her gown of deep rose brocade.

'Let me do that, you've got it all twisted,' Jessie scolded, and snatched the lacing from her fingers.

'Don't be cross with me, Jessie,' she said and, leaning forward, gently kissed the woman's cheek. 'I've said nothing to you that I wouldn't repeat directly to the earl.'

A tear came to the woman's eyes as she deftly arranged the laces. 'Mayhap I spoke out too hasty, like. I'm sorry, Miss Adams. Master wouldn't like me speaking sharp to a guest in his home.'

'Then we'll forget it happened.' She picked up a brooch decorated with tiny pearls from a tray. 'Would this look pretty pinned on my cap?'

'Bless you, no, 'tis a lover's knot and meant to be pinned over the heart if your interest in the suitor who presented it is returned.'

'But I'm promised to the earl's cousin.'

'The master knows that, don't he? Like as not he don't realize the significance of the brooch, him never having been a serious courtin' man, as yet. And it's not as if the earl would deliberately set his cap at you. He probably thought it a pretty piece to set amongst the female fripperies.'

Chagrined by the reminder that she was not of good enough stock for the earl to be bothered with, she snapped, 'I don't suppose he would set his cap at me when I'm a nobody, and therefore beneath his notice. And even if I liked him enough to offer him encouragement, which I don't, for he's too fond of his own way, I'm promised to his cousin, John Lamartine, and must honour the agreement brokered between us. Damn it, Jessie, his cousin John sounds like the most unlikely partner for me.'

Jessie gave a bit of a grin and an infuriating, 'Hmmm.' Drawing a filmy fichu around her shoulders she secured it with the brooch in the middle of her bosom. 'Looks real pretty, it do. Now off you go for your breakfast, and take your shawl. It be right cold out there in the corridors. There's some more snow on the way, I shouldn't wonder.'

Graine was glad of the shawl. The cold had given her hunger a sharp edge, and the smell of food made her hasten her steps towards the dining hall.

Saville was already there, awaiting her presence before he broke his own fast. A glance at the little french clock on the mantel showed she was late. She dropped a curtsy and said mischievously, 'I apologize for my lateness. I was woken from my slumber by a barking dog and its master, and overslept as a result.'

'Did it take you long to return to your dreaming, my lady of the moonlight?'

'Only as long as it took Rebel to return to sentry duty.'

'He's taken a great liking to you.' His warm smile drew an instant one from herself. 'We have a guest for breakfast; Captain Josiah Harrison. No doubt you will remember him.'

Graine's heart sank into her slippers. Was her deceit to be uncovered so soon? She wanted to run from the room and hide, but was paralysed by her own fear. How she kept her smile in place she didn't know as she said ineffectually, 'I must return to my chamber, for I've forgotten my handkerchief.'

'You shall have mine,' he said, pressing a monogrammed square of white linen into her hand. He gazed at the brooch and his smile became more intimate. 'A pretty thing. It's a love knot.'

She lowered her eyes from his. 'Does that have some significance?'

'My father gave it to my mamma when he courted her.'

She felt like striking him. How insensitive to give a woman a love token which signified another couple's affection. She bit down on a hasty retort. 'Then I'll make sure I look after it, for it must hold precious memories for you. I thought it would look well with this gown.'

'It fades to insignificance when measured against the beauty of the wearer. You, my dearest Eve, are a gem beyond compare.'

His compliment made her tremble, for soon he would despise her. She placed her hand on his arm. ' Saville, there's something I wish say to you.'

Her hand was turned over for her palm to receive the most tender of kisses. 'And I have something to tell you. A most surprising thing has occurred—'

He gave her a rueful look and dropped her hand when the door was opened. 'Ah, Josiah. You slept well, I hope.'

With great trepidation, Graine turned to see a man who was a stranger to her. Of medium height and getting on in years, he was grey-bearded and of a weathered appearance. Bright blue eyes surveyed her with a certain amount of uncertainty.

Expecting to be denounced, Graine held her breath until her heart thumped a protest against her bodice.

Then the uncertainty was replaced by a wide smile as the man growled softly, 'I'll be damned. When you was ten you were the living image of your mamma, God rest her soul. Be danged if you ain't Seth's daughter through and through, now. You've grown up to be a beauty, Evelyn.'

The relief she felt, rendered her weak at the knees. What name had Saville called him by?

'I can see you don't remember auld Josiah Harrison. Can't say I blames you. You was only a sprat the last time we met and all fixed to go to a neighbour's picnic. Could hardly sit still with the excitement of it.'

On the occasions Graine had managed to escape from the attention of the ever vigilant nuns, Graine had observed many a plantation picnic. She'd enviously watched the plantation owners' children from the safety of the sugar canes as they enjoyed pony rides, songs and games. Possibly, Evelyn had been amongst them.

The adults had gazed indolently and fondly on their offspring from under sun shades. They'd talked of some far off land they called home, and drank rum distilled from the sugar they grew. Later in the day, the men would wrestle and the women laugh and flirt.

She'd envied the freedom those children had enjoyed, and envied more the love and attention lavished on them by their parents.

It was from such picnics that marriages were arranged so estates would merge. Although she had been invited and tolerated, poor Evelyn had not figured in such grand plans for the future. Her father was too notorious, she too lumpy and dull.

Leaving the past behind she pulled a smile to her face. 'Of course I remember you, Captain Harrison. How nice to see you again.' She allowed him the liberty of a brief hug. His beard smelled of salt and tobacco.

'What was it you wanted to tell me?' Saville asked her, when they seated themselves at the table.

Graine searched her mind for something plausible, but could pluck nothing of significance from it. It seemed as if she was sinking deeper and deeper into this pit of lies she'd created for herself, but she couldn't think of any way to stop herself. She snatched at the first thought that entered into her head.

'I just wanted to thank you for your hospitality, I believe.'

His eyes engaged hers and his smile robbed her of breath. 'My dearest Evelyn. I'm not being hospitable, I'm being totally selfish. I'm savouring every precious moment of your company, so don't be at all surprised if I keep you here for ever.'

Captain Harrison gave a chuckle when she blushed. 'Now there's a pretty thought. Your father's blood runs in your veins, after all.'

'Be assured that it does,' Saville murmured.

Drowning in his deep regard, Graine could only wish such a thing was possible.

5

Graine knew she'd had a narrow escape. Thank God Josiah Harrison had allowed his memory to absorb her as Evelyn. She thought long and deeply about the position she'd dared to assume. She must be on her guard, for all she knew of Evelyn's life was the four years she'd spent as her companion.

But Saville and John Lamartine knew even less, she told herself. Evelyn had never met either of them, and her own unease stemmed from nothing but guilt. It wasn't her fault that Evelyn had perished, and it wasn't as if she was a complete stranger. She and Evelyn had been bonded by strong blood ties through their father. But without her mother's letter, Graine knew she had no way of proving the relationship existed between them and the letter was now at the bottom of the Atlantic ocean.

She quaked at her own temerity. If the fraud was discovered the penalty would be severe. She'd probably be sent to prison.

Josiah Harrison had come as a complete shock to her. Evelyn had rarely spoken of her childhood or parentage. That struck Graine as slightly odd now, and she knew she must prepare herself for more surprises of that nature. Luckily, the captain had grasped on the similarity between them instead of the differences, and those were inherited from Seth Adams.

Fetching her cloak, she headed downstairs. Saville and Josiah were sequestered in the library. The low rumble of their voices reached her as she walked past. She was halfway down the stairs when Rebel gave a short, sharp yelp. The library door opened and the dog bounded past her, waiting at the bottom of the stairs with an expectant look on his face.

She glanced up to discover Saville looking over the balustrade at the top. He smiled. 'It seems as though you have a companion on your walk. Don't go too far, or stay out too long. You're not used to the cold weather.'

His concern for her welfare was touching. 'I'll never acclimatize myself if you do not allow me to venture out.'

'Proceed with all caution then.' But the warning was said with laughter in his voice.

'Of what should I beware? Is there a pack of hungry wolves waiting in the bushes to devour me?'

'Perhaps one wolf, alone in his wintery den.'

'And is that wolf dangerous, or does he possess a growl more ferocious than his bite?'

Saville's answer was to bound down the stairs. Reaching out, he gently arranged the cowl over her head. 'How exquisite you look framed all in fur.'

She laughed, charmed by his smile and the warmth in the depths of his eyes. 'Thank you, my lord.'

They stared at each other for a few moments, then Saville brushed a thumb gently over her lips. 'It would not do for me to kiss you now.'

Graine thought it would do very nicely to be kissed by him now. 'Why not?' she said lightly. 'Is there a special time set aside for kissing in England?'

He chuckled, but the expression in his eyes was watchful. 'You're my guest, and at the moment are promised to my cousin. Do not tempt me.'

Was she being a temptress? Her smile faded and she nodded as she confessed, 'I'd quite forgotten about John Lamartine.'

'Had you? But that's why you journeyed here. To find a husband.'

'To wed the husband you found for me,' she corrected. 'What if you've made a mistake, Saville Lamartine? Must I spend the rest of my life paying for it?'

'I admit it's a possibility, but still, we must treat John's petition with some respect. He has feelings too, and pride is one of them. It would not do to make him a laughing stock.' His hands were still cradling the sides of her face, his body a scant few inches from hers. The warmth of him pulsated against her, making her glow. All she had to do was lean forward.

His hands dropped to his side and he took a step back, putting distance between them. 'I have sent a message to John. Amongst other things, I've informed him of your safe arrival and advised him that we'll be travelling to London in the spring. In the meantime, we must observe convention.'

'Yes, we must, but I'm unfamiliar with this convention of yours,' she said, her heart thumping painfully now she knew she'd fallen in love with him. But he was an earl, and too far above her for serious consideration. She had no intention of following in her mother's footsteps and taking a lover, but she was dismayed to discover she'd inherited her traits. Was this tumultuous clamour of feeling she had for this man as entirely carnal and wicked as it felt?

Oh yes, she knew all about her mother. Hadn't the abbess lectured her on the perils of giving into temptation before she'd left the orphanage?

'My dear,' Mother Beatrice had pontificated, 'you're unfortunate in having inherited bad blood from both your parents. Your father was dishonourable; your mother was a temptress who lured men from the path of righteousness. Such a pity you lack the disposition and fortitude for a life of prayer and self-sacrifice. We must be grateful that Miss Adams is in need of a companion. You must atone for your parents' sins by working hard and casting out lustful thoughts. Keep yourself pure in body and soul and seek solace in prayer as you've been taught. Then you will come to no harm.'

She'd not known who her parents were then, only of their sinful natures. The mother superior had taken it upon herself to inform her of her maternal side. Her mother's family had owned one of the larger plantations. Once again, the mother superior impressed on her young mind the need to curb any sinful impulses inherited from her.

'Blanche Seaton brought shame on her family and was cast out, disinherited and disowned. The Seatons want nothing to do with you, the child planted by sin in her womb.'

They'd given her a bundle of her mother's possessions when she'd left. There was a gold brooch fashioned in the shape of a heart. Inside, it contained her mother's initials, BS. There was also the word, 'love'. Both were picked out in tiny rubies, and concealed inside the heart by a lid which slid to one side. Inside an inscribed Bible, the cover of which was decorated by an ivory cross, she found the letter from her mother to Seth Adams.

The heavy burden of her sinful parentage had lightened as soon as she'd left the orphanage to be taken under Evelyn's wing. Her sister, grateful for her company and pleased she had someone to whom she could relate at a personal level, had been so kind and loving. They'd soon become firm friends.

From Evelyn, Graine had learned how to behave in company, though it was hard to remain demure in the company of men whose thoughts were all too apparent in their manner towards her. It had seemed to her that Blanche Seaton's daughter was fair game for adventurers. But Evelyn had guarded her well.

But the sinful thoughts which came to haunt Graine now were not so easily set aside. Saville Lamartine had come to represent protection, love and fulfilment to her, which was something she'd had precious little of in her life.

Her eyes glinted with tears as she turned and walked away from him. How unfortunate to fall in love with a man she could never wed. She could only hope that John Lamartine was a little like his cousin. Perhaps then, she could fall in love with him as well.

Outside the protection of his home, the air was colder than she imagined it could be. Heavy clouds had moved in from the sea. The ground underfoot crunched as her boots flattened the thick frost. Although her toes soon became numb, inside her muff, her hands were as cosy as a pair of rabbits in a burrow.

Without thinking, she followed after Rebel through the copse of trees and skirted the lake, now glassy with thin ice. Through a densely wooded copse and out the other side, she arrived at a walled-in orchard. There was no gate. Rebel disappeared through the gap and rushed across to the other side, where he pushed open the door to an outbuilding with his nose, and disappeared inside.

Graine followed, inhaling the smell of apples appreciatively. She could hear Rebel whining and scrabbling at the floor. When she called him he took no notice. The inner room was full of drying herbs and cobwebs. Rebel was attempting to dig up the floor in a corner.

Grabbing the dog by the collar she said sternly, 'Behave yourself, there's nothing in here but herbs and mice.' She dragged the reluctant dog out through the building, closing the door firmly behind her.

She'd taken only a few steps when she heard it open again. She turned to see Edmund Scanlon come out of the building and lock it carefully behind him. Appearing agitated, he jumped when he turned to find her there, saying sharply, 'What're you doing here, Miss Adams?'

'I'm out walking and Rebel went into the outbuilding. I didn't see you in there when I went in to get him.'

His eyes hooded over a little. 'Aye, most likely I was behind one of the racks. I'll escort you back to the house, miss.'

It wasn't likely at all, but Graine didn't bother to argue with him. It was entirely possible there was another room she'd missed, she thought as she turned back towards the copse.

She had a job to keep up with Edmund Scanlon on the way through the trees. 'How deep is the lake,' she said, almost out of breath.

'The edges are shallow for several yards, then it shelves deeply and goes underground before being filtered into the sea. Trout and eels can be fished for, but if we get too many they're netted and sent off to market.' He threw her a warning glance. 'Best not to swim in it.'

She gave a breathless giggle. 'I'm hardly likely to do that in this weather, Mr Scanlon. Besides, the earl said it's not usual for ladies to swim in this country. I shall do as I please, of course.'

He managed a distracted smile. 'Until he decrees otherwise, though the earl is the first to set aside convention in the privacy of his own estate, when the occasion arises.'

Her chest had begun to ache from constant inhalation of cold air, her side had cramped into a painful stitch. 'I'm afraid I must slow down, Mr Scanlon. It's obvious you have urgent business to attend to, so please go on ahead. I'll be quite all right when I've rested.'

Immediately, he halted. 'My apologies Miss Adams. I'd overlooked the fact that you couldn't match my stride. I must admit, I'm in rather a hurry.'

'Then go. I have Rebel to escort me in.' Indeed she had, for the hound had brought her a stick to throw. Seated directly in her path, his tail creating a storm of its own, the hound looked alert, expectant and extremely pleased with himself.

She watched the steward lope off, covering the ground at twice the pace he'd been going before. Goodness, he *was* in a hurry. But not from something in the outbuilding. Apples going mouldy wouldn't send him scurrying with such urgency. If she hadn't been feeling the cold so keenly she would have gone back to investigate the outbuilding further. Some other time, perhaps.

She picked up the stick and threw it, laughing when Rebel overshot it and did a clumsy somersault before coming back for it.

Thus, they made there way back to the house, dog and woman a companionable pair.

Despite the seriousness of the situation, Saville couldn't stop himself from smiling at the sight of them coming across the garden. 'She saw us come back last night, Edmund. I don't want her getting lost down there when she figures things out and her curiosity gets the better of her.'

Edmund grinned to himself. 'I like the girl. She's got spirit.'

Saville's grin was wider, and smug with the comfort of his discovery as he thought. *I love her.* He looked at his companions to make sure he hadn't said it out loud.

Josiah gave a cackle of laughter. 'She's got a strong streak of her pa in her, that's for sure. She's a different girl altogether than the one I remember. The change has surprised me. Now, what are we going to do about the runaway slaves? They won't get far in *Nellie Jane.*'

Saville had turned away to watch Evelyn again. 'There's nothing we can do. Those slaves have headed straight into the snow clouds. They'll lose all direction when it snows. If they don't freeze to death or get caught first, the boat will probably sink under them and they'll drown.'

Josiah joined him at the window. 'I'll have to get back to Bristol overland. Can you lend me a horse?'

'I'll supply you with one if you like. He'll be my retirement gift for you. He's a little past his prime, but is sound of wind still, and sturdy enough to pull a cart if needed. I'll provide you with papers to say you bought the beast, which will also give you an alibi if you need one. All I ask of you is that you treat him kindly.' He patted Josiah on the back. 'Enjoy your retirement, Josiah. I hope we'll meet again some day.'

'What about the female slaves?'

'At least the women had the sense to stay put. I'll give it a day or two in case someone comes looking for them, then bring them up to the house. Room can be made in the servants' quarters and they can learn domestic skills. It will help them find employment later on. I don't know what we shall do with the infant when it comes, though.'

Evelyn disappeared from his view. He heard her footsteps patter-patter up the stairs, and rang for a maid. 'Take Miss Adams some hot chocolate to warm her, then ask her to join us in the drawing-room. Tell her that Captain Harrison is about to depart and wishes to say goodbye to her. Also, tell Cook to supply a flask of brandy and a food hamper for Captain Harrison's journey in some saddle-bags.'

Edmund headed for the door. 'I'll get the sale papers ready for Brutus and see that he's saddled.'

The departure was executed with a minimum of delay, for Josiah had a long journey before him with the weather closing in.

As he turned on to the road, Josiah was pleased to have discovered that Evelyn Adams was looking so well. He'd always felt sorry for her, but now his mind had been put at rest.

And it wasn't until he was well into the journey that he found the purse of golden guineas amongst his belongings. There was a note from the earl. '*Many thanks, Josiah. This is compensation for the boat.*' Saville's father would never have been so generous.

He grinned to himself as his mind turned to Evelyn Adams. It was apparent that Saville was besotted with the girl. 'Now there's a situation,' he said to his new acquisition. 'Will the earl let her go to John Lamartine, or will he keep her for himself.'

At that moment, Saville was on his knees in front of his guest.

Blushing prettily, she was protesting. 'You're an earl, you cannot act as a foot warmer. It's not dignified.'

'Then I'll be undignified.' She had exquisitely shaped feet encased in pink, silk stockings. They fitted snugly into his hands as he gently chafed them back to warmth.

'If I'd known you were going to do this, I wouldn't have mentioned that my feet were frozen,' she said crossly.

'Then your toes would have turned black and dropped off.'

She shuddered, her eyes rounding at the thought. 'Is that what happens?'

'If they're frozen long enough.' He glanced up, caught her glance and grinned. 'I will not allow it to happen to you. Did you enjoy your walk?'

'It was interesting. I ran into your steward.'

Saville's eyes sharpened, but he said nothing, just waited for her to continue.

'He came from an outbuilding in the orchard. It was odd. I didn't see him when I went in.'

'I expect he was behind the apple racks.'

'That's what he said.' Her eyes assumed a slightly wounded expression, as if she knew she was being lied to. 'He's a tall man: I would have seen him.'

'Perhaps he was bending.' He kissed her foot and placed it back into its slipper, hating lying to her. So he must tell her the truth, he could do no less. Ruefully, he smiled. 'To be truthful, the building conceals a trapdoor which leads to a network of tunnels and caves. We have runaway slaves concealed in them.'

Instantly, her eyes lightened with amusement and she began to laugh. 'You must not expect me to believe a magistrate would indulge in such a practice.'

He grinned, mostly because her laughter was infectious, but partly because he hadn't been believed. 'You have odd ideas. I'm a man first and a magistrate second. Sometimes, I'm a foot warmer.' He kissed the toes of her second foot and put it away. 'Is that better?'

'They're glowing.'

'You are glowing. You warm my senses.'

'And you're too extravagant in your praise of me.' Tears glistened in her eyes and she whispered, 'I'm unused to the attention of men. I don't know how to respond to it, or to you.'

'Evelyn—'

'No, let me finish please, Saville. Sometimes you draw me to you, then you push me away. I have . . . *feelings*. I beg you, please stop playing games with my heart, for I'm afraid I am weak, and might allow you to break it in two.'

Face grave, he gazed into her eyes and murmured, 'My dearest heart.'

Though longing to declare his love for her, Saville knew that he couldn't, in all fairness, encourage such feelings in her until he received an answer to the missive he'd sent to John. She was too unworldly. A girl. Not the mature woman he'd been expecting.

He stood and, drawing on his will-power, bowed almost formally and turned away from her. 'It will be as you request, Miss Adams. I shall observe all propriety. You must excuse me now. I have to go through the accounts with my clerk.'

Rebel stood, gazing from one to the other. When Saville moved towards the door he flopped back down before the comfort of the fire.

After he'd gone, the drawing-room seemed to assume a chill. Yet the fire still burned brightly. For a long while Graine sat and stared into the flames, listening to the clock tick. She felt quite bereft, and totally alone.

Ignoring the accounts, Saville fetched his warmest cloak and headed for the stables to saddle his gelding. The foal, Dancer, was nuzzling at her mother's teat. The mare gazed at him through half hooded and contented eyes.

He stroked her soft muzzle, sighed, and whispered, 'Life is complicated for us human beings. I would have Evelyn gazing at me with the same love and trust as I see in your eyes. I have a desire to see my infant sons and daughters nuzzling against her breast, and would guard and cherish them whilst my body drew breath.'

Talking to a horse! Was he turning into the village idiot? He gazed around him, grinning to himself as he hoped his foolishness hadn't been observed. The stable lad was at the far end of the stable, tugging at the girth on his saddle to tighten it.

The air outside was bitter. Saville took the cliff path, cantering the animal at an easy pace. He was thinking of Evelyn Adams suckling his son. More pleasurable at this point was the means of getting that infant on her. She was at the peak of innocent desirability, with enough awareness to enjoy her conquering. Her mouth was a crushed peach for him to sip the juice from. Her thrusting little breasts would snuggle into his palms, the nubs tilted up towards his teasing tongue. When his body began to react to his thoughts, he sighed and deliberately directed his mind to something safer but less pleasurable.

The dense cloud bank had moved closer. There was no sign of Josiah Harrison's fishing boat. It was as if the sea had swallowed it up. He pitied the slaves who had commandeered it. It was bad enough that they'd been torn from their families and homes, without perishing in such a manner. He'd compensated Josiah for its loss, for the man had been useful in his endeavours over several years and Saville had no intention of encouraging a fraudulent insurance claim.

He reined his horse in on the top of a hill where he could look down over his estate. Over to his far left was the village of Rushford. It was well kept, each labourer's cottage allocated a yard for chickens and a pig. Behind the village there was an acre of communal ground for growing seasonal vegetables.

Every year, his labourers were given a pair of stout boots and two yards of drabbet cloth with which to make working smocks. A pound each of flour, barley and oats, and a sack of coal each week in the winter, supplemented their wages. He knew each villager by name and kept a jeroboam of metheglin on tap at the local inn, so they could celebrate special occasions such as the birth of a new baby. The spiced mead was a popular drink on such occasions.

On the advice of the local doctor, he'd had the cesspits moved so they were away from the village and below the water well. Since then, the health of the villagers had improved.

Saville treated his labourers well compared to other estates. As a result, they worked hard and caused no trouble. He rewarded them with a feast in the grounds of Rushford House after the harvest was gathered.

He grinned at a recollection of past disorderly gatherings. Men and women, both drank the local scrumpy then, and danced to a couple of fiddlers hired for the occasion. Usually, they slept where they fell and staggered home with sore heads the next morning. Invariably, come June, a fine crop of infants were birthed and put to the breast.

He turned and headed back to the house, giving his mount its head. It was blowing hard when he reached the stable. Steam rose from its flanks. He called for the stable boy, who came running.

'Mr Scanlon bin lookin' for you, milord. He said to tell thee he'll be in his office.'

'Thanks, Rob. Make sure the horse is rubbed down well and cooled slowly.'

Edmund looked relieved when he joined him in his office. 'The slave girl is about to drop her brat. She's scared stiff and needs help, the other one doesn't know what to do.'

'What about Jessie?'

Edmund shook his head. 'Says she knows nothing about birthing babies, and nothing would make her go down those tunnels even if she did.'

'Well, we can't call in the new doctor, not until he's settled in and I can sound him out. It will give the game away.' Evelyn came into his mind. She'd tended his coach-driver's arm most competently, and had sewed up Clem's leg without the flicker of an eyelid.

He found her in the library, her nose buried in a book of heraldry. She looked up, gave him a remote smile, then avoiding his eyes, returned to her reading. He'd hurt her feelings and, understandably, she was annoyed with him.

He remembered Theodore Chambers listing one of her feminine attributes as a love of embroidery and tapestry. Not that the man's judgement was faultless, he noticed. Still, he had the feeling there was a tapestry frame, some canvas and a box of silk thread stored away in a cupboard. He would ask Jessie to find them so she would have something to employ her fingers as well as her mind.

Evelyn wasn't reading now, simply staring at the page. The atmosphere was strained and she quivered with the tension his presence had generated in her. What a sensitive little creature she was.

He crossed to where she stood and took the book from her lap. 'Do you know how to deliver babies?'

She looked up then, her tawny eyes wide with surprise. 'Why yes . . . I have assisted women to give birth.'

He grinned, and only just managed to abstain from giving her a relieved hug. 'Remember those slaves I told you about? One of them is giving birth. She's very young, and frightened. Can you help?'

'You were telling the truth, then?'

Must she sound so astonished? He nodded. 'I always tell the truth. It compensates for the dishonesty of my forebears.'

She smiled a little at that, and rose, her face composed. 'I'll fetch my cloak and boots.'

'I'll send Jessie with some breeches and hose to wear under your cloak. It will be easier to navigate the tunnels.'

He was pleased she remained incurious, for he had no inclination to answer questions about his activities. Either she accepted the situation as nothing out of the ordinary, or she didn't.

Now it was her turn to nod. 'Do we have any shawls, or a crib for the infant.'

'There are blankets to wrap the child in and there's a large basket to use as a crib. Edmund will go on ahead with them.'

The breeches and hose must have survived Saville's youth, Graine thought, a few minutes later as she pulled them on, for they wouldn't have fit him now. They didn't fit her either. She had to tie them to her waist with a scarf to keep them from falling down.

'Fancy dressing you like a boy? Of all the crazy ideas he comes up with,' Jessie grumbled.

'He said it would make it easier for me to navigate the tunnels.'

Jessie shuddered. 'Mayhap, but you wouldn't catch me going into the tunnels. One of the servants was lost down there in the late earl's time. His body was never found. Another was drowned when he was carried off by water flooding through the tunnels.'

Graine shivered. 'I'm sure the earl wouldn't take me down there if he didn't think it was safe.'

Jessie's eyes speculated on her face for a moment. 'There's that, of course. He wouldn't let you come to no harm. Anyone can see he's fair mazed by you.'

Warmth trickled into her cheeks. 'I'm sure that's not true, Jessie.'

Jessie cackled. 'Sure is as sure ain't and truth is in the eye of the beholder. The pair of you be moonstruck, for all the world to see. He be on his best behaviour, but a body can see the wolf prowling in him. And you be on your'n, like as not, but blushing like a rose every time he sets his eyes on you with that man look of his. You'll be mistress of this place afore too long. Just you wait and see.'

'Nonsense. The Earl of Sedgley is too far above me in social standing.'

'Yon earl doesn't set much stock on such notions.'

'I'm promised to his cousin,' she reminded Jessie.

'Aye, there's that, but a girl like you has too much spirit for John Lamartine. I reckons the master knows that. Much as he's trying to behave like a gentleman, deep down he's taken your measure. I reckon he'll keep you for hisself.'

Graine recalled the routing Saville had served her with earlier in the day. Her ears burned at the thought that she'd more or less indicated she was his for the asking. If he had cared for her he'd have taken advantage of that moment.

'You're wrong, and I might have something to say about that,' she said more briskly than she felt. 'He's being charming to me because I'm his guest. He's being a perfect gentleman in fact.'

'Earl's got his father's hot blood in him,' Jessie said with a snort. 'He could charm the Devil out of Hell if'n he put his mind to the task. He's all man when he needs to be, and you'd do well to keep that in mind.'

'You're being too familiar about your master,' she told her.

Jessie grinned as she removed Graine's cap to sprinkle a few drops of perfume against her scalp. The length of her hair was fashioned into a loose braid down her back and tied with a pink ribbon. 'There, my dear. You look right pretty, despite the breeches.'

Which are light and unrestricting, affording me a certain amount of freedom, Graine thought, as she ran down the stairs to where Saville was waiting for her.

Excitement grew in her as they made their way to the outbuilding in the orchard. Saville locked the door behind them. When he threw open a trapdoor in the herb room she bit her lip at the sight of the steps leading down into darkness.

Saville picked up the lantern, which had been left burning for them. 'There are twenty two steps and they are almost vertical. I'll go down first and wait for you at the bottom. You'll be able to see the glow from the lantern.'

'Promise you'll wait.'

He grazed his knuckles gently against her cheek and smiled. 'Don't go faint-hearted on me, my Eve. I'm depending on you.' With that, he swung himself into the hole and disappeared.

She followed more slowly, her heart thumping painfully against her ribs, for she liked not the feeling of enclosure that the quietness of the earth pressing around her brought. She emerged into a tiny chamber and gave a small glad cry to see Saville so soon again.

'Good girl,' he said, the planes of his face brought into relief by the lantern so he looked slightly devilish.

They were standing so close that their bodies were almost touching. Indeed, the place was so small she began to feel entombed. 'I like it not down here, Saville,' she admitted, her voice trembling with the panic she was trying to hold in check.

'And must never come down here without me. Come, take my hand. The caves will get bigger as we proceed, and you will feel less closed in.'

But sometimes, the caves grew smaller and the tunnels darker. Often though, the roof was so far above that the light couldn't penetrate. In places the walls twinkled and shone with such beauty she just wanted to stop and stare in wonder at this world hidden beneath the ground. Often, water dripped, or puddles appeared in front of them. Dark tunnels went off in every direction, so she marvelled that Saville knew where to go – until she noticed a rope slung from spikes which served as a handrail.

After a while the air gradually became fresher. Now and again, a low keening noise reached her ears. Saville stopped to listen and she bumped into the back of him. 'What's that noise?' she said.

He turned in the confined space, his eyes glittering. 'The mother is very young and is probably frightened of what's ahead.'

72

Without her skirt as a barrier, Graine found herself more in contact with his body than was good for her. Or him, it seemed, for he took a hasty half step backwards. His head hit the roof and he cursed when he dropped the lantern to the floor. He apologized immediately, his voice filled with laughter.

But Graine couldn't laugh. Darkness had crowded in on her. She gave a mew of fright as she reached out for him. Immediately, she was drawn into his arms and against his body. 'Don't be frightened. We have only a short way to go now.'

She clung to him, her heart racing, gasping for breath as his nearness overwhelmed her.

Saville's mouth was soft against her ear as he murmured, 'Alas, I'm only a man. I cannot have my senses filled so completely with you and remain strong in my resolve. Forgive me for this liberty.' When his mouth captured hers in a kiss of prolonged tenderness, her knees lost all strength. She sagged against him, savouring the caress of his mouth against hers whilst he took his measure of the pleasure she afforded him. His breath was a husky intake when he let her go. 'I have tasted of your sweetness and will be forever your slave.'

'Saville, this cannot be, I'm promised to John,' she murmured, weakly.

'Perhaps we could lie to my cousin, tell him that you're not Evelyn Adams, after all. We could tell him Evelyn Adams was drowned in the ocean and you set yourself in her place.'

In the darkness, Graine's eyes widened, and her body jerked with the shock she felt. 'We cannot.'

He gave a bitter laugh. 'Of course we cannot. Not only would it be dishonest, it would appear as if we'd conspired to steal your estate in the first place.'

Which was exactly what she had done, if a person could conspire with oneself.

As another frightened groan reached their ears she sucked in a deep breath. They must put all that was personal between them aside. 'We must make all haste.'

'Of course we must. Forgive me, Eve, your presence makes me forget all else. Here, take my hand.'

She wished she could undo the past as they moved cautiously

forward in the dark. Tears of remorse filled her eyes. If he ever discovered the truth of his words, he'd despise her now.

6

The spaciousness of the cavern stunned Graine. Easily the size of the entrance hall of Rushford House, it was furnished with a table and stools. Lanterns provided lighting and a kettle hung steaming from a tripod over a fire.

A rope ladder with wooden rungs hung over the edge of the sheer drop, and the reason for her breeches became clear when Saville said, 'Can you manage to descend by yourself? I'll be at the bottom to catch you if you fall.'

Her mouth dried a little as she nodded. 'I'll try.'

Being unhampered by a skirt made negotiating the ladder easier, but it had a tendency to twist sideways until she learned to co-ordinate her hand and feet movements. She was nervous of heights and completed the exercise slowly, her heart banging against her ribs. Saville lifted her the last few rungs and she clung to the safety of him for a moment, conscious of the warmth of his hands spanning her waist as he whispered, 'Brave girl.'

Edmund Scanlon grinned at the sight of her in breeches, then nodded towards a side chamber. 'The mother is in there.'

The young slave girl had been made private by a screen covered in pleated linen placed at the entrance. Her eyes were dull, her face expressed fear. Mixed with the fright was an oddly resigned expression, as if she'd reconciled herself to the inevitable. Huddled on a straw palliasse, she hugged her stomach with her hands and moaned softly. The other woman squatted on her haunches by the mattress. She moved aside when Graine approached. Both females were mulattos, the younger one, several generations so, for her African blood was well diluted.

The older woman began to croon a dirge low in her throat. Her glance slid assessingly over Saville and her eyes hooded as she offered him a smile. Graine tried to ignore the dart of jealously she felt when Saville grinned. This one knew her way around men. There were women like her plying their trade all over the world. She had probably been born on a plantation, become the mistress of the owner and had been sold on when he'd tired of her. It was a common enough story.

Graine asked Saville to leave, then examined the girl. Amy's contractions were evenly spaced, the infant in the correct position for birth. Her hips were a little on the narrow side, for she had not fully developed as a woman yet. An ear against the girl's distended stomach revealed the infant had a strong heartbeat. Graine smiled reassuringly at her and took her hand. 'Try to relax. I'll stay with you and help you through it.'

The dull resignation remained in her eyes. Now and again she gave a low, animal-sounding moan, which made the hairs of Graine's neck rise.

The older woman stopped crooning to gaze at her. 'Amy don't want no baby to look after.'

'I know, but she has no choice.'

Graine became the subject of an inscrutable look. 'Amy has a choice. She consulted with the obeah man. She and the baby will die, you wait'n see. Her ma will come to take her from her pain and misery. That's what she wants.' The woman closed her eyes and started singing under her breath again.

Her words brought Graine's anger flaming to the surface. 'I've heard that slave obeah nonsense before. It's superstition. Now stop that noise and make yourself useful. Fetch me some warm water in a bowl so I can sponge Amy down and make her comfortable.'

'I'm a myla woman. The girl's taught in the way of the obeah, so I can do nothing to help her, and neither can you.' The woman blazed a challenge into her eyes for a moment then, when Graine's eyes didn't flinch from hers, it faded.

'Do as I ask, please. At least she can be made comfortable.'

The slave shrugged as she rose to her feet and pulled the screen aside. Gently, she said, 'What the men do to Amy isn't my fault, missy, and it won't be my singing that kills her. The obeah man has gone with the boat and will never return. Seems to me that Amy don't intend to live, and there's nothing you or I can do about it. She'll be better off if she doesn't, for now she's broken in, there can only be more of the same for her. D'you think she wants that? Would you?'

Graine didn't want to think about what had happened to this child, or speculate on her future. She'd grown up surrounded by the oppression of slavery all around her. Amy's was a common enough story. She'd helped the nuns nurse the victims of the slave trade. She'd watched them become crippled, or die, from tumours and infection caused by the tropical yaws, diseased lungs, over-work, or simply the lack of will to continue living. From self-preservation she'd become detached from their hardship, for it was something she was powerless to prevent. Field slaves rarely lived more than a few years in the West Indies. These two would be trained house slaves who were no longer needed and so had been traded on. The obeah and myla woman would have been troublemakers who had unsettled the others.

She sighed, more in anger than in sorrow. She thought she'd left this cruelty behind her, but had forgotten the many British ship owners amongst the opportunists exploiting the weak. Her father had been one of those opportunists. Now she would use the profit he made to buy herself a husband and respectability in this cold land. That, because she needed to live herself, and to respect the memory of her dead sister, whose only dream had been to have a family of her own.

'Tsk!' She made an exclamation of annoyance at the thought of subjecting herself to a man she didn't love in pursuit of such a reward, when it was obvious from her own circumstance that men were so careless about their offspring.

She set about washing Amy, who was surrounded by the musky odour of fear. She talked soothingly to her in the slave patois she'd been banned from using by the nuns, but knew the girl closed her ears and mind to her words.

'The language is guttural to the ear and vulgar sounding. You will communicate, always using properly enunciated King's English,' the mother superior had ordered when she'd first heard her use it. The second time she'd heard her she'd suffered several strokes of a cane across her buttocks. The only time she'd used it after that was when she was sure she wasn't being overheard, which wasn't often.

Just the thought of having someone at hand to look after her seemed to calm Amy, for when the next contraction rippled over her distended stomach she made hardly a sound.

Graine smiled encouragingly at her, refusing to pander to the girl's superstitious belief in the coming of death. Nature would soon prove her wrong. 'It will take a little while yet. Soon, the pains will come one on top of the other and there will be strong pressure. When that happens, the infant will shortly be born. You might like to crouch, or position yourself on your hands and knees when that time comes. It will make delivery of your child easier.'

Indeed, the birth did seem to go well. The infant was a boy. Pale-skinned and of a good size, despite that, when he slid from Amy's body it was obvious he was stillborn. Trying to massage some life into him did no good at all. When Graine gazed with despair at the limp little body, a lump came to her throat. Amy didn't even look at her child. She just turned her face towards the wall.

Wrapping the child tightly in a cloth with the afterbirth, Graine set it to one side and cleaned Amy up. The girl lay quietly, staring upwards.

Graine went out to talk to Saville. 'The child didn't survive.'

He nodded. 'Edmund will dispose of the body.'

She placed a hand on his arm as he turned away. 'The girl is too heartsick over what has happened to her. She longs for her mother and home and has lost the will to live. I believe she has conspired with the obeah man to bring about her own death. If so, she will not survive the night.'

His eyes mirrored the pain she already felt. 'Damn superstition. Is there anything we can do?'

Graine shook her head.

He called to Sheba, who sauntered over, her eyes lowered in submission.

'Can anything be done to help the girl?'

'No, mastah. Obeah is all powerful.'

'Then we'll wait.'

It didn't take long. Amy died with quiet dignity, her last breath a barely heard sigh.

Tears trickled down Graine's cheeks as Saville and Edmund sewed Amy and her infant in a piece of canvas.

'What are you going to do with her body?'

'The soil in the churchyard is too frozen to dig a grave in. We'll weigh it down and bury her at sea. There's a deep spot—'

She muffled her ears with her hands, wishing she hadn't been so curious. She didn't want to imagine Amy and her baby in their watery grave. Graine didn't ask him anything more. Accepting as he was of the situation, she sensed a deep anger in him over the incident. She guessed he felt as impotent as herself over the slave issue. 'What will happen to Sheba?'

'Don't you worry none about Sheba, missy,' the woman said calmly. 'Sheba can take care of herself.'

'But you can't stay here alone.'

The woman shrugged. 'This is a good place. The spirits won't frighten Sheba. They be her friends.'

So they left the woman there. Graine spent a restless night thinking of her all alone in that place.

Over breakfast the next morning Saville told her that Sheba had gone.

Eyes widening she stared at him. 'Gone where?'

'Who knows? She must have left shortly after we got back to the house last night because there's been a light fall of snow and when we looked for her, we found no footprints.' He crossed to where she stood. 'Try not to worry about her. The woman's a survivor and she's taken a warm blanket and some food. Is there anything you want to ask me about last night?'

She gently touched his cheek. 'You're doing what you can, and I know exactly how you feel for I feel the same. I admire you for it, Saville and will not abuse your trust. One day, when enough men of compassion and conscience band together, they will put a stop to the trafficking in human misery.'

'I'm surprised you have such a sympathetic attitude when you were raised on a sugar plantation.'

Although she was no longer hungry, Graine avoided his eyes and helped herself to a wafer of bread, spreading it with honey to give

herself time to think. 'I didn't have much to do with the plantation. It was run by an overseer. Theodore Chambers considered
the plantation to be an unhealthy environment for a young girl
lacking parents. We lived in a house in St John's.'

The honey ran from the edge of the bread and across her finger.
She licked it clean with one sweep of her tongue, then remembered a real lady would resist such impulses. Sliding a glance at
Saville she caught the amused look in his eyes and giggled. 'I
suppose you're used to females who are prickly with manners, like
those hedgehogs I saw in a book in your library.'

Laughter grumbled out of him. 'I can't recall ever setting eyes
on a woman such as that. I should imagine everyone relaxes when
out of the public eye. I'm jealous because your tongue is so very
long, and it got to the honey before mine did.'

Her face warmed at the intimacy of his answer. Another stream
of honey ran down her finger and into her palm. Placing the bread
on her plate she was about to pick up her napkin when Saville took
her hand in his. His tongue slid moistly against her palm, sending
a delicious quiver of goosebumps skittering up her arm to her
shoulder. She couldn't prevent the small sigh of pleasure escaping
her mouth before she snatched her hand away.

He gazed at her, his eyes an ocean of provocation. 'I should not
have done that, for it makes me less than a gentleman. My only
consolation, I'll have the sweet taste of your palm on my tongue
through all eternity.'

A sudden and tumultuous pounding from the hallway below,
brought Rebel to the alert. The dog gave a deep, baying bark and
his hackles ridged magnificently along his back. Saville drew in a
deep breath and muttered, 'What in hell's name is going on?'

They found out a few seconds later when a manservant handed
Saville a card. His gaze skimmed over it and his eyes hardened as
he gritted out, 'Captain William Younger has honoured us with a
visit. I wonder why?'

'Who's Captain William Younger?'

'A ship owner and black-birder. He sails out of Bristol.' He sent
the servant to fetch Edmund Scanlon.

Clearly, they heard a woman cry out in pain.

'That sounded like Sheba,' Graine breathed.

Saville placed a restraining hand on her arm when she would have run from the room. 'Be careful not to give anything away. We don't know what she's told him.' They went down together, united as one.

There were two of them, cloaked and booted against the harsh weather. An aura of cold surrounded them. Obviously father and son, they were dark-eyed, dark-haired and hard-faced.

Sheba was huddled on the floor, her chest heaving as she struggled to regain her breath. Blood trickled from her nose and she was bruised about the face. Her skirt was torn and bloodied and her shoes had fallen off. Her feet were shredded. There was a rope around her waist, the other end was attached to the older man, who jerked her cruelly to her feet.

'The slave says she belong here, my lord. I can't remember you having a slave in your household, so thought I'd better check her papers.'

Graine stepped forward and, with as much indignation as she felt, said, 'That is my slave, sir. Who are you to demand to see her papers?'

Rebel slid in front of her and sat at her feet.

The man inclined his head. 'I'm Captain William Younger, this is my son Thomas. I'm certain this girl is one of several slaves who absconded from my care a few days ago. And who may you be?'

Saville scowled at him. 'This is my guest, Miss Adams, lately of Antigua.'

'Ah . . . Seth Adams's daughter.'

'You knew him?' she said with some astonishment, for it seemed to her that everyone but herself had known her father.

'Oh aye. I had a few dealings with him in his time. Knew you when you was a young-un, too.' He stepped forward, his glance darting over her face. Rebel gave an impressive warning growl with teeth bared and the whites of his eyes showing. The man stepped back again hastily, saying ungraciously, 'Your looks have improved some.'

'You are being impertinent, sir.'

'My pardon.' He eyed the gold brooch pinned to her bodice and his eyelids hooded over slightly. 'I guess you don't remember me.'

'Should I?' she said flatly.

81

Thomas Younger, who was openly admiring her, laughed. 'Pa said you sang and danced for him. I guess a girl who growed up on a sugar plantation had to make her own amusements.'

'One needs to do that anywhere.'

He inclined his head. 'I dropped in to pay my respects when you turned seventeen. Your guardian said you were attending a neighbour's wedding. It was a well-run plantation, as I recall. It must have brought in a pretty penny when you sold it. I put in a bid that day for you, seeing as nobody had seen fit to make you a wife. I guess your guardian didn't think I was a good enough a catch. Likely, he wanted a peer of the realm.'

'That's entirely probable, since he had to be careful of adventurers who were after my fortune,' she said hastily, as Saville's breath hissed angrily in his throat. She drew in a deep breath and resisted the urge to say anything more to the man's surly statement. 'Will you release my servant, please, Captain Younger. It looks as if she's been dragged behind your horse.'

Rebel was still giving prolonged warning rumbles. She placed her hand over the end of his snout and he licked her palm. The dog was like the master, she thought, a bubble of laughter growing inside her.

'She needed a bit of discipline. Making them run soon takes the spark out of them,' he growled. 'She had a blanket and food on her. Stole them and was on the run, no doubt.'

'Not at all,' Saville interjected smoothly. 'She was taking them to a sick woman in the village at my request.'

Sheba's head jerked slightly when Edmund Scanlon came into the room and nodded to the assembled company. Rebel's tail lashed back and forth, whipping against her skirt and causing a draught. Graine's hand closed around it, stilling its motion, though the tension in it was hard to contain.

'Do you have papers for the slave, Miss Adams?' William Younger's eyes darkened when the dog snarled at the sound of his voice.

'Don't be a fool, man,' Saville blistered. 'All her chattels were lost when her ship foundered. She was lucky to escape with her life. You'll just have to accept my word for my guest's integrity, Younger. It should be good enough for you.'

'Of course, my lord.'

Sheba scrambled to her side when she was released. The dog pushed between them.

Feigning annoyance, Graine slapped the woman's face lightly. 'You stupid girl. How do you expect to become a lady's maid when you can't carry out the simplest task properly? Go and clean yourself up before I decide to give you another whipping.'

'Yes, mistress.' Bursting into tears, Sheba scuttled painfully up the stairs.

Graine managed a shrug for the two men and, even whilst knowing she hadn't fooled them for a minute, said with a smile, 'I'm sorry she caused you so much trouble. The girl has yet to learn her place.'

Saville was not so gracious. He dismissed the two men with a curt, 'You look as if you could do with some breakfast. My steward will take you to the servants' quarters.'

William Younger's face flushed at the put down. 'Thank you, my lord, but it won't be necessary. We'll be staying at the inn for a couple of days to see if we can catch the other runaways.'

'If they absconded from Bristol, I see no reason why they should be in the area.'

'According to Josiah Harrison, they stole his boat from the wharf and, as there's rumours of some caves on your estate, they might be holed up for the winter. Would you mind if we inspected them?'

Saville's eyes narrowed. 'Are you referring to the caves my father and grandfather used for their smuggling ventures?'

'There have been rumours of illegal use in the past.'

Saville sighed. 'It's not rumour: it's a fact. As you will, then. Edmund, take Captain Younger and his son to inspect the caves my father used in his smuggling days, then escort them to the road.'

Edmund smiled slightly. 'Yes, my lord. This way, gentlemen. The tide is on the ebb and by the time we get there the entrance should be accessible.'

As the men moved out of sight, she whispered, 'What if they find the bedding?'

'Don't worry. There's nothing to find. There's more than one set of caves.' He gazed at her thoughtfully. 'You think quickly.'

83

She could have looked into his eyes all day long. 'And I must go and find Sheba and tend to her. Will you mind if she stays?'

'Not if that's what she wants. I'll find room for her in the servants' quarters. Tell her she can travel safely with us to London in the spring, where I can find her a situation.'

Graine's face fell. 'I hope spring never comes. I'm not looking forward to going to London.'

His face softened. 'Do you like it here so much?'

She nodded and fondled the dog's head. 'The countryside has a pleasant feel to it, now I'm becoming acclimatized to the cold. The servants are happy and willing, which says a lot for you as their employer.'

'But we must still go to London. The arrangement brokered between yourself and my cousin must be discussed, and a closure satisfying to all those involved, reached.'

'Yes. I suppose it must,' she said dully, for she'd now reached an unwelcome conclusion. Saville might indulge in a mild dalliance with her for the sake of his amusement, but he had no intention of allowing any serious involvement to grow between them. He was a man of honour. She was destined to be the wife of his cousin, and John Lamartine was the person he'd deliver her to. Covered with shame, because her own naïveté was suddenly exposed to her, she turned and walked away from him, tears stinging her eyes.

Saville went into the drawing-room and threw himself in a chair after she left. The wounded expression in her eyes had been almost too hard to bear. He couldn't declare himself to her, as he so badly wanted to do. The speed with which his feelings for her had developed astounded him. He knew she returned them, her every feeling was expressed on her face, her unsureness, her hopes and her fears. Yet she had guts and courage.

Lazily, he recalled the way she'd negotiated the rope ladder, clinging on for dear life as she tried to keep it from twisting. Her long, slim legs had been outlined against her breeches and her buttocks had been taut against the material. He smiled with the pleasure she'd unknowingly afforded him.

The situation had to be explained to John before he acted, though. Even though John might not be happy about it, he wouldn't hold Evelyn to the contract if he thought Saville's affections were involved. He knew he wouldn't let her go, anyway. Telling John would simply be a courtesy.

Sheba had been flayed, her back bore bloody whip marks. Her legs were grazed from top to bottom and embedded with splinters and gravel from where she'd been dragged. Some of the nails were torn from her toes. Her feet were puffy and bruised.

Jessie gave a shocked murmur. 'Those men need a good flogging.'

'Get out the bath tub and fill it please, Jessie. Add some lavender oil. We'll have to soak those cuts to clean out the dirt, then pick out every bit of gravel. If we coat her legs with honey and bind them with linen strips for a couple of days it will help them to heal and prevent infection and scarring.'

After Jessie had left she turned to Sheba. 'Why did you run off? We would have looked after you.'

The woman murmured, 'I was scared you were like the others, mistress.'

'Well, we're not. The earl said you can stay in the servants' quarters, and we'll take you to London when we visit in the spring. He'll find a safe place for you.'

Sheba took her hand and there was an absence of bravado in her voice now. 'I cannot be servant to another, again. You give Sheba a piece of paper setting her free. I'll rent myself a house and sell charms and love potions to the society women.'

'Your freedom is not mine to give you.'

Angrily, she said, 'Yes it is, mistress. For it's the Adams plantation I worked on, as did my mother and my grandmother before me. Since the age of two, when I was taken from my mother's side to pick up leaves from the yard, to the day I worked in the field gangs, I've been your slave. Then my breasts grew and I was noticed by the overseer. Being his mistress weren't no better than being a slave. He sold me on, but I was *your* slave, not his.'

Graine sighed. Although she felt sorry for Sheba's plight, to tell the truth, she'd like to be rid of the woman right now. Sheba had an unsettling effect on her, and her conscience was being unfairly pricked. 'Where will you find the money to rent a house and start your business?'

Sheba's eyes became opaque. 'From you, mistress. You're kind, and you remind me of Seth Adams's white bastard, the one who worked for the nuns. I heard tell that she drowned.' Sheba smiled when Graine started. 'I don't need much, and you will never hear from me again, unless you need me. Then I will know, and I will come.'

Shaken to the core, Graine thought, the woman's no fool. She nodded. 'I'll ask the earl to advise me about setting you free. He's a magistrate.'

Sheba kissed her hand. 'Thank you. I won't wait until spring though, but will go as soon as I can. Watch out for the seafarer father and son, missy. They're bad, hard men, especially the father. Although they fear the earl, they're no respecter of women and will not forget you crossed them.' She fell quiet when a troop of servants came in carrying a tub and hot water.

They soon had Sheba cleaned up. When her wounds had been tended to, warm clothes were found and she was borne away to a servant's room to rest.

'Cook's going to put a chair in the kitchen so she can watch the comings and goings. When she feels better she can help with clearing things away,' Jessie said. 'I'll keep an eye on her now. It's only scratches and stuff, and it ain't fitting for you tend to her. After all, she be in no danger.'

'Jessie,' she said with a smile, 'you need not imagine I'm a frail English lady. I've been brought up to be useful, and I'm used to unpleasant tasks.'

'You be the earl's own guest, but I'll call you if you be needed,' Jessie said firmly.

Later, Graine went in search of Saville and told him of what had been done. He smiled with approval at her, but it changed to a frown when she said, 'Sheba used to work on the Adams plantation and has asked for a paper giving her freedom.'

He crossed to the fireplace. 'I have a feeling that William Younger has her papers. He'll come back with them.'

'I doubt if. . . ?' She bit down on her lip. 'I can't remember signing her away.'

'Theodore Chambers would have signed the bill of sale, I expect.'

'Then I'll have to forge some papers. Do you know what they look like?'

A sign of exasperation reached her ears. 'I cannot conspire with you to commit a crime. There's really no need to forge anything. Whilst she remains in England, Sheba is a free citizen.'

'Then how can a set of false papers be classed as a crime. She's asked me for money to establish herself in business in London.'

His eyes sharpened. 'What exactly is the nature of this business?'

'Oh, telling fortunes and selling love potions and charms to the gullible.'

He chuckled. 'She's so beautiful and exotic that she'll draw men and women alike. This money: has she any intention of repaying it?'

'I thought it should be a gift,' she said, the guilt she felt over lying to him apparent in her voice. 'After all, she's worked on the South Winds plantation for nothing since she was quite small.'

'Which, no doubt, she reminded you of, hmmm?'

She laughed. 'She did, but I would have done the same.'

'As well as being exquisite, she's clever,' he mused.

Graine said crossly, for a quiver of jealously had lodged in her heart, 'It sounds as though you admire her.'

He smiled at her. 'A man always admires a woman of beauty. I like her spirit. She has courage and determination, and has remained strong despite her trials.' He crossed to the bureau and unlocked a drawer. Drawing forth a wad of papers he shuffled through them and murmured, 'Sometimes, certain documents fall into my hands. I rarely find them useful, but on this occasion . . .' He removed a paper and handed it to her.

Her brow creased in puzzlement. 'Why, this is a bill of freedom. It's signed by Theodore Chambers and back-dated two years. It's for one Eliza Jones, lately of South Winds sugar plantation in Antigua.'

'So it is.' A leather purse was placed on top of it. 'Weather permitting, Edmund will be visiting his mother in Poole next month. Sheba can join a group of travelling players who winter there. Her fortune telling will be an asset to them.'

The papers and escape route had been prepared in advance.

Saville's involvement was deeper than he let on, and he'd outguessed her. She grinned at him widely. 'Thank you, Saville.'

He ran a finger down her nose, growling, 'You mustn't thank me, but accept my apologies, instead. I shouldn't have involved you in the first place, for I regret placing you in a position where you were forced to be untruthful.'

'There's no need to apologize, Saville. I'm enjoying the adventure of it.'

He laughed. 'Be off with you. I have book work to do and you're a distraction.'

'I'm going to visit Ebony.'

He nodded. 'Keep Rebel with you.'

'He'll probably persuade me to take him for a walk.'

'Wear a warm cloak and boots, then,' he said, advice which was followed by his final instruction, 'And don't stay out too long.'

'Yes, my lord,' she muttered as she left.

A smile crept across Saville's face when the door closed and he blew a kiss after her.

7

The sky was low and dense, the earth so meltingly white that the sharp edges of the landscape had been blunted. Where earth and sky met on the horizon they merged into one. The sky was low, pressing down on her, so Graine felt as if she was layered between that and the earth.

Dancer greeted her with a flirt of eyelashes and a delicate pawing of her forelegs, as if she was showing off her dancing skills. Her mother watched carefully when Graine edged closer to stroke the filly's velvety muzzle, moving between them when she felt enough attention had been afforded her offspring.

Thrusting her hand into her pocket, she brought out a twist of paper containing some sugar and, sprinkling some on her hand, held it out to the mare. The mare's nostrils twitched as she slowly stretched out her neck to whuffle at her palm.

'You're a lovely creature,' Graine told her with a smile. 'However, I haven't come to visit you. I'm here to make Ebony's acquaintance. Your master said I should visit her often, so she will become familiar with my smell. Though how I shall learn to ride her if I'm married to John Lamartine and living in London, I do not know.'

From the adjoining stall, Ebony gave an impatient and proprietorial snort.

Concealed in the trees beyond the lake, William Younger watched through his spyglass as Graine emerged from the stables.

'She has the dog with her,' he muttered. 'But she's unaccompanied and on foot.'

Thomas drew a pistol from under his coat.

William gave him a scathing look. 'Don't be a fool. One shot will bring the entire household down on us.' He took a bosun's whistle from his jacket. 'I'll draw off the dog, whilst you talk to the girl. Don't be too rough. Just put the fear of God into her.'

'She's a pretty little piece of baggage,' Thomas said almost absently.

'Aye. She could make a man forget he had a wife waiting at home.'

Thomas grinned. 'It wouldn't be the first time you'd forgotten that, you horny old goat.'

William gave a soft cackle. 'What your stepmother doesn't know about, doesn't bother her. Besides, when a man's been at sea for a spell, it's only natural to sail his ship into the first port available to him.'

'Not in this weather, it ain't. Besides, yon maid's little harbour hasn't opened for business yet, if you ask me. She looks as innocent as a lamb.'

'Looks are deceiving. She might still be intact, but she's a devious little minx. You can break her in when she's used to dancing to our tune.' He moved towards his horse. 'Make sure she understands what's at stake, Tom. I'll meet you over by the road.'

Thomas trained the spyglass on the girl again and swore. Snow had begun to drift from the sky. She was three-quarters of the way around the lake now. She stopped to gaze up at the sky, then poking out her tongue allowed a few flakes to settle on it and melt.

Only a child would do that, he thought sourly. Then he remembered her pert breasts and tiny waist. He grinned. He liked them small and feisty.

He looked for the dog. It was a little way behind her, lifting its leg at every clump of grass. Tom heard his father signal to the animal. The whistle sounded like a bird's fluting call. The dog stopped, and his ears pricked up. Suddenly, he headed off across the ice on the lake.

The girl didn't even notice. Head down, she kept on coming towards him.

Reaching up, he plucked an icicle from a branch. He sucked it for a few moments, so the vapour of his breath disappeared and wouldn't give him away.

Graine's feet were beginning to numb. She pulled her cloak around her, holding it across her chest. I'll walk to the trees then turn back, she told herself, gazing around her for Rebel. She could hear him barking, somewhere in the distance.

The snowflakes had become larger, the fall heavier. Behind her, her footprints were almost obliterated. The snow settled on her shoulders in a powdery layer and muffled the sound of the barking, so she couldn't quite tell from which direction the noise was coming.

Reaching the trees, she was about to call Rebel to her side when an arm snaked around her from behind.

Graine's yelp of fright was muffled by the hand clamped over her mouth. An automatic jerk of her leg and her heel connected with a knee. A grunt was followed by a curse. Her teeth sank into the hand and the next moment she was sent sprawling on to her back. A foot came down on her waist. It heeled her into the earth and forced most of the breath from her body so she couldn't shout for Rebel.

'You,' she squeaked at the sight of Thomas Younger. 'What do you think you're doing?'

He smiled. 'Not what I'd like to do, believe me.' The foot was removed. He pulled her upright and back against his body. His fingers exerted pressure against her windpipe. 'Don't try and call the dog else I'll break your devious little neck.'

Over the thump of her own heart Graine could hear his as it pulsed against her back. She wished it would stop. Why had he lain in wait for her? What did he want?

'The earl will kill you when he hears of this,' she threatened.

His voice was a sibilant hiss against her ear. 'Only if he believes you. And once he discovers what a lying little bitch you are, he ain't likely to, is he?'

'I don't know what you mean?'

'You know exactly what I mean.' His free hand found its way under her cloak to close around the brooch at her bosom. There was a ripping sound as he tore it away. He held it before her eyes.

91

'Seth Adams gave this to his whore, Blanche Seaton. My father was with him when he had it made. You're not Evelyn Adams: you're Blanche Seaton's bastard.'

Graine muttered, 'The Seaton girl was my companion. She lent me the brooch. I was wearing it when the ship went down.'

His laughter was loathsome. 'You're a liar, girl. My father visited Evelyn Adams to try and arrange a marriage between us. You're not the girl he saw.'

'You cannot prove that.'

'We wouldn't have to. The rumour would be enough for you to be sent packing.'

'Then I'd have nothing and wouldn't be worth pursuing, would I?' The snowfall was heavier now, Graine could almost hear its soft thud as it quickly coated the ground.

'Now you're thinking.'

She was ahead of him, but her relaxed muscles did nothing to give her away. 'How much do you want?'

His hold on her slackened. 'One thousand guineas to start with, and one thousand the next time I'm in port.'

She laughed. 'You're crazy. The earl has control of my money.'

'If he hears you're impersonating Evelyn Adams you won't have any money for him to control. He'll throw you out into the snow.'

The horse behind him stamped and whickered under the shelter of a pine tree as she glared at him. 'He won't believe you, and if I tell him you tried to blackmail me he'll slit your poxy throat.'

'But he'll investigate the claim and discover the truth, for he's a magistrate, and that's his nature. You'll be charged and sent to gaol.'

Glaring at him she held out her hand and ordered, 'Give me back my brooch or it's you who'll be imprisoned.'

He dangled it between his thumb and forefinger. 'I'll exchange it for the first payment. I'll be back in two weeks for it.' His dark eyes scrutinized her face and his breath quickened. 'By hell and fury, why am I bothering? I'll just take you for a wife, that way I can have you as well.'

'I wouldn't wed a scab like you if you were the last man left alive,' she yelled, hoping the dog would hear her.

'I could arrange it so you'd have to wed me. Let's see if you take after the whore who gave birth to you.' Suddenly she was pulled against him, his mouth crushed against hers. Skin crawling she sank her teeth into his lip in a savage bite. Blood spurted, her brooch fell into the snow and was trodden underfoot. He tripped backwards over a log and sprawled on his back.

She laughed, but not for long, for he sprang to his feet.

'You bitch! Now you're going to get what you're asking for.'

When he slapped her she staggered backwards with the force of it. Instead of trying to run, she sprang back at him, her fingers hooked to rake down his face. The unexpected attack threw him off guard and the punch he threw, which would have caused her considerable damage had it landed, went wide.

Before he could retaliate, she turned and ran, screaming out for Rebel. Relief filled her when she heard him give an answering bark. As she fled, Thomas Younger cried out with pain. She glanced back to see Rebel upon him in a flurry of ferocious snarls and bites that sent the man staggering backwards. William Younger ran from the trees and levelled his pistol at the dog.

Saville stared through the window at the whirling snowfall. He could barely see the trees at the other side of the lake. The visibility was closing in faster than he'd expected. He was worried. as he gazed at the clock ticking on the mantel. He turned to Jessie.

'How long has Miss Adams been gone?'

'Two hours, my lord. She said she was going round the lake.'

'And Rebel?'

'He hasn't returned either.'

Saville experienced a moment of relief. At least the dog was still with her. Would she have gone into the caves? No, the door to the outbuilding was locked now, and she was aware of the dangers. Evelyn might be unworldly for her age, but she certainly wasn't stupid, however much to the contrary her guardian had suggested.

There was the sound of a muffled shot. Poachers? No, they'd know better than try for game in this weather. A feeling of unease settled on him.

'I'd better go and look for her. If the snowfall thickens she might become lost and disorientated. Tell Jackson to bring me my cloak and hat please, Jessie.'

Not long after Jessie left he heard a faint bark. He crossed to the window again, in time to see Evelyn running pell-mell on to the ice. Rebel was chasing after her.

'No!' he shouted out in some alarm, even knowing she couldn't hear him. 'Fetch help,' he yelled to the astonished manservant who'd appeared, and within seconds had pushed past him to charge at top speed towards the lake.

He heard the crack before he reached the lake's edge, saw the ice star outwards from the middle and heard Evelyn give a terrified scream before she slid into the dark patch of water. For a moment her fingers scrabbled at the shifting ice, then she was gone. Rebel slipped and scrabbled around, barking furiously at the hole as he tried to understand where she'd suddenly gone. Saville's marrow chilled in his bones.

Beneath the surface of the water, Graine struggled for her life. It was cold, and so terribly dark. The fresh water pulled her down, whereas, the sea water had pushed her up. That was frightening. It took her a moment or two to realize her skirt had floated up over her head. She tried to kick herself upwards, but her sodden cloak and skirt wrapped around her legs and dragged her down.

She managed to reach the clasp and the cloak floated free. The skirt of her gown was another matter. It clung against her body, and her fingers were too numb to undo the ties. Was she destined to drown, after all? Had she cheated death in the ocean only to be pursued by the grim reaper to this very spot?

Everything about her ached as she floated in the murky half light. As the warmth leached from her body so did her breath, bubbling out bit by bit until she could hold it inside no more. It left her suddenly, with a noisy swoosh of sound. Her ears popped. Faintly, she heard Rebel barking.

She opened her mouth to say some comforting words to him and water rushed in. Her throat seemed to swell, as if determined to keep it out. Her heart boomed in her chest, then fluttered frantically. She reached up, only to touch a cold mirror of ice. She struggled for a few moments, then a great lassitude crept over her and she began to sink slowly into the depths. No longer cold, she thought, I'll rest for just a few moments . . .

'Got her!' Saville yelled, as his hands closed around some fabric. But when he hauled it to the surface it was only her cloak. If her cloak had floated to the surface she must be beneath it, he reasoned. Ignoring Edmund's warning, he dragged in some air and made his next dive deeper. His groping hand closed around something that felt like rope. Chest bursting, he hauled it to the surface.

Hair! He had her hair in his fist. Her head broke free of the water and she bobbed upwards, her breasts pale moons above her pink gown. How pale she was. How relaxed. Her petticoats spread about her like the sodden petals of a rose, her hair was a dark, water-slicked centre of stamens. Amber eyes open, she gazed at him with infinite and unseeing intensity from narrowed pupils. Her eyelashes were spiked and trembling with droplets. Blue ringed, her lips were set slightly apart, the corners set upwards so she wore a tiny smile.

'Dear God, don't let me be too late!' he almost sobbed, and signalled to Edmund. The rope around his middle tightened. Gradually, he was dragged with his burden across the ice to be received by a bank of reeds, stiffened with frost and razor tipped with ice. He lay there, gasping, whilst Edmund wrapped his cloak around her.

When his breathing gained a comfortable pace he pushed Edmund aside and knelt over her limp body. Ear to her mouth, he realized she'd stopped breathing. He applied pressure to her stomach. 'Eve, my angel. Breathe for me, for God's sake!'

'I think Miss Adams is dead, sir,' Edmund said slowly.

'No . . . no! Death cannot have her! I'll not permit her to come into my life, then have her snatched from me. I won't have it, d'you hear? Let's get her back to the house and warm her.'

He picked her up in his arms and staggered off towards the house, his strength almost spent, refusing to believe what his instincts told him. Her head lolled to one side and water trickled from her mouth with his uneven gait. Then unbelievingly, she swooped in a painful, rattling breath and began to cough.

Thank God! Thank God! Saville fell to his knees, holding her head whilst she involuntarily relieved her stomach of the water she'd swallowed. When she was comfortable he wiped her face and brought her up against his shoulder, where he rocked her back and forth, pressing kisses against her cold, pale face and murmuring, 'My dearest one, my love. You're alive.'

She made a little murmur of protest. 'I'm so cold and tired.'

'We must get her to bed, my lord.'

Tears ran down his cheeks when he gazed up at Edmund, but he didn't care. 'I thought I'd lost her, Edmund.'

'I know, my lord. But now you must regain control of yourself. Let me carry Miss Adams the rest of the way. We must get you inside where it's warm, because your strength is nearly spent.' But Saville couldn't bear to hand her over. He managed to push himself upright and draw on a final reserve.

The servants had come out to meet them, all a-babble. Amidst mixed exclamations of horror and congratulations they were half pushed, half carried inside, where Saville collapsed on to the nearest seat.

Relieved of his sweet burden, he watched anxiously as she was borne away in a blanket held by some half-a-dozen chattering maids. A dejected Rebel trailed after them.

Jessie bossily shouted instructions to them on the way up the stairs. 'Mind the newel post, you stupid lammokins. Lift her head higher, Mary Tapley. What's the matter with you, girl, you'm all of a pucker? I'd pack you off to the hiring fair come February, 'cept'n you haven't got enough wit to sell a ha'peth of fire-scroff for a living.'

'When I see'd that magpie all alone I told thee it would bring bad luck down upon the house,' Mary answered back.

'You be fair mazed, girl,' Jessie scoffed. 'That'd be a year back, and the steward broke his arm shortly after. Wouldn't have happened if you hadn't encouraged the thing, allus feeding it and such. Fat lot of good trying to tame it did. The kitchen cat made a good meal of it and that was bad luck on the magpie, if you asks me. Hey, you! Dog. Don't think you be sneaking in here all cosy like. Go and find your master, and be quick about it!'

Saville managed a weak grin as Rebel came slinking back down, his ears flattened and his tail hanging between his legs. There were traces of blood on his snout, but a cursory examination revealed no wound. He must have caught a rat. The women's voices faded away.

Saville was shivering uncontrollably, despite the fact that some-one had draped a blanket around his shoulders. Edmund thrust a glass of neat brandy into his hands. 'She's in good hands now, sir. Drink that, then you must change into dry clothes, rest, and warm yourself.'

'Sometimes you fuss like an old hen, Edmund. There's enough liquor in this glass to fell a cart horse.'

Edmund chuckled. 'Nonsense. Your father could down twice the amount in one gulp.'

'I'm not about to compete with him.' Teeth chattering against the glass, Saville swallowed half of the brandy and grimaced at the fiery sting of the liquid. He handed the glass back to his steward. 'The rest is yours, Edmund. I'm off to bathe and change. I want to know the very minute Miss Adams is ready to receive visitors.'

Graine was seated in a tub of lukewarm water and Jessie was massaging lavender-scented soap through her hair.

Another maid warmed her bed with coals in a warming pan. The fire was heaped with extra coals to encourage it to flame up the chimney and warm the room even further.

Graine wasn't listening to the chatter going on. Her mind seemed to be filled with darkness, her body was numb, her limbs heavy and her tongue mute. There was an awful, deadening exhaustion inside her. She said nothing as she was dried and bundled into a flannel night gown. Jessie brushed her hair into shining dryness. Fashioning the sides into two thin braids to circle her head, the rest was left hanging free. Graine didn't resist as she was helped into bed.

'Go and fetch the broth, Mary. The rest of you can empty the bath water and go about your business.'

Graine didn't want to eat the broth. Her teeth were chattering too much to eat. At least Jessie didn't argue with her when she pushed it away. When she turned her head aside, Jessie got up and left, closing the door behind her.

The room was blissfully quiet. All Graine could hear was the fire crackling in the grate, the little clock ticking on the mantel and the black thoughts churning in her head. Her lie had come back to haunt her. God was punishing her for her deception.

When she heard the door open and close she pretended to be asleep. Saville's breath against her ear, his voice telling her to wake, ignited a deep glow of contentment inside her. Quickly, she opened her eyes. He had a determined look on his face and the bowl of broth in his hands as he sat on the side of the bed. The damp, spiky darkness of his hair made her want to smile, but she couldn't summon up the energy.

'I'm here to feed you this broth,' he said quietly. 'If you refuse it I shall pinch your nose until you open your mouth, then pour it in. Do you understand?' He gave a small smile when she nodded.

Rebel came over to watch. His great head lay on the bed, his eyebrows waggled up and down as he watched each movement of the spoon from bowl to mouth. The broth trickled warmly into her body. When the bowl was empty, Saville dabbed at her mouth with a napkin and smiled. 'Good, now you're looking a little less pinched. Can you tell me why you were running across the lake?'

She could tell him, but she wouldn't. Miserably, she shook her head, setting free the tears gathering at the corner of her eyes. How could she tell him now, when she had nowhere else to go? She'd just have to find some money with which to pay Thomas Younger. A sob tore from her throat.

When he gathered her into his arms she snuggled her head into his shoulder. Taking her hand he kissed the cold palm, then tucked it inside his velvet waistcoat to snuggle back to warmth. His heart was a warm, living pulse against her hand. He ran his fingers through her hair, releasing a fragrance of lavender.

How tender and caring a man Saville was. How content she'd be if she could stay with him instead of marrying some stranger. But even if he wanted her to, she couldn't contemplate such a thing, not with Thomas and William Younger in charge of her secret, and she might end up married to Thomas Younger if she didn't pay his price. She shuddered.

'What's bothering you, my angel?'

'Nothing,' she murmured, feeling an overwhelming desire to tell him everything. But the words stuck in her throat. Turning a strained smile his way she discovered his mouth a scant inch away from hers. For a moment they gazed at each other, then he kissed her gently and thoroughly. It healed the repugnance of the kiss

Thomas Younger had forced on her mouth. Her body quivered with a response, and there was nothing cold about that.

'This cannot be,' she said afterwards, her voice shaking with the tension inside her.

'What cannot be?'

'Us.'

'Ah . . . I see.' The laughter in his voice brought a rush of heat into her face. His finger grazed down her cheek. 'See how warm you've become. You must stay here in this bed for a little while longer, for it's doing you good.'

And she did stay there, forgetting her troubles in the comforting safety of his arms.

When Jessie returned it was to find the earl propped against the pillows asleep, with Evelyn Adams snuggled against his chest. At least the earl was on top of the covers, she noted approvingly. A real gentleman, the earl, even if he had allowed her hand to stray inside his waistcoat and had his own on top of it to keep it there.

The dog was on the other side, stretched along her back.

Jessie scratched her head, sent the animal a frown and the couple a smile. 'I'll be blowed if them two aren't in love, and why disturb them when they be as snug and content with each other as two turtle doves?' she whispered, and tip-toed away.

Whilst the pair slept, outside the window the sky released a drifting white mantel to fall upon the land and the air took on a new hush.

Graine woke heavy-eyed, and with her throat on fire.

'Glory be,' Jessie said, taking a look at her. 'Your cheeks be as red as a rooster's crop. You be going down with a dose of something, my bonny, else my name ain't Jessie. I told the master he shouldn't take you down those tunnels. You never know what infections them darkies be bringing with 'em. Not that it be their fault, poor souls, but all the same, 'tis better to be careful.'

'They were perfectly healthy,' Graine rasped. 'I've got a sore throat from falling in the lake, that's all. I'm not used to the cold. I'll soon recover when I'm up and about.'

But she didn't recover; her condition grew worse. By evening, she could hardly speak and Saville gazed at her with some concern. 'You must go to bed and stay there. As soon as the snow clears I'll send for the doctor. In the meantime, Jessie will look after you.'

'I don't want to be any trouble to anyone,' she whispered.

'You'll cause me less trouble confined to your chamber.' He took her hand in his. 'You shall get the best attention I can offer, and shall soon be well again, my Eve.'

But she grew worse. Within the week she couldn't stop coughing, and a week after that her body grew so heated she could hardly bear the bed covers against her skin. Perspiration soaked through her night gown and the sheets, and her throat parched with thirst. Yet when she threw the covers aside she cooled rapidly and began to shake uncontrollably.

She grew so weak she lost the energy to drink. Her head ached constantly and her limbs grew heavy. Hallucinations came to haunt her. Great dogs with slavering mouths who made her cry out in fright. The slave girl who'd died came to stand at her bedside. She was carrying a child with the weatherbeaten face and the dark eyes of Thomas Younger. Graine lashed out at him, screaming for him to go away.

Saville came often. There was great concern on his face. He spoke soothingly to her and coaxed her to drink from the cup he held to her mouth. She tried to please him, but she couldn't swallow and the liquid ran from the corner of her mouth. Exhausted, she fell back on the pillows and closed her eyes.

'You must get better,' he whispered, 'For I love you dearly.'

She smiled a little at that. How could he love a woman who'd told him so many falsehoods? She was a liar and a thief and wasn't fit to clean his boots. Not that it mattered. Graine knew she was very ill, and was now so lethargic she didn't care if she lived or died.

One night she heard a low-pitched singing. Sheba stood at the end of her bed. The slave's dark eyes glowed like rubies in the firelight. When she'd finished her song she came to stand by the pillow.'

'Who are you?' Graine whispered fearfully. 'Are you obeah?'

'I'm a myla woman, missy, stronger than the obeah to those of the faith. Listen to my song, it will strengthen you against evil.'

Their glances joined and Graine felt a force pass between them as the myla sang. Sheba closed her lids with her fingertips. 'Rest well now, little one.'

Peace filled her. She slept deeply, with only the sound of Sheba's song to keep her company. Then the song stopped. Graine opened her eyes to find Saville standing by her bed.

'At last,' he murmured. 'Your fever left you a week ago and you've been sleeping ever since.'

'How long have I been ill?'

'Four weeks. You were suffering from a lung infection.' He took her hand in his. 'Now you must gain strength, for in a few short weeks we must leave for London.'

She must have imagined his declaration of love, for he still intended to hand her over to John Lamartine.

Then she remembered Thomas Younger and tears filled her eyes. Two weeks, the sea captain had said, and already four had passed. But perhaps the snow had prevented him calling.

'Have there been any visitors for me?' she asked him anxiously.

His smile was faintly amused. 'Even if you expected any, it would have been impossible for them to reach the house. The snow has been too deep.'

'And it has not cleared?' she said, less anxious now.

'It's just begun to thaw, and today I saw some snowdrops by the stable, a sure sign that spring is nearly here. I've picked you some.'

The delicate white blooms were arranged amongst their spiked leaves in a small china vase. He placed them on her bedside table.

'Thank you, they're so pretty.' But she couldn't meet his eyes as she hoped it would snow again, for even John Lamartine wouldn't want her after the truth got out.

8

Saville's relief when Evelyn had awoken to the world was so heady, he could have put his dignity aside and danced around her chamber.

She was extremely pale and thin, and her hair and eyes lacked lustre. After their initial conversation, she managed a pale smile when he lifted her hand to his lips to kiss it in celebration. For some reason he couldn't fathom, she started to weep. Nothing he could say or do would stop her, and his heart nearly broke into a thousand pieces when she weakly turned her head away from him.

'Away with you, now,' Jessie scolded, as she bustled forward to take her charge in her arms, a comfort Saville would have been pleased to provide himself. 'You know nothing at all about women if you thinks Miss Adams wants to be gawked at, especially when she's not looking or feeling her best. And would you please take the dog with you, my lord,' she said, as he ambled reluctantly towards the door. 'The sick-room is no place for an animal and I can't move for the pair of you mooning about.'

Chastened, he and Rebel went down to the library to skulk amongst the books for a day or two. There, he caught up with his correspondence, sending a missive to his sister Charlotte, begging her to visit and act as companion to his invalid guest. *She has need of a woman to confide in, I think*, he wrote.

Feeling happier, he then settled down to discuss seasonal preparations for the estate with Edmund Scanlon. The thaw had started, and once the snow had gone he intended to occupy himself with the training of Ebony. Over the last few months he'd already accustomed the filly to the use of bit and bridle. Now, she must accept

102

a saddle and rider and learn to respond to command. He didn't envisage any trouble with her. She had a quiet nature, like her mother.

The snow cleared enough to send a message to the new physician, who'd wintered in Poole waiting for the snow to clear. He'd taken up residence the previous week, or so Saville had heard. He waited an impatient hour whilst the man examined Evelyn.

Henry Rideout spoke softly, with the accent of a man from the north. The man had not yet reached middle age, but he was not far off. Slightly dour in manner, he'd also been trained in surgery techniques.

He came down to the library just as Saville was about to storm upstairs. The doctor's countenance was grave. 'It's obvious that Miss Adams has been very ill.'

'I don't need you to inform me of that, man,' Saville said testily. 'I feared for her life at one stage.'

'As well you might have, my lord. She could so easily have lost it, for her lungs are congested.' A thoughtful frown creased his forehead. 'It also seems Miss Adams has been delirious.'

'In what way?'

'She told me a slave woman stood by her bed every night to sing the evil spirits away. Do you have any notion of that to which she refers?'

Saville had a suspicion of one. His skin prickled. 'Miss Adams grew up in Antigua. It's probably some native superstition she picked up as a child. Perhaps the thought of extra protection aided her recovery.'

'Ah, yes.' Rideout drew his mouth into a straight line and his features took on a stern set. 'However, it would be unhealthy to encourage the young lady in such beliefs. People have been interrogated and committed to Bedlam for believing in the manifestation of such demons.'

Saville frowned at him for even hinting at such a suggestion. 'I assure you, Miss Adams is of sound mind. Anyone who cares to dispute that, will have me to deal with, Doctor Rideout.'

'Yes, yes, of course, my lord,' the doctor said hastily. 'I'm suggesting it would be better if such beliefs were not aired by the patient. The minds of the young are susceptible. Once superstition takes root it can be hard to shift and sometimes, rigorous treatment is needed. Perhaps Miss Adams should be encouraged to pray to the Lord, which will strengthen her mind.'

Saville grinned. 'Miss Adams's mind is sufficiently strong enough as it is, as you will realize once she has regained her health. As for her beliefs being aired. I trust you'll bear in mind that my guest's confidence is exactly that, and the slave woman was a part of her fevered delirium.'

Henry Rideout's face assumed an offended expression at being taught his business. 'Which concurs exactly with my own diagnosis, my lord. As for her physical condition, the illness has taken its toll of her, but she's over the worst. She will cough for some time to come and tire easily. Her appetite will be small to start with. Keep her warm, and tempt her with nourishing broths so her strength will be regained. I'll leave you a tonic with which to enrich her blood and will call again in a day or two to check on her progress.' He managed a wintery smile and said with heavy gallantry, 'Miss Adams seems to be a charming young woman.'

Saville's attitude towards him softened. 'Miss Adams is more than charming. She's entirely delightful and—' He shrugged and toned down the enthusiasm evident in his voice as he crossed to the bell pull. 'The morning is brisk. You'll take some refreshment with me before you go, Doctor. Perhaps you'd care to fill me in on events taking place in the district. It will save me waiting until the Candlemas Day hiring fair.'

'Thank you, my lord; there's some gossip you may find interesting. Boat wreckage and the bodies of some escaped slaves washed ashore up the coast three days ago . . .'

Saville's eyes sharpened. 'From where did they originate?'

'Captain William Younger of Bristol was looking for runaways in the district recently, I believe.'

'Ah yes. I allowed them to search my caves. Surely they're not in the district, still?'

'The father has returned to Bristol, where he has business to attend to. I visited the son at the inn just yesterday. He's being cared for by the innkeeper's wife for a consideration.' Rideout's eyes hooded over as he said blandly, 'But far be it for me to discuss his condition.'

Saville gave him a sharp look. 'The man is on my land. If he has a communicable infection, I need to know it.'

'Seafarers often suffer from communicable diseases, especially those weakened by moral lassitude. However, one can't classify infected bite marks on the face in such a way. They have every appearance of being inflicted by a large dog or a wolf, and will not heal. He's in danger of brain inflammation from the poisons being released into his bloodstream.'

Rebel lifted his head and managed a casual yawn. Saville's eyes narrowed on him. 'When did he get these bites?'

'It was the day your guest fell through the ice on the lake, I believe he said.'

Saville gazed at him. 'How the devil could he have known of that?'

'I believe he was a witness to it. He seems to be under the impression that Miss Adams perished. In fact, the thought seems to prey on his mind.' Rideout accepted a glass of steaming chocolate from a manservant and cupped his hands around it. 'This may be a coincidence, but the man mentioned he was being haunted by the apparition of a slave woman.'

'The Younger family is well known for their ill-treatment of the slaves they ship. They would be familiar with the concept of obeah. It's possible that fear of it may have a bearing on his conscience, and therefore affect the ability of his wounds to heal satisfactorily.'

'There are some who embrace such outlandish theories.' Rideout shrugged. 'Utter nonsense, of course, for it cannot be proved scientifically.'

'Neither can obeah. Yet I believe it works amongst the West Indian slaves. We, of course, embrace the Christian church, placing our faith in something equally intangible.'

Rideout ignored the latter. 'It sounds as if you're acquainted with slave culture, my lord.'

'Good grief! Does it?'

The doctor's glance met his and he gave a faint smile. 'I'm not entirely stupid, sir. Thomas Younger said much in his delirium.'

'None of which can be proved, of course.'

'Of course. And none of which will be aired outside of these four walls. My discretion can be relied on, my services called on. From now on, Younger will be kept sedated, for if there are any runaways in the district I would not have them hunted down and driven to their deaths. As a matter of interest, I gave shelter to a woman a few nights ago. I've put her on a cart to London, as was my Christian duty. Her name was Eliza Jones. I have one or two acquaintances in the capital who will help settle her there, and wondered if they are mutual.'

'Do you, by God.' Warming to him, Saville leaned forward, his eyes astute. 'Pray, tell me their names.'

After the doctor departed, Saville fetched his cloak and made his way around the lake, now an innocuous ripple of cloud reflection, and with only a few patches of cracked ice still clinging to the reeds on the shoreline. He shuddered when he realized how close Evelyn had been to death.

Underfoot, the ground was soggy with mud and sodden leaf litter. The indentations his feet made filled slowly with water after he passed. Ahead, the snow still lay in patches under the trees. The pines were dark, saturated shapes, their branches weighed down by dripping slush. When he reached them, he squatted on his haunches and lined the house up across the lake. Evelyn would have started running from about here.

Under the trees were signs where two horses had been concealed. A burn on the tree bark indicated where one had been tethered. The minimum of investigation revealed the remains of some dung, and snow-filled hoof prints.

It didn't take Saville long to discover the signs of the scuffle. Here were the prints of one man, and smaller marks made by a woman. Here were the scuff marks in the ground, the confusion of prints where she'd turned and began to run. Here were Rebel's paw prints.

He followed the smaller footprint towards the lake, then turned to look back, trying to imagine what had taken place. Just then, the sun momentarily emerged from behind a cloud and his eyes were drawn by a glint of gold.

It took him but a second to push aside the leaf litter with his cane. He stooped to retrieve a heart-shaped brooch. It was dented badly now, but the clasp still held it firm to a scrap of pink fabric.

Why hadn't she said she'd been attacked? And why hadn't she told him it had been William Younger who'd attacked her?

As he ran a thumb over the heart the top came off its hinge. Tiny rubies picked out the initials, B and S, and the word 'love', in the two halves.

'B and S,' he said out loud and his brow furrowed. Seth Adams was Evelyn's father, but for the life of him he couldn't remember what her mother had been called. It was probably her initial. Placing the brooch in his coat pocket he whistled for Rebel and headed back to the house.

Candlemas came and went and along with it, the hiring fare. Saville needed no labourers or servants, but attended with Edmund to exchange gossip with landowners from neighbouring districts to discuss harvest yields and the probable profits to be made with tenant farmers.

At the inn, he and Edmund ate a succulent rabbit pie between them, washing it down with a jug of ale. There was talk of the black slaves who'd been washed up with the boat wreckage.

'Gave old Robbie a turn, I can tell thee,' one local said. 'All plimmed up with water, and frozen solid, every one. Robbie was all of a pucker for days after.'

'Don't take much to confuse Robbie these days. I hear tell they was so frozen that the gulls were bending their beaks trying to pick the darkies' eyes out of their heads,' said another, and gave a raucous laugh. 'The horned man made a good harvest of them heathens, if you asks me.'

'Nobody did ask you as far as I can see, so don't you be talkin' such mischief in here,' the landlady shouted at him. 'I've got enough to cope with, with that Bristol black-birder upstairs givin' me the willies. It gives me the fair shudders, it do, talking about poor folk being drowned in a cold sea. It will call down the Devil's attention upon us and he'll cause mischief in the district, just see if he don't. So don't blame me if that daughter'n yours gets a puddin inside her.'

He laughed. 'How could I do that, unless you got something up your skirt you ain't be tellin' us about. Give us a look see, then. Could be you have a cork stuck in the neck of your bottle.'

'And could be you should find out who's sticking his cork in your daughter's bottle.'

Saville exchanged a grin with Edmund when a sopping cloth whistled across the bar and wrapped around the labourer's head.

Fishing in his pocket for coin with which to pay the innkeeper, he came across the brooch again. He rotated the top half between his fore-finger and thumb, watching the rubies glint. 'Can you remember the name of Seth Adams's wife, Edmund?'

'Patricia.'

'Are you sure? I thought her name began with a B.'

'The name of his mistress did. It was Blanche Seaton.'

He pocketed the ornament. Had the brooch belonged to her? B&S. Blanche and Seth? Or was it simply her name? If so, how had the brooch come to be in Evelyn's possession? Obviously, he couldn't ask her until she was fully recovered. On the way home he dropped it off at a jeweller's shop to be repaired.

February became a breezy March sending clouds scudding across the sky and the reeds at the lakes edge whispering.

Recovery was a slow process. Doctor Rideout left nothing to chance. Determined to regain her strength as soon as possible, Graine ate what she was told, even when she didn't feel hungry. She swallowed his foul-tasting elixirs and slept a great deal when she wasn't being woken for bathing, having the tangles brushed from her hair, or for physical examination.

It was two weeks before she was given permission to take her first steps. Her initial excitement fled when she realized her legs felt like frail stems. With hardly the strength to carry her own weight, she tottered to the window and clung to the sill to catch her breath.

The world outside seemed to have taken on a new verdancy. She gazed with some perplexity at this metamorphosis. What had once been white was now painted in shades of ochre and delicate green. The trees had little green buds decorating their branches, like candles. One was adorned with a scattering of the palest of pink blossoms. Clouds raced in ragged streamers across the heavens, seagulls wheeled in the currents and the wind sent ripples chasing across the lake. She turned to beam with pleasure at the doctor. 'Is it spring?'

He blinked, then managed a drawn-out mumble, which could have meant anything.

'My pardon, but I did not catch your words.'

A wintry smile touched his mouth and he said with heavy gallantry, 'I said, if it was not spring, your smile would make it so.' He turned a severe look on Jessie when she snorted. 'A little more practice will be needed to strengthen those legs of hers.'

Graine took a deep breath and followed his advice by venturing once more across the floor. Her efforts to regain her bed drew forth a coughing fit which left her feeling weak. Her knees began to buckle. Frustrated tears filled her eyes when both Jessie and the doctor rushed forward to support her.

'There, there, my dear,' Henry Rideout said kindly, as Jessie tucked her back into bed. 'Remember that you've been very ill. Please be assured though, you're the best patient I've ever had the fortune to attend. If you continue to follow my advice you'll make rapid progress and will be dancing in no time.'

Graine would have snorted as loud as Jessie if she could have found the breath, for she felt as frail as a newly born kitten. There was something she liked about the doctor, though. Even if he was blunt in his manner, he was thorough and caring and clean in his practices. He would leave his instructions regarding her with Saville, she knew, which was a little irksome considering they were not related and it was *her* health and not Saville's which had brought him here. However, Saville visited her on a daily basis, visits she looked forward to.

'You're a good doctor,' she said to him, as he was preparing to leave.

He appeared to be pleased by the praise, if a little embarrassed. 'How can you possibly judge that, young lady?'

'You are fastidious in your habits. You clean your instruments and hands thoroughly with soap and vinegar so infection cannot be passed on to others, and your apron is always spotlessly clean.'

'The praise for the latter belongs to my good wife, who cannot abide a stain and boils them in an iron pot until they are clean. She would do the same with me if she could.'

Graine gave a little giggle at the thought of him being boiled with his aprons. 'She looks after her husband, then.'

109

'As all good wives should,' he agreed, and she could sense the amusement in him.

'But you digress, Doctor. We were talking about you, were we not?'

'You were being inquisitive, I believe. I'm not a very interesting subject for conversation. I understand you have surgical skills yourself. At the earl's request I have examined your emergency treatment. Where did you learn to suture wounds so skilfully?'

'At the convent clinic in Antigua, which was run by an order of nuns.'

His face took on a slightly scandalized expression. 'My dear child, as worthy as such a pursuit is, I'm surprised your guardian indulged you in such a risky pastime.' He sighed and shook his head. 'But I must not lecture you on the propriety of such activities when applied to unmarried women, for the labourer, Clem, would probably have bled to death without your intervention.'

'And I would have died without yours. Had I been born a man I think I would be a doctor too, for there's something wonderful about saving a life.'

'There is. But it's not quite so wonderful when your skills are to no avail.'

With sadness, she remembered the slave girl and her baby. 'To stand by and do nothing is worse. I must insist that you stop arguing with me, Doctor. I'm determined to have the last word regarding your worthiness and it will be bad for my health if you continue to try and convince me otherwise.'

He chuckled at that. 'Then I shall accept your praise and thank you for it . . . and before you decide to confer sainthood on me, I'll say good day to you, Miss Adams.' He left with a smile on his face, the last word clearly his.

A week later, Saville visited Dorchester to sit on the judicial bench at the quarterly assizes. For once the workload was light, the cold weather having kept people indoors and out of mischief. Before him appeared several people accused of petty thievery, much of which was related to hunger.

Many of the stealing offences carried the death sentence, but Saville dealt with them in his usual manner, taking into account the offender's circumstances. Poachers were fined if they could afford it, or given a spell in the local watch house. The worst case was a man he sentenced to death by hanging – a man who'd violated a shopkeeper's wife in front of her children. A pillow had been placed over the woman's face to muffle her screams, and she'd suffocated to death during the assault. A servant caught stealing from his master was sentenced to transportation to the West Indies.

A man accused of stealing a horse received his full attention. The man had borrowed the beast to get home from an inn, and said that snow had prevented him from returning it. The beast had been wintered in his parlour, enjoying the same meals as his family.

'It didn't half pong, m'lord,' the man said respectfully, all the while twisting his hat in his hand, 'My Maisie was right put out, shovelling up after it all winter.'

'The truth be, I'll never get rid of that stink if I scrubs my fingers to the bone,' Maisie grumbled, standing up amongst the public spectators with her nose twitching at the thought. 'So if Your Worship can find it in your heart to forgive my man, Jimmy Lunn, who was in his cups at the time, and whose goodness to dumb creatures be as well knowed as his brain be small, I'd be mightily relieved. That beast lived like a king with us. It ate all our provisions and if my Jimmy ain't free to work for his living our cheils will surely go hungry.'

The cheils in question, who were flanked either side of her like a row of urchin soldiers, turned large brown eyes their father's way and began to snivel and whimper at the thought. And Saville knew straight away that he couldn't find it in his heart to allow their children to starve.

Jimmy Lunn was looking suitably distressed. 'Sorry, our Maisie, but I didn't know what else to do with it and couldn't let the poor creature freeze to death, even though a bit of horse flesh makes a tasty stew.' Spreading his hands, the man appealed to him. 'I took it back to its rightful owner as soon as I be able, Yer Worship, when my Maisie could've made a fine meal or two out've the old nag, and none the wiser. So how was that stealing?'

Laughing to himself at the ingenious plea of this duo, Saville dismissed the case and ordered the plaintiff to reimburse eight shillings to the Lunn family for the food the horse had consumed.

Mood uplifted, he left the courtroom and visited the jeweller, where he collected the brooch he'd left there. Expertly repaired, and showing no sign of the damage inflicted on it, the gold had been polished to a soft glow. On impulse, he bought a circlet of creamy pearls with matching ear-rings, a gift to be presented when a propitious moment occurred.

He'd reached the inn on the way home, when the landlord's wife came rushing out. She was red-faced and out of breath. 'Beggin' your pardon, my lord, but that black-birder sea captain has taken a turn for the worst. He's got the rattles. My man had gone to fetch Doctor Rideout, but I be all alone and need help, for I have to cater for my customers.'

Saville hadn't given Thomas Younger much thought. The man's appearance shocked him. Pale and wasted, his face was a mass of scabs. Muttering to himself, the man's head thrashed back and forth and he twitched uncontrollably. His eyes were staring, his skin hot and dry and the death rattle was an unnerving and constant sound as he laboured for breath.

Even knowing it was too late, Saville sent the woman for a bowl of water and a cloth, then sent her about her business and began to bathe Thomas Younger's forehead. 'Try and calm yourself,' he soothed.

Saville didn't know whether his presence brought the man comfort or not, because although the bodily agitation stopped, the rattle remained constant. Towards the end of the hour there was a moment when the man's eyes seemed to focus on him. His mouth contorted and he strained to speak. '*Evelyn . . . Adams.*'

So he *had* been involved in Evelyn's accident. Saville's blood pounded against his temples as he stooped to catch any statement the dying man wanted to make. 'Do you wish to clear your conscience over the matter?'

The hair of his neck and arms stood on end when the man stared beyond his shoulder and almost screamed, 'Get away from me, she devil!'

Saville couldn't help but turn his head and look behind him. For a moment, he could have sworn he saw movement in the corner of the room, but it was only a shadow of a cloud shifting across the window, for immediately it lightened. There came a moment when time seemed to stop, because suddenly the room was filled with an absolute silence.

Saville turned back to the bed to gently smooth the lids down over the man's eyes and cross his hands on his chest. Normal sound intruded on the silence: the landlady humming as she bustled about in the kitchen below; his horse pocking a hoof against the earth and the clicks and creaks of its leathers. How quickly and easily life left the body, he thought, looking down at the corpse of Thomas Younger.

Just then came the sound of the doctor's carriage. Saville met him at the door. 'Thomas Younger has died.'

'I was expecting it. The undertaker is on his way with his cart. I'll have him buried in the grounds of the local church.'

'Is there anything I can do to help?'

'Send a messenger to inform his stepmother, perhaps. His father will be at sea.' The doctor's eyes came up to search his. 'Did he say anything before he died?'

'He mentioned Miss Adams. I believe he was trying to clear his conscience about her accident when he died.'

Henry Rideout nodded. 'More than likely. Was that all he said?'

Mentioning the devil woman to Rideout would be unwise. 'He was unable to speak for long. I'll compose some words to bring comfort to his father, for he would have been thinking of him at the end, I expect. I could have his effects delivered back to Bristol, if you wish.'

Henry acknowledged his words with an ironic smile. 'An occasion when a small digression from the truth will be forgiven by the Lord, I should imagine. His horse is in the stable, and I will gather together his personal effects, if I can but delay you for a few minutes longer. How is my delightful patient?'

Saville smiled, because the thought of Evelyn always had that effect on him. 'You can inform me of that when you call on her the day after tomorrow.'

Saville refreshed himself with a tumbler of mulled wine before taking possession of Thomas Younger's horse and personal goods. There wasn't much: a pocket watch, a pistol, and a money belt with enough coinage inside to bury his corpse and pay the landlady and doctor for their efforts. Saville took the precaution of obtaining receipts for the cash.

When he arrived home it was to immediately visit Evelyn. He took the stairs three at a time with Rebel at his heels. Seated in a chair by the fire and propped against some cushions, she looked pale and drawn.

She managed a smile for him – a smile so small and troubled that his heart turned over.

Taking her brooch from his pocket he offered it to her. For a moment she stared at it glinting on his palm, then she gave a small cry of alarm. Immediately, he took her in his arms, holding her against his chest in comfort.

'You needn't worry, my Eve. I know Thomas Younger attacked you on that day you fell through the ice. He cannot harm you now, for he is dead.'

She lifted her head and gazed at him, horrified. 'You didn't—'

He smiled and assured her, 'Of course not. He died from an illness.' He smoothed the tawny hair back from her brow. 'Hurry up and get better, for I cannot bear to think of you suffering.' He gazed around him. 'Where's Jessie?'

'She was needed elsewhere.'

He stole a small kiss from her lips then placed his mouth against her hairline and whispered, 'We should not be alone like this, for I cannot trust myself with you.'

'Saville, there is something I must tell you.'

He placed her back against the cushions and sprang to his feet when a knock came at the door. By the time she bid the caller enter he'd moved to the other side of the fireplace.

'Charlotte, you've arrived at last,' he cried out, when his sister swept in. She was followed by Jessie, who carried a tray containing cups and a jug of fragrant, steaming chocolate.

'Of course I've arrived, and three hours since, making all haste through the muck on the highways, since your message said it was urgent. But I can stay no more than six weeks. I am here to make the acquaintance of Miss Adams now. As for you, you rogue, you should know better than be in here alone with her. What were you thinking of, Saville?'

He smiled as he moved towards the door, speaking softly so Eve wouldn't hear. 'What I've been thinking since I first met her, is that she's too good to give away to John and I should keep her for myself.'

She gave him a long, steady look. 'I took a good look at her whilst she was asleep. The girl looks to be a poor scrap of a thing.'

'Usually, she's more robust, and she's a precious little scrap to me.' He took her in a hug. 'Be kind to her, Charlotte. She's been through a lot.'

'Have you declared yourself to her?'

'Not directly and with intent. John's feelings must be taken into consideration. I must bring the matter to his attention as soon as possible, else he will be a laughing stock if it gets out. We will go to London as soon as Evelyn is well enough to travel.'

He might as well have declared himself, Charlotte thought, observing the unguarded adoration in the girl's eyes as she watched Saville move off. Saville's last glance was filled with such tenderness that she smiled.

This was something entirely unexpected. She'd been nagging her brother to wed for years, and over that time she and her husband had introduced him to a countless number of healthy and eligible girls. Now he'd fallen in love with this delicate miss, who had no family name or breeding to speak of – a girl destined for his cousin.

Such deviation from social expectations was untypical of her sensible brother, yet she loved this stray quirk of character he'd unconsciously revealed. It indicated he was emotionally vulnerable. Now he'd made his choice, she knew he'd allow nothing to stop him from attaining that which his heart desired.

She began to laugh, she couldn't help it.

9

Charlotte, wife to the Marquess of Falhampton and mother of two daughters, was tall and elegant, blue of eyes and dark of hair. She was also the possessor of a direct manner.

She was striking to look at. To a certain extent she resembled Saville, but her features were softened by femininity. Her mouth drew a softer curve, her nose and brows were less pronounced and her skin was of a finer texture.

She took charge of the household servants with an assuredness that left Graine completely in awe of her. Rebel was banned from entering the bedchamber, and sent packing from the rug outside the door. He slunk off downstairs to find his master, his tail between his legs.

'Now, my dear,' she said, her charming smile contradicting the ring of authority in her voice. 'Saville has asked me to act as your companion whilst you're under his roof. I admit, I had not expected to find you in such poor health, but I'm assured your illness is of a temporary nature and you are convalescing satisfactorily. I do hope my brother is being a good host.'

A little easier in her mind now Thomas Younger was no longer a threat, Graine's cheeks began to glow at just the mention of Saville's name. 'The earl has been wonderfully kind.'

'He can be no less than kind to his cousin's betrothed.'

Graine felt the spark drain from her. She plucked restlessly at the thread on the bed cover. 'Yes . . . of course. I am to wed John Lamartine. I had almost forgotten.'

'I have noticed that you appear to hold my brother in high regard,' said Charlotte, her eyes a steady blue gaze. 'Men are not constant when women freely offer their affection. Such looks as you bestow on him could draw the wrong conclusion from him. In its turn, that would attract gossip and your reputation would be blemished beyond retrieval.'

Graine blushed, saying with some heat. 'Any looks I bestow on the earl are occasioned by gratitude. I'm too far below him to warrant consideration, and the earl has been a perfect gentleman.' She chose to discount his kisses, knowing she'd been shamelessly eager to accept what she suspected was little more than a casual and affectionate gesture from him.

'He has been trained to be gentlemanly, and I would expect no less of him, even though you have been living under his roof unchaperoned for some time. But even the most civilized of men have a limit, which once breached, robs them of all control. Do you understand to which I refer?'

'Most certainly,' she said, albeit a little breathlessly, because nobody had been this frank with her since she'd left the convent.

'That's good.' Charlotte patted her hand. 'I understand you've lacked a mother to guide you in these matters, which is why I offer such advice. It is kindly intended.'

'Thank you, my lady. I'm appreciative.'

'You will find London society difficult after a lifetime spent in the West Indies. John Lamartine, and especially his mother, will expect socially acceptable behaviour. Aunt Harriet will not want a wife for her son who proves to be an embarrassment.' Her lips pursed for a moment of reflection before she added, 'Even though her own behaviour can be tiresome on occasion.'

Graine tried to hide her resentment. 'A man who reaches John Lamartine's age and heeds his mother's advice instead of his own, is an embarrassment unto himself. The more I hear of this man and his mother, the less I find to admire in them and the more to despise. Indeed, it's more than probable the inclination to wed him will desert me altogether, for I do not intend to spend the rest of my life on my knees, seeking forgiveness for every small sin I commit.'

Charlotte laughed. 'Saville has been teasing you, I see. My brother's sense of humour often reflects the quirkiness of his nature. John is devout, but he has a kind heart. He is a scholar by nature, and would have been content to remain a bachelor if my brother had not talked him into this match, for John swore he would not wed for fortune alone. He probably regrets his decision by now, but his nature is such that he'll not back down from it unless he's offered a good reason.'

Her pillows were energetically punched into shape by Charlotte's fists. 'We must find something to occupy your time whilst you recuperate. Jessie told me there's a tapestry frame and some silks. You can sit in the window seat and embroider for a while. And I will find some brushes and water-colours for painting. I understand you like to read, too. Shall bring something light up from the library. Daniel Defoe's, *Moll Flanders*, perhaps. Have you read it?' Charlotte's grin was a replica of Saville's when Graine shook her head. 'Then I hope you are not too easily shocked, for it's about a woman of ill-repute who prospers when she repents her ways.'

Graine flushed as she was forced to think of her mother, who hadn't lived long enough to repent. She took a deep, steadying breath, reminding herself that Charlotte knew nothing of her background. 'I can read and mend, but I've never embroidered and do not know how to paint.'

'Then I must teach you. I shall consult with your physician, and we will soon have every hour of your day accounted for. Thus, you will not suffer from boredom.'

'You're already tiring me out,' she grumbled.

Charlotte sent her a smile. 'I have a managing nature, on which you must not waste argument. If you are good, and if we have a warm day, I will arrange a short outing in the carriage next week. Breathing the sea air will strengthen your lungs.'

Graine nearly wept with joy at the thought of such a reward when Charlotte stooped to kiss her cheek, and from that moment on, her health began to improve rapidly.

He'd taken the correct course in sending for Charlotte. Saville was gratified to see his lady love's cheeks regain some colour, and her eyes their shine.

Spring had brought a certain bustle with it, as if the March winds had energized the body and minds of people. He was often absent from home now, the work associated with the assizes dividing his time equally between the county hall in Dorchester, where the sessions were being held this quarter, and the estate.

Even with the competent Edmund Scanlon in charge, there was a variety of sowing, threshing and mucking to be discussed and the breeding of cattle and sheep to be attended to. The pastures for the stock had to be prepared, the fences inspected and the tenant farmers visited.

The cottages in the village were brightened with a coat of lime wash, and any defects reported were dealt with, for Saville found it cheaper to maintain, rather than let repairs accumulate. The women spring cleaned. They polished their pots and windows, and hung their bedding out to air. Children chased through the activities, oblivious to the warnings of their mothers and the occasional slap around the ear. Their men stoically tramped to work, wearing in the new issue of squeaking boots, and wincing at the crop of blisters they raised.

A couple of runaways arrived, straight off one of William Younger's ships. Saville had the doctor check the men over, then sent them on their way to the capital.

He never saw Evelyn alone now. Always, the watchful Charlotte was present. The conversation was polite, but was never allowed to become personal. Just the sight of her made Saville's blood heat, and the distance that chaperonage placed between them, only served to incite his ardour. He ached if a day passed when he didn't see her.

It was his joy to be home when she arrived back from her first outing. Her smile filled his senses. Without consulting Charlotte, he swung her up in his arms and carried her up to her chamber, his sister protesting loudly at every step he took. He speeded up, leaving her behind.

He could feel the quiver of tension in Evelyn, brought on by their proximity. He could smell her perfume and hear the whispery feathers of her breath fanning against his cheek. All he had to do was turn his head, and. . . ?

Action followed thought, and the next second there was a pair of tawny eyes gazing deliciously into his. He heard her breath catch in her throat, and his followed suit. They exchanged a smile,

119

almost rueful in the unspoken knowledge they shared. He had an urge to ravage her exquisitely soft mouth when the pink tip of her tongue emerged to moisten her lips.

He kicked open the door and strode to the bed with her. One day he'd join her amongst the brocade hangings, tear away her frills and flounces and make her part of him. Beneath the sensuous blue silk wrappings her flesh was warm and unawakened. It was waiting to be uncovered, to be spread naked for his delight, to be teased and tickled, feasted on and consumed. How eagerly he would exploit its pleasures and plunder its treasures. His thumb brushed under the lace of her bodice to graze lightly across the nub of her breast and bring it thrusting against her bodice. There was a tiny noise deep in her throat, a cross between a growl and a gasp.

Her eyes darkened to a sensuous liquid honey. His name purred from her mouth on a quivering little breath as she smiled. 'Saville,' she whispered. He was jubilant. It was meant for his ears alone, and he knew without a doubt now that she returned his feelings.

Charlotte poked him in the back. 'You may put Evelyn down and leave us now, Saville,' she said, the amusement in her voice clear, though she could have seen and heard nothing. 'Didn't you say you were going to train a horse today?'

Gathering his wits together he lowered his sweet burden to the bed, brought her hand to his mouth and kissed her tender little palm. 'It's the horse I gifted to Evelyn. I will train her under the window so her mistress can watch.'

Firmly, Charlotte shooed him to the door. 'I'm afraid not, Saville. Evelyn is tired from her outing and will be resting this morning. You may visit her this evening for fifteen minutes before dinner.' He was pushed from the room, and the door closed behind him with a determined thud.

He stood in the corridor for a moment, smiling to himself as the lusts of spring rushed through his body in a turbulent stream. From a pocket against his heart he took her scarf, and held its perfumed silkiness against his cheek. Pulsing hard against his linens, he was ready for the duties of loving with a vengeance. He whistled to himself as he thrust the filmy scrap back in his pocket and headed for the stables.

*

April arrived in a soft shower of rain. One spiky daffodil bloomed, it was joined by another, then spread to become a countless patch. Gradually, they spread over the grass, where they bobbed about in the wind like gossiping women in yellow bonnets. Saville brought her a vase filled with them. He set them on a table near the widow, where she sat practising her embroidery.

He gazed at it long and hard, grinning.

'I'm sorry,' she said, whispering because Charlotte was napping in the chair. 'I'm not very good at embroidery.'

'It's beautiful because it's yours.' She knew he was lying and giggled.

He sent a swift look at the sleeping Charlotte, then took the circlet of pearls he'd purchased for her from his pocket to fasten around her neck. When she gasped with delight at the unexpected gift, he turned her face up to his to be kissed. This was not a kiss to be taken lightly, but an ardent caress, full of passion and intent.

Being in love made Graine feel reckless. Love made her forget she was a penniless orphan child who could not remember affection, and had relied on the charity of others in the past. She forgot she was a liar, impersonator and thief in this moment of togetherness with him. She could not withstand such an onslaught on her senses, and responded to it, allowing his tongue the little intimacies it so desired. The sin of it was a delicious flowering inside her, as if she was a plant opening to his sun.

'I must have you,' he groaned,when he'd taken what he needed to sustain him for that moment. He ran his thumb gently across the mouth he'd just kissed, then turned on his heel and left, leaving a flat box in her lap. Pearl ear-drops nestled inside.

Charlotte jerked awake as the door closed. 'Who was that?'

'Your brother. He brought us some daffodils.'

'Hmm.' Her companion gazed at the clock and smiled. 'Time for your rest, I think.'

Calmly, Graine told her, 'I don't feel much like resting today. I feel like going for a walk around the garden.'

'But the good doctor is due to visit.'

'I feel perfectly well now, Charlotte. Doctor Rideout said I could go out any time I wished.'

'You look flushed, my dear.'

Graine reached up to touch the necklet, her smile more dreamy than she knew. 'I'm flushed because Saville gave me this precious gift. I've fallen in love with him, Charlotte, and I think he loves me in return.'

'If he does, you must wait until he formally declares himself. Only then can you be sure of his intentions.'

Graine engaged her companion's eyes. 'He kissed me and told me he wanted me.'

Charlotte frowned. 'Oh, my dear, be very careful. There's a wide gulf between a man wanting a women and loving her. Men say such things as a means to an end.'

'Are you telling me your brother is less than honourable?'

'I'm telling you he's a man like any other, with all the impulses and needs of a man. Men believe what they say in the heat of a moment. I love my brother, and I've grown to like you. I'm asking you to be careful, for I don't want to see either of you hurt.'

'Saville wouldn't hurt me. He's too fine a person,' she said, and nobody was going to convince her that he was any different.

The sound of a cantering horse heralded the arrival of Henry Rideout. Soon, Graine was pronounced fit.

'That's wonderful,' Saville told her, his smile warm with regard, 'For I need to be in London in the first week of May. I have urgent business, which can be put off no longer.'

Her heart sank, but his glance reassured her that the business was to set things right with his cousin concerning her. 'Now you are fit again I will take you to see the countryside, so you can try out your horse. She's beautifully behaved.'

'I don't think I will ride very well, for I've only ever ridden on a cart horse,' she said.

'Theodore Chambers informed me you could ride well.' The frown he gave was relieved by a perplexed smile. 'The man was obviously given to exaggeration of the wildest sort, for you are not what he said you were.' He shrugged. 'No matter, I will teach you to ride myself.'

Charlotte gazed from one to the other as if she was about to say something, then seemed to change her mind. 'I will travel with you to London, for my husband and children will be in residence there. I take it we will not be taking the coaches all the way.'

'No, the roads will be rutted and boggy after the winter. It'll be too hard on the horses. We'll take the coaches as far as Poole, then yours can proceed on to Kent with your outriders.'

Riding was easier than Graine expected. She found her brown taffeta riding habit, with its bell skirt, jacket, waistcoat and tricorn hat, to be slightly cumbersome. But the side-saddle proved to be comfortable, and she felt safe with her knee tucked over the horn.

Charlotte too, had relaxed her vigilance a little, for Saville was teaching her in full view of the house. One fine morning, however, the stable boy brought Saville his gelding. Immediately, he sprang into the saddle. 'You're doing so well I thought we'd ride further out today. I'll take you through the woodlands and show you my favourite place. Keep the horse at a steady canter if you can. It will be less tiring for both of you.' He glanced back at the house. 'Let's be off before anybody notices, for there's something I wish to say to you privately.'

They exchanged a conspiratorial smile.

Jessie noticed them leaving and drew Charlotte's attention to the fact. Charlotte merely smiled. 'No doubt, my brother wanted a private moment alone with Miss Adams. It's probable that he's counselling her, so she knows what to expect from John Lamartine. Besides, the earl has an appointment with his steward in half an hour.'

Jessie snorted. 'Don't think you've got me fooled with your scheming, Miss Charlotte, I've known you for too long. If that their brother of your'n keeps that appointment I'll wag my tail and bark, for he asked Cook to pack some vittles for the pair of them and that tells me he intends that they should spend the day in each other's company. If you asks me, it's more likely that he'll get down on his knees and ask for her hand in marriage.'

'It's more likely that he will wait until he's spoken to our cousin, John Lamartine.' She grinned at the maid. 'Do you think Miss Evelyn Adams would make a suitable mistress for Rushford, Jessie?'

Jessie slanted her head to one side. 'God knows, the girl has no pretensions to grandeur and she's well liked by those who've met her. Even you, Miss Charlotte, who is a bit too fussy for her own

123

good at times, even if it isn't my place to say so.'

'What nonsense, I'm not in the least bit fussy. If she makes my brother happy, then of course I like her. The earl is not a shallow man who would give his heart lightly. He has the heart of a man of the land and knows the ways of nature. He is content here, but lonely, and this is the first time I've seen him show anything but a passing interest in a woman. He needs a wife he can care for, one who loves him in return and who doesn't crave for the glitter of life in London. I believe they truly love one another.'

'Anyone with half an eye can see that, for they cannot take their eyes off each other when they're together. It was her neshness that first appealed to him, I think. Though he put on a good face, he was worried sick when she was taken ill.'

'Her delicacy hides an inner strength, Jessie. She survived a lung infection which would have felled most people. My brother and his guest deserve a little relaxation so they can speak of what's in their minds.'

' 'Tisn't what they be saying that's got me worried, 'tis what they be doing. Despite her age, that girl be an innocent lambkin where men be concerned, and the earl be all man.'

A little while later, Charlotte was called to the window again. A man on horseback was coming up the carriageway.

'A villainous-looking fellow,' Charlotte muttered.

' 'Tis the black-birder, Captain Younger,' Jessie said with a scowl, 'Him whose son died with a devil in his soul.'

'Stop talking nonsense,' Charlotte snapped. 'The doctor said the man died from blood poisoning.'

'A lot he knows,' Jessie mumbled. 'It be Satan who caused the blood to be poisoned in the first place.'

'I expect the captain has come to thank the earl for looking after his son.' Crossing to the bell pull Charlotte gave it a jerk, saying to the manservant who appeared, 'Advise the visitor that the earl is absent, and tell him to leave his card.'

'He wanted to leave a note, so the steward is seeing to him, my lady.'

'Good, good. Tell Mr Scanlon the earl is not yet back from his ride and he should go about his normal business. It's not much use

him waiting. The earl will send for him when he arrives home, no
doubt.'

Just at that moment the earl was leading his love through the
woodlands. Overhead, the trees were filled with birdsong, a joyous
sound amongst the soughing leaves.

Saville's mind was occupied wholly with the woman beside him.
She filled his senses so completely that his skin tingled when he
was near her, his eyes mourned her loss when they were withdrawn from her fair countenance, and his nose twitched when he
could no longer inhale her perfume.

He was gloriously, irretrievably in love, full to bursting with it –
and he liked the feeling. This women would become his countess.
She would accept him into her body as husband, take his seed unto
her and grow him a crop of strong sons and daughters. He sent her
a smile, adoring her. Nothing would ever come between them, and
he knew he'd love her for ever.

They'd slowed to a walk. He allowed her horse to come up
beside his, then reached out to take her hand. He bore it to his lips
to be kissed and said tenderly, 'I have tried not to declare myself
prematurely, but cannot keep quiet any longer. I adore you, my
Eve.'

How her eyes shone at his words, how delicately pink her
cheeks became. He laughed and, bringing their mounts to a halt,
dismounted. He reached up for her, his hands spanned her waist
and he lifted her from the saddle. Lowering her against his body,
he kissed her willing mouth with such passionate intent that she
began to tremble.

He gazed down at her, said fiercely, 'John can't have you. I'll tell
him so. Tell me you love me, for I can't live another minute without hearing it directly from your sweet lips.'

The place took on a magical timelessness for Graine. His ardour
scared her a little, for she didn't know exactly how to handle it.
'You're not mistaken. I do love you, Saville. But I'm not good
enough for you.'

'Let me be the judge of that, my dearest.'

'But Saville—' She was allowed to say no more for his lips
were on hers again, loving her and coaxing her so sweetly that

125

she had no recourse but to allow him the liberty. Her arms slid up around his neck and his body lay in sweet, hard possession against hers.

Gradually, he backed her up against the gently sloping trunk of a tree, so she was half reclining along its length. 'My sweeting,' he whispered against her ear, 'you're causing me so much torture that I, who pride myself on my control and good sense, find it slipping away from me.'

His fingers brushed against her bodice and circled the hardening nubs. 'I want to kiss them, my sweet Eve. I want to run my tongue over your flesh and taste the sweetness of you.'

Something nudged against the apex of her thighs. Her eyes widened when he nudged her legs apart and snuggled himself between them. She grew so moist and giving that her breath came in small gasps of delight. Wanting more of him, she unconsciously arched towards him.

He gazed at her, smoky-eyed with passion. 'I ache from needing to love you. One day I intend to incite the demons that lurk in this sweet body of yours with my hands and tongue, and tame those same demons with my possession of you. To hear you cry out in the throes of passion, begging me for release, will be my reward for your surrender. I will show you all the ways of loving for all the days of my life, and have you love me in return.'

'Let us love each other then, for that's what I want, too.'

'Oh, Evelyn.' He withdrew from her and, pulling her upright, smoothed the creases from her skirt. 'Only a rogue would take advantage of such innocence.'

'Can that be so important when we love one another?'

'Yes, for a man of experience will say anything to a maid to slake his appetites, and how do you, in your innocence, know I'm not lying?'

'Am I unable to trust you then, Saville?'

'God, yes,' he said almost vehemently. 'I would die rather than cause harm to you in any way.'

She smiled dreamily at him. 'You love me that much? What if I was not what I seemed? Would you love me still?'

'Love cannot be switched off and on at will.'

She leaned her head against his shoulder. 'I hope that's true for, if you discovered I was not what I seemed, I couldn't bear to lose you now.'

'What nonsense you talk? How can you not be what you seem? Nothing will part us, my Eve,' he said tenderly. 'Come, let me lift you on to your mount before I forget myself again.' And only a brief kiss was her reward before they were on their way again – but a kiss with a possessive little bite in the middle to let her know what lay beneath it.

He took her to the top of the highest hill.

His arm described an arc across an undulating plain lying to their north, and containing clusters of trees, villages and farms. Beyond the downs, a range of hills were a misty blue smudge against the sky. 'Beautiful, isn't it?'

His pride in his homeland was justified, for the little she'd seen of it was surprisingly pretty, and diverse in its landscape. It had a solidness about it, a sense of strength and rightness. That fact was evident in Saville's eyes, in the quiet pride of his smile.

'It seems that an Englishman needs nothing but rustic England to sustain him,' she teased. 'You offer me a treasure, indeed. Now, I would be offered a little refreshment, for we have come a long way and I'm hungry and thirsty. Is there a farmhouse nearby where we can beg refreshment.'

He laughed, his face all at once self-deprecating. He astonished her by taking a flask of wine and a kerchief containing bread, cheese and apples, from a bag tied to his saddle.

They sat on a flat rock and refreshed themselves whilst the horses munched contentedly at the grasses. The breeze was a soft sigh.

On the horizon, the sea was a glittering silver ribbon between land and sky. A narrow strip of grey pebbles curved towards a grim-looking island, which thrust steeply upwards from a churning sea.

'That's the Isle of Portland,' he told her. 'Some of the finest buildings in London are built from the limestone quarried there. There is a courtship tradition there, that the woman is got with child before the wedding takes place. When Graine gasped, he laughed. 'It proves the couple can produce issue. Isn't that interesting?'

She avoided his laughing eyes and changed the subject. 'It's very pretty here, I'm glad you brought me.' Rushford Hall was nowhere to be seen, hidden as it was in a secret valley sloping between hills stepping down to the sea. They had come a long way, further than she was ready for, she thought, for the ride had chafed blisters on her rear and she had tired.

He smiled lazily when she gazed at him. 'I'm glad you like it.' Somewhere, a lark began to sing. Presently she grew sleepy and rested her head against his shoulder, soaking in the lush landscape through half-closed eyes. His arm came around her for support, his fingers brushed gently through her hair, relaxing her. The world faded to a distant hum.

She woke to find him gazing at her still. She smiled, reassured by his presence. He brushed a kiss across her mouth. 'We must go, my love, for there's a long journey ahead of us on the morrow.'

She no longer feared that journey into the unknown, for her future would be here, with Saville. 'Thank you for giving me this perfect day,' she said, they hugged each other for a few, precious moments.

They arrived back to Rushford at sunset. Charlotte was waiting for them, her face stern. 'I was just going to organize a search party. Really, Saville. Evelyn has just recovered from a serious illness.'

'It was the best day of my life,' she said simply. 'I'm not in the least bit tired.' Evelyn's face was glowing, her eyes were filled with dreams. Charlotte felt a lump in her throat. How wonderfully reassuring that her brother could make a woman look as happy as Evelyn did at that moment.

As she gazed from one smiling face to the other, she began to smile herself. 'Do you have something to tell me, then?'

Saville's laugh was full-throated. 'You will be the first to know, after I have seen John.'

'Should I arrange a ball in London with you and Evelyn as guests of honour?'

'That would be a very good idea, Charlotte.' He kissed the top of her head. 'Now we must change for dinner, else we'll be late. Is there anything that needs my attention?'

'Nothing urgent. Captain William Younger called. He left a

message for you on the table. I think he wanted to thank you for attending his son's death-bed.'

Picking up the note, he was about to open it when Evelyn gave a tiny gasp. Her face had assumed an ashen hue.

'What is it, my angel?'

'I'm sorry,' she said, for she had a dread that her deceit was about to be exposed and, despite Saville's sincerely expressed words of everlasting love, she feared his reaction and the distaste he would surely feel for her. The hallway began to shift and dim.

Hastily, Saville shoved the note in his pocket and stepped forward to catch her when she buckled at the knees.

10

Graine recovered quickly from her faint, reassuring the earl and his sister that she was able to travel. That same evening she wrote Saville a note, thanking him for the perfect day they'd spent together and professing her love for him in a much more eloquent and poetic manner than she could have told him. She asked his servant to hand it to him in private before they left in the morning.

The moon was full, its bright, white light keeping her awake. When she heard a dog bark she ran to the window. Dressed only in breeches, a brocade robe tied carelessly at the waist, Saville was siting on the terrace wall below. He was gazing out over the grounds, which were touched with strands of silver moonlight. Nose to the ground, Rebel ran from place to place, his tail swiping at the air.

'Saville,' she whispered softly, bringing his gaze up to hers.

His smile melted her. 'Well met, my lady of the moonlight. The night has enchanted me, so I cannot sleep.'

'Nor I.'

'Then come down and join me, until Rebel tires of chasing hares.'

Pulling a silk shawl about her shoulders she made her way downstairs, not needing a candle in such luminosity as filtered through the windows.

The night had a chilly edge to it. 'I'll get into trouble with Charlotte if she finds out.'

'She won't find out if we don't tell her.' He pulled the night-cap from her head, tossing it to one side. 'Your hair is too beautiful to hide under such a garment. When you're truly mine you'll be ordered not to wear this cap.'

'One order I'll be glad to obey, but do not think I shall allow you to have your own way over everything, my lord.'

He chuckled, as if the thought amused him. 'Shall I not, sweeting?'

He resumed his seat on the wall and, with his arms in possession of her waist pulled her back into his body. He kissed her ear, his breath a small caress that sent a cascade of shivers racing along the curve of her neck. Everything inside her flamed into life.

'Oh, that was most unfair of you,' she murmured. *And sensuous*, she thought, grinning with the unexpected delight of it. *If this is what carnal sinning is all about. I shall apply myself to such business between us with pleasure.*

He chuckled and rested his chin on her scalp. They stayed like that for a few minutes, their eyes absorbing the magical night, then he lifted her hair and allowed it to trickle through his fingers. 'It's like silk.'

She took his hands and brought them back around her body, holding him there with her hands. 'I like being in your arms, like this. You make me feel loved.'

'You are loved.' His thumbs brushed gently against the undersides of her breasts. When she let his hands go free it was an invitation, and he slid them upwards to cup her in his palms.

She made a frustrated little sound deep in her throat, wishing there was no material between his hands and her body. Softly, she quoted a few lines from the *Merchant of Venice*:

> *How sweet the moonlight sleeps upon this bank!*
> *Here we will sit, and let the sounds of music,*
> *Creep in our ears: soft stillness and the night*
> *Becomes the touches of sweet harmony.*

Immediately, his hands were withdrawn. 'My pardon, I'm making the situation between us almost unbearable. Go back to bed, my Eve.'

'But I cannot, for you have me held prisoner to your heart.'

'Go, before it's too late.'

She twisted to face him. 'And if I don't want to go?'

'I'll have to take you to your chamber, but I cannot guarantee I'll leave.' He kissed her, his mouth a tender caress against her trembling bottom lip. 'Go, I beg of you,' and there was a finality in his voice, now. 'Anything less could bring about your downfall.'

She didn't push the situation for she suddenly remembered that her mother's sinful nature had brought about *her* downfall. She had left her only child an orphan, without the protection of a father's name and carrying the sin of her parentage on her shoulders. Even the Seaton family had found her mother too corrupt to acknowledge. How unfair the rules of society were. Blanche Seaton had been buried in an unmarked grave, and her baby daughter disowned.

The shame of her background was acute sometimes, as if the blood relationship between herself and her mother had turned her into a soiled creature, who was worth nothing as a human being. When Evelyn had drowned, Graine had lost the only person who'd ever shown her true affection. Now Saville had offered her his love and protection, not knowing she was worth less than the dust beneath his feet. She must not do anything to incur his distaste.

She realized it would be impossible to tell him the truth, for then she'd lose everything. She must not allow the sin she'd inherited from her parents to overcome her good sense, but must remain chaste and modest, however hard it seemed. Lying in Saville's arms in the moonlight was definitely not good sense.

Women had to exert the most rigid discipline on themselves, the reverend mother had told her, for as the Bible demonstrated, men were easily led into sin by the temptress, Eve. And didn't Saville always refer to her as his Eve?

Giving a cry of awareness at her own wanton behaviour, she gathered her shawl around her and ran into the house. Reaching her chamber, she fell to her knees and prayed to the Lord to save her from the temptation of sin.

Despite her prayers, Graine slept badly, her conscience troubling her. She could see no end to the problem she'd made for herself. If she told Saville the truth now, she was damned. If she didn't tell him, there was a possibility that William Younger would – or already had.

It was a long night of tossing and turning between snatches of sleep. At breakfast, she found it hard to appear rested, but Saville didn't seem to notice. His smile was slightly preoccupied, but loving nevertheless, and his eyes warm with his regard for her. Charlotte was out of sorts with the early hour and grumbled like a bear roused prematurely from hibernation as she picked at her food.

They departed Rushford in a gold-tinted dawn shimmering with mist – two coaches, three personal servants and four outriders, all armed.

Rebel, held fast to the side of Edmund Scanlon by a short leash, struggled and howled disconsolately as the coaches rolled down the carriageway and out of his sight.

'Damned dog, Saville spoils him,' Charlotte said grumpily and, tucking a cushion under her head, reclined into a corner and fell instantly asleep. Not so Graine, for this ethereal start to the morning had entranced her, and continued to entrance her until the mist was dispersed by the heat of the sun to disappear into a blue, cloudless sky.

Saville was on horseback. He cut a dashing figure in his blue, single-breasted frock coat, dark breeches and knee length roqualaure cape. His calves and feet were encased in a comfortable pair of half-jack boots.

As the carriage wheels measured the miles, Graine began to relax. If Captain Younger had informed Saville of what he knew, he would have said something by now.

Saville had forgotten all about William Younger's note, but he'd memorized every word of Evelyn's love letter. His fingertips carried a kiss from his lips to the pocket over his heart. Her letter had made him smile a little, for the parchment had been tied with a pink ribbon bow, and Evelyn had sounded like a lovesick girl in it, instead of a mature young lady of twenty-six years. He couldn't help being flattered at the thought of being so adored, though.

My dearest love
I cannot believe the truth my heart presents me with, that a man so generous of nature, humble of heart and honest in his

ways, holds this most humble of females most precious to his heart.

I am afraid, Saville, fearful I will wake to discover your affection for me was merely a dream, an illusion which sprang from the mind of one who loves you truly, and for all of eternity.

Worse, would be to discover that the regard you display towards me is a whimsey, or have it changed into disdain by circumstance, for now I've been uplifted by the sweetness of your love, nothing can ever dislodge you from my heart.
Your Eve

Something bothered him about the letter, and it wasn't her uncertainty, which not only made his heart ache, but also heightened the tender feelings of protectiveness he felt for her. He wondered though, what made her think he was so fickle of nature that his love might become disdain?

He tried to put it from his mind during the tedious journey to Poole. Although he'd made sure the road was kept in good repair to the boundary of his land, beyond, it was full of ruts and potholes. Of necessity, for Saville didn't want to risk injury to his coach horses, they were forced to slow down. Even so, the coaches were jolted this way and that, forcing the two women inside to hang on tightly.

They encountered no trouble boarding a ship at Poole, and they headed out past Brownsea Island to sail leisurely around the coast and into the mouth of the river Thames.

Charlotte was affected badly by the motion on the ship, and lay on her bunk, day and night, looking pale and sickly. 'It's not motion sickness, for I have felt this way on several occasions of late, and my courses have not arrived. I think I'm with child,' Charlotte told her in a matter-of-fact voice and, managing a wan smile when Graine exclaimed with delight, added, 'I hope to present my husband with a son, this time.'

Saville managed to snatch only one private moment with Graine. They took the air on deck together, where he gently kissed the palm of her hand and told her he loved her. 'How are you coping with Charlotte?'

'She doesn't like being fussed over and suspects her sickness is caused by other than the motion of the ship.'

'Ah . . . I understand. I'm to become an uncle again.' He thought about it for a few moments, then grinned at her, saying softly, 'I would enjoy being a father, I think.'

A delicate blush stained her cheeks and she couldn't quite meet his eyes. 'I'm glad, for some men seem indifferent to the existence of their offspring.'

The sadness in her voice touched him. 'It sounds as if you speak from experience. Was Seth Adams such a man?'

She nibbled on her bottom lip for a moment, then said so quietly that he had to strain to hear her above the slapping sea and hissing wind, 'The man was never a father to me.' She glanced up at him then, her eyes startled and wide, her face draining of colour. 'I meant, of course, that he died when I was young, so I cannot really remember him being paternal.'

'I understand. My own father died when I was young, too.' For some reason, the elusive puzzle her letter had presented him, suddenly resolved itself. There had been no sign of the awkward phrases or spelling mistakes of her earlier one. It was as if it had been written by a different person. In fact, he could almost swear it had been written by a different hand altogether. Unfortunately, he didn't have the earlier one to compare it with.

'Evelyn,' he said, 'do you remember the letter you wrote to me when I was negotiating on behalf of John Lamartine?'

She started slightly and her eyes darted to the hatch leading to below deck. 'Of course I remember. I must get back to Charlotte. She's not looking at all well.'

He detained her with a hand on her arm. 'Did you write that letter?'

There was a watchful stillness about her now. 'Why do you ask?'

'Your writing has improved considerably and I wondered if the same person had penned both notes.'

She gazed at him for a moment, then gave an odd, breathless sort of laugh and mumbled, 'As I recall, I was unwell at the time and I dictated it to my companion.'

'Ah yes, poor Graine,' he said, 'Such an unusual and pretty name. It must have caused her much amusement to have written about herself in such a manner.'

Tears glistened in his companion's eyes. 'Graine found much in life to amuse her, despite her circumstances. But she is gone and cannot be brought back. You will excuse me now, for to think of her causes me much distress.' And she was discovering that being someone else, was a responsibility difficult to maintain.

'I'm sorry, my love. I won't mention her again. Thank you for your note. I was touched by it, and will keep it close to my heart. Rest assured, the love I feel for you will remain constant, whatever circumstances may arise.'

Graine prayed his constancy would never be put it to the test as she hurried away.

Indistinguishable from its adjoining neighbours, Saville's London home was situated in Hanover Square. The house fronts were protected by posts and chains. People paraded in their finery on this narrow strip. Beyond was the road, where carriages and horses came and went, and then the square in the middle, where vendors sold goods of many varieties.

Her mind was already exhausted by the colourful crowds, smells and sights of London, and Graine was grateful to step inside a hall of quiet serenity. Blue and white were the predominant colours, with touches of gold in the candle sconces, the chandelier and the wall panelling.

Charlotte immediately headed upstairs, with her maid hurrying after. Saville was drawn to one side by a male servant in livery and, giving her an apologetic look, preceded him into the nearest room.

Graine sank on to a velvet chair with gilt legs and watched the servants scurry here and there, hauling their luggage upstairs.

Jessie assumed a rather haughty manner as she told one of them to take Miss Adams's luggage to the best guest chamber at the front, and she'd come up and inspect it to make sure it was clean.

Which she did. There was the sound of scolding. A couple of maids scurried downstairs, long of face, only to dash upstairs again with dusters and clean bed linens in their arms.

A little while later, the maids came back down again, looking all flustered. Jessie was behind them, grinning all over her face. She watched them move out of ear-shot and whispered, 'Those harping cats have nothing to do for half the year, then think they can give me a length of their tongues when I asks them to put the room to rights. They needs a cane across their—'

Saville came out of the room and smiled at her. 'I'm sorry you've had to wait. The servants didn't know we were coming. I hope you're looking after her, Jessie?'

The maids slunk past Jessie with steaming jugs of water and headed up the stairs.

'I've allocated Miss Adams the guest chamber at the front.' Saville grinned, and they exchanged a glance of mutual amusement when Jessie sent a shrivelling look after the maids and raised her voice. 'I'll take Miss Adams up and she can rest whilst her bath is being prepared.'

'Good . . . good, I'll see you at dinner then, Evelyn. You'll have to excuse me now. I have some urgent business I must attend to.'

And Graine guessed that the business was a quiet glass of wine in the solitude of the study whilst the domestic issues were being sorted out.

She followed Jessie upstairs to a room overlooking the street. It had a little dressing-room in which there was a truckle bed. Jessie gazed at it in some satisfaction. 'We shall be right comfortable here, I can tell thee. At least I won't be stuck in with that pair of London mop squeezers. They couldn't raise a breeze with a broom if they tried.'

The pair in question were filling the bath and exchanging grimaces and grins. 'You can stop making those silly faces and fetch Miss Adams some tea when you've finished filling the tub,' Jessie said to them.

They giggled and dropped Jessie a curtsy. 'Yes, your ladyship.'

'Cheeky madams.'

Graine couldn't stifle a smile. 'I think there's enough water in the tub. What are your names?'

The taller one said, 'We're Millie and Mollie Perkins, miss. We're sisters.'

'You're very much alike. I doubt if I'll remember which one is which.'

'We'll have no airs and graces from them. They can both answer to Perkins,' Jessie said, the name tripping from her mouth with some scorn, 'And a right lazy pair of Perkins they be, too.'

Graine sent them a rueful smile. 'I'm sure you're not.'

'No, miss, it's just . . . well, everyone arriving at once and shouting for this and that put the household in a bit of a stir.'

'From now on address his lordship's guest as Miss Adams, else you'll be hearing it from the earl, hisself,' Jessie hissed.

The younger Perkins sniffed and the older one tossed her head. Off they went without another word, their eyes glittering with affront.

'You were too sharp with them, Jessie,' Graine admonished, when they were alone. 'They're doing their best. I don't like feelings to be hurt for no reason. It causes resentment and brings tension to a house.'

The snap went out of the maid. 'I be worn to a frazzle after that journey, that's for certain.'

'Then go and rest. I can see to myself.'

A stubborn glint came into her eyes. 'Not whilst I've got breath left in my body, for the earl hisself put you in my charge. I'll rest after you've bathed and changed, and not a moment afore.'

So Graine was forced to hurry when she would have relaxed and lingered, and Jessie's fingers were clumsy with fatigue as she hurriedly dressed her hair. The maid fell asleep almost as soon as she lay on the truckle.

Graine had chosen a gown of bronze-tinted satin to wear, with deep embroidered cuff sleeves and bodice, over lace flounces. The sea air had leant a healthy bloom to her cheeks. Her hair was untidy, with wisps escaping from under her cap. She frowned and, pulling off her cap, shook it loose.

The taller Perkins came in with refreshment for her. The girl handed her a posy of red peonies. 'The earl asked me to give you this. He bought them himself from a street vendor.'

'Thank you, Millie.'

The girl grinned. 'It's Mollie, Miss Adams.' Her glance swept over her loose hair. 'You have lovely hair. Let me dress it for you. I could fashion a pretty pom-pom from the flowers and ribbons.'

So her hair was expertly dressed in a prettier style than Jessie could manage, with finger ringlets curling at her ears and the nape of her neck. The style was enhanced by a frivolous pom-pom of peonies and ribbons worn at the crown of her head. A single flower was attached to the pearl necklace around her throat. It sat moistly in the small hollow, where the warmth of her pulse beating against it released a subtle fragrance.

Graine smiled gratefully at her. 'I must apologize for Jessie. She's tired after the journey.'

'We won't pay her no mind, for she's getting on in years and is set in her ways. If you want to look special for an occasion, you ask for me to attend you, Miss Adams, for I study all the latest fashions and know where gowns and accessories can be bought in a hurry at any time of night or day.'

'Thank you, Mollie.'

'The earl said that when you're ready he'd be honoured if you'd join him in the drawing-room until dinner is served.'

'I'd enjoy that,' she said dreamily, and followed the girl downstairs.

Saville was in black trimmed with silver braid, his waistcoat was of patterned brocade the colour of burgundy, and his dark hair was tied at the nape of his neck with a black ribbon. He wasn't a slavish follower of fashion. Jessie had told her he didn't favour wigs, and Graine had never seen him in one.

The admiration in his eyes as his glance went to the flower at her throat was too blatant, his smile too wide to be ignored. She found herself all of a blush.

'Come here,' he growled, when Mollie closed the door behind her. Pulled into his arms, she became the recipient of a long and hungry kiss, then he stooped to kiss the flower scented hollow in her throat. He gazed at her face afterwards, laughing. 'I cannot resist such provocation.'

'Then I must provoke you more often.'

'You most certainly must.' He slid his finger down the length of her nose. 'Charlotte has decided to stay in her chamber, so we only have each other for company. Would you like a glass of wine?'

'Just a little, for too much makes me sleepy.'

He filled a glass and brought it up to her lips whilst she drank, then took a sip or two from the place where her mouth had rested. 'I have never tasted wine so sweet,' he said, and handed the glass back to her. 'I've sent a message to John, telling him we're in town

139

and will call on him in the morning.'

Her smile faded a little.

'You need not worry, my love. I'm looking forward to straightening the matter out, for deceit does not sit easy with me.'

'Yes, it must be straightened out.' She tried to ignore the feeling of dread lodged in her heart, but it persisted, spoiling the intimate dinner they shared. She hardly tasted the tender-fleshed chicken, which had been cooked in a mixture of wine and delicately flavoured herbs, or the variety of steamed vegetables which accompanied it. The apple pie with its sweet, crispy pastry, tasted like ashes in her mouth.

'You will not regain your strength if you do not eat,' Saville said, observing the amount of food still left on her plate. 'Won't you swallow a little more for me, my sweet?' She nearly choked on tears at the tender concern on his face, managing a few more mouthfuls just to see him smile.

When the dishes had been cleared away and it was time for her to go to bed, she hugged him tight for a few precious moments. 'Remember always that I love you, Saville.'

'My angel, what is it?'

'I just wanted you to know.' A final hug and she was gone, her way to her chamber lit by candles flickering in wall sconces. Jessie was still asleep, but someone had lit the candles and her night clothes had been laid out.

Undressing, she slipped under the covers and lay there in the dark, inhaling the scent of the peony on the table at her bedside. She was thinking of Saville and how much she loved him, and how one small slip on her part or that of another, could bring her happiness tumbling down around her.

The sounds of the house gradually quieted and she drifted between sleep and wakefulness. But she must have slept, for she jerked awake to a grey, overcast dawn, and to the sound of someone knocking at the door in the street below.

Then Jessie came in with water to wash with, and the ritual of her toilette began, so she could ready herself for the day.

'Folks keep funny hours in London,' Jessie grumbled, as she shook the folds from a dark-blue gown. 'Fancy sending a message round at this time of morning, when quality folk are still rising from their beds and 'tis only nine of the clock. Best wear the velvet pentenlair with the fur trim over this,' she muttered, 'the weather can't make up its mind whether it be winter or spring today.'

Jessie's energy had renewed itself overnight, for the brush was applied with vigour and her hair was pulled so tight it tugged painfully at her scalp. Braided, it was swept up under a cap. A lace fichu was placed around her shoulders, tucked under the pentenlair at the front, and pinned by her mother's brooch to her bodice. The ornament looked new now it had been polished.

Mollie came in with a beaker of steaming chocolate just as Jessie walked out with the chamber pot. 'And about time too,' she sniffed, as they swept past each other.

Mollie called after her. 'Cook said you didn't come down for your dinner last night, and if you don't want to miss breakfast as well, you'd better go to the kitchen for it now. I'll tidy up in here whilst you're gone.'

Whilst Graine drank the chocolate, Mollie rebraided her hair, threading a blue ribbon through it and tying it with a bow at the bottom and another at the nape of her neck. She teased some ringlets from it, giving the style a much softer appearance and changed the round cap for a frivolous one of lace and ruffles.

'There, that looks better, Miss Adams. That Jessie had nearly pulled it out by the roots. It would have given you a fine old headache by the end of the day. The earl is waiting for you to go down to breakfast. Better not keep him waiting. A messenger brought a message from John Lamartine, and he's out of sorts this morning. He's already had words with Miss Charlotte. She's in a right old pother, and has instructed her maid to ready her to leave.'

Saville hardly raised a smile when she went down, but she caught his glance on her often as they broke fast. She had almost finished eating when he said abruptly. 'That brooch you wear. I meant to ask you before: where did you get it?'

Her hand began to tremble and she placed her knife carefully on the plate. 'It was my mother's brooch. Why do you ask?'

It seemed as though he was about to say something more, but he changed his mind. Rising, he crossed to the window, where he stared out into the garden. 'No reason. Did you sleep well?'

141

'I was a little restless.'

'Good,' he said, clearly preoccupied.

'Has something upset you, Saville? Was it that note from Captain Younger.'

He turned, looking puzzled. 'Captain Younger?'

'The note he left for you at Rushford . . .' She faltered, for she'd made a mistake in pointing out to him what he'd clearly forgotten.

'Oh, that.' He fished around in his pocket and came out with a piece of screwed-up paper. Flattening it, he read the contents. His eyes widened with disbelief. 'Damn him for a thieving knave!'

Quaking a little, she said in a tiny voice, 'What is it!'

'He's asking for ten thousand pounds as recompense for his son's death. He said it was my dog which caused Thomas Younger his injuries.'

Her hand went to her mouth. 'Oh, Saville. Will you pay him?'

His eyes lit on her. 'It seems, my dear Evelyn Adams, that people take me for a fool. Of course I will not pay him. He was trespassing on my property when he'd been warned not to. He nearly caused the death of a guest of mine, namely you.' His smile had a bitter edge to it. 'Unless, of course . . . but no, you were surely not conspiring with him to defraud me.'

She shuddered when she thought of the icy water dragging her down. 'If I wanted to defraud you, would I have drowned myself in the attempt?' She crossed to place a hand on his arm, the hurt in her voice evident, for such a suggestion had wounded her badly. 'Saville, do you really think I'd steal from you?'

He gazed at her for a moment, then smiled, self-deprecating. 'I accuse you of stealing the most precious thing I own. My heart. I pray you, do not break it in two. Go and get your cloak, my Eve. We have an appointment with destiny to keep.'

An odd choice of words, she thought, as she hurried to do his bidding.

11

Once they'd negotiated the busiest part of the city the density began to thin. Saville took over the reins of the carriage himself. More and more countryside appeared and they passed prosperous looking houses set in spacious gardens.

John Lamartine lived in Chiswick. His residence was a square, solid, red-brick house standing in wooded grounds, with no pretence at being anything but the master's residence for the school it was first designed to be. The residence and the school-house, which was concealed by trees occupied a large tract of land sloping down to the river.

The property belonged to the Lamartine Estate. It had been built by Saville's grandfather to provide his younger son with gain-ful employment. The schoolhouse itself legitimately served a purpose as storage for a merchant who thoroughly disapproved of the inhumanity of the slave trade and spoke openly against it. He gladly arranged accommodation and employment for the slaves who'd escaped from their so-called masters. The river gave access to the secluded buildings by boat. It was a pursuit of which John was fully aware and thoroughly approved – whilst Harriet was kept in ignorance of it for the sake of peace and quiet.

Saville had been taught his lessons there by his uncle, along with a sprinkling of other boys whose parents had the means to pay for the excellent education his uncle provided. When the man had died the school had died with him, for John Lamartine, although learned, was a scholar by nature, and had not the inclination to step into his more practical father's footsteps. Instead, the small church he officiated over made him feel gainfully employed, whilst all his spare time was spent in the library. John was content to exist on the stipend his calling provided, and was a man who had not displayed much ambition, so far.

His mother, Harriet, having ruled over her only son since birth, had no intention of relaxing her hold on him. She'd always wanted more for John than he could produce. Although it was written in John's hand, Saville sensed Aunt Harriet's input in the note he'd received.

The strident accusation and demands for vengeance were unmistakable. John's was the voice of reason, the voice of doubt. He imagined Harriet standing over his poor cousin, dictating to him in her demanding voice.

He brought the carriage slowly to a halt. Eight small windows at the front gazed sightlessly over a sizeable, but slightly unkempt, country garden. An attempt had been made to soften the ugliness of its façade with a honeysuckle rambling over the porch. He inspected the house, remembering snatches of his youth, anything, to keep himself occupied, to distract him from the problem of Evelyn Adams.

It didn't work. He was totally aware of the presence of his exquisite heart-breaker, his fair pretender. His curtness had wounded her this morning. He'd meant it to, the savagery in him had been barely under control after John's message had arrived. He'd wanted to crush her. The odd, unworthy thought had surfaced that he should have taken what she'd offered the night before. At least he would have known her and his lust would have been satisfied. Instead, he remained unfulfilled, and his body still hungered at the sight of her.

The courage to ask her outright at breakfast if she was imper-sonating Evelyn Adams, had deserted him at the time. Something had held him back. He hadn't wanted to know the answer. Still didn't, in fact. He'd suspected for some time that she wasn't who she seemed. She was the antithesis of the dull spinster of his expec-tations. Her vibrancy, her wit and her vulnerability had fooled him, her beauty had dazzled him, her love had captured him.

So who was she? Indeed, was she an impostor, at all? John's letter had been agitated, but expressive in its uncertainty. How undecided I am, Saville thought. A pitiful fool clutching at straws, trying to convince myself of the best, when logic tells me the truth.

His Eve knew something momentous was about to happen. There was an air about her, a slight droop to her shoulders, a half-hopeless, half-hopeful look in her eyes. She reminded him of a dog with its tail tucked under its body, dreading an expected beating, but hoping it wouldn't happen.

He felt sickened by his own cruelty. It didn't have to be this way. He could turn the carriage around and take her back to Rushford. He could keep her there and leave himself in blessed ignorance. But a union based on lies was a union without trust, and without trust, love would wither and eventually die.

So he drew the carriage to a halt, jumped down from the driver's seat and, opening the door, held out his hand to her. 'We've arrived.'

'Yes,' she said simply. Her eyes met his, unsure. Her lips trembled as if she was about to say more, but she didn't. She just gazed at him, her eyes the colour of autumn reflected in water. She would like autumn at Rushford, he thought inconsequently.

Feeling like her executioner, he avoided that gaze, avoided the hurt and the slight accusation in them. It was as if he'd betrayed her, not the other way around. The thought refreshed his anger.

But her guilt is not proven yet.

He closed his eyes and prayed for her innocence, savoured the kiss she brushed against his lips. It felt like goodbye to him.

There was a dragging reluctance in Graine as she followed Saville to the door. She kept telling herself that the feeling of presentiment in her was nothing to do with Saville's attitude, but rather by the task he faced in explaining the situation to the man she was betrothed to.

At Saville's knock, the door was opened by a women in apron, who bobbed a curtsy. The quick glance Graine received was followed by a thinning of her lips as she invited them into the hall.

'I'll fetch the Reverend Lamartine,' she said, and waddled off to the back of the house.

Bewigged, a small pair of glasses perched on the end of his nose, John Lamartine appeared agitated as he advanced toward them. His voice was soft, but had a pleasing timbre to it. 'Ah, Saville. It's good of you to come so promptly.'

'I'd like to introduce Miss Evelyn Adams,' Saville said.

John stared at her for a moment or two. His eyes were a paler blue than Saville's, introspective, but with a depth of intelligence. There was a vaguely academic air about him. He gave a small, embarrassed, cough, saying very gently. 'Yes, yes, quite. Welcome to my home, Miss, er . . .' He turned to Saville. 'Oh dear, I think it would be wise not to prolong the issue at hand, though I like it not at all. Mama is quite distressed, as you can imagine, so we had best not keep her waiting.'

'Of course,' Saville murmured, and motioned her forward up the staircase.

With each step Graine took, the feeling of imminent disaster increased. Then they were standing outside a room to the left of the upstairs landing. John Lamartine took a handkerchief from his pocket and wiped his brow before grasping the doorknob. He gazed at Saville, who nodded reluctantly.

Their eyes met and she saw shame in the damning blue depths of his. He knew! She lowered her eyes and felt her heart break as the door swung open with a muted squeak of the hinges.

Graine's breath became an anguished gasp. Nothing could have prepared her for the scene which met her eyes. On the far side of the room, Evelyn was seated in a chair by the window, working at an embroidery frame. She gave a small cry of thankfulness. Somehow, her sister had escaped from the clutches of the deep!

'Allow me to introduce you,' Saville whispered savagely against her ear. 'This lady has presented herself to my cousin as Miss Evelyn Adams from Antigua. Is she uttering falsehood?'

'No.' The muscles in her throat constricted as she tried to murmur Evelyn's name. Evelyn glanced up, a smile forming on her lips. It froze there as they stared in complete shock at one another. Tremors ran through Graine's body.

A woman rose from the armchair. She was short, her portliness emphasized by fussy frills adorning a gown of eye-catching purple. Her face wore a disagreeable expression, her mouth was as pursed as a badly darned hole in hosiery, and her eyes as sharp as needle-points.

'See how the girl shakes,' she screamed out in triumph. 'She has guilt written all over her and should be hanged from the highest gallows. You have been duped, Saville. We all have.'

Graine only half heard the woman's words, for Evelyn's smile had lit her features. 'Graine, my dearest. I'd quite despaired of ever seeing you again. I've missed you so.'

Graine took a step towards her. 'And not a day has passed when I haven't grieved your loss and prayed for your soul.'

Tears began to trickle down Evelyn's cheeks and she held out her arms. 'Come here and hug me, for I cannot believe you are less than an apparition until I can touch you to make sure.'

Graine needed no urging. Heart beating erratically, she flew across the room into Evelyn's embrace, weeping tears of joy. *'Thank God, thank God!'*

'Thank you, John,' Evelyn murmured over her shoulder. 'This is a most wonderful, wonderful surprise. I'm indebted to you.'

John blinked, moistened his lips with his tongue and gazed guiltily at Saville.

'Wonderful?' Harriet shrieked. 'The girl is a trickster. She has falsely represented herself as you in an attempt to marry my son. She has tried to cheat us all out of the fortune that would rightfully belong to us when you marry, and has accepted bed and board from the earl under false pretences. She must be given a good beating and sent to gaol!' To emphasize her point, the virago flew across the room and slapped her viciously about the head.

Crying out with the vicious suddenness of it, she turned her face into Evelyn's comforting shoulder.

'Mama!' John said, sounding shocked as he pulled her away. 'There is no need for such violence.'

'Is there not? This girl is Evelyn's servant. She needs a good beating and I'm the very one to give it to her. Afterwards, she can be locked in the cellar with the rats overnight, then in the morning she must be taken to the watch house and charged.'

'We will do no such thing, Harriet,' Evelyn said firmly, and it was the first time Graine had ever heard her raise her voice.

'Pray, who are you, miss, to tell me what to do in my own home? Nothing but a spinster lady, who, I might add, has my son to thank for the fortuitous change due in her status. Well, you are not wed to him yet. As a guest in my home, you should mind your manners and your business. Take the girl to the cellar, John. I will lay your father's cane across her back. That will teach her to try and steal a fortune.'

'Graine is welcome to the fortune. She is my sister, and therefore my heir.'

Graine gazed at her wonderingly. 'All this time, you knew of our familial relationship?'

'Of course I knew. That's why I insisted Theodore Chambers hire you as my companion. I wanted you under my protection. He agreed, as long as I swore never to tell you.' She managed an ironic little smile. 'He had no right to insist you be kept in ignorance, but I was too weak to defy him whilst he lived. I had determined to inform you of our relationship when we reached England. How silly, when it's obvious you knew all the time. We must never keep secrets from each other again.'

Saville gave a bitter laugh. The humiliation in his eyes was being overtaken by a growing anger, and it damned her to hell. His mouth twisted in scorn when her eyes pleaded with his for understanding. His eyes became ice.

'Saville, my dear,' Harriet said, and the look she aimed at Evelyn was designed to crush. 'You are most grievously wronged in this matter. Out of the kindness of your heart, this devious creature has been allowed to shelter under your roof, and has supped at your table. Who knows what treasures she may have stolen? You must search her bags, and she must be made to pay for her crimes against you.'

Saville contemplated her for a moment or two, his eyes half-hooded. 'Have you stolen such treasures from me, my Eve?'

She knew that which he referred to. Tears squeezed from beneath her lids. She'd stolen only the one thing she'd ever wanted from life and that was the most precious thing he had to offer her. His love. As if it had been worth nothing, she'd accepted it, then crushed it and tossed it aside.

'Yes,' she whispered, the agony she experienced excruciating. 'I'm sorry . . . so sorry, Saville. I should have told you. I thought you'd turn me from your door. I knew nobody in this country and had no means, and nowhere else to go.'

'See!' Harriet shrieked. 'With her own lips she's admitted her guilt. I demand that you have her charged and thrown into a cell.'

Saville's voice was a whiplash. 'Please be quiet, Aunt Harriet. You're in no position to demand anything of me.' He crossed to where they stood and smiled at Evelyn. 'I'm pleased you survived the storm, Miss Adams, for your sister appears to have sincerely grieved for you. There is another storm ahead of you. Stay strong, but beware: Graine will need somebody to lean on, and she has a sly way of creeping into your heart.'

Graine hung her head at his condemnation.

Evelyn placed her hand on his arm. 'Perhaps you would wait for a few moments, my lord, for I have something I wish to say.'

He nodded, and withdrew to a spot near the door. Not one glance did he afford her, as if she no longer existed for him.

'Saville,' Graine whispered, in quiet supplication, but the plea didn't reach his ears.

Harriet, puffed up and purple, advanced on her son. 'Well, don't just stand there, John. Insist that the girl be thrown out.'

John's face flushed. 'I don't think there's much I can do, Mama. She has committed no crime against us and Evelyn seems to want her to stay.'

'The girl is an undesirable creature to have in our home.' Her glance impaled Evelyn. 'My dear, you are being disagreeably obdurate over the matter. As you know, our connections are impeccable. We are God-fearing people. What will people say if we give the girl room? She is illegitimate, her mother was a loose woman, so who knows who fathered her.'

Evelyn didn't argue with the notion, just gazed at John. 'What are your thoughts on this matter, John?'

John appeared uncomfortable at being pinned down. 'Mother is right, of course. We cannot be sure of her parentage. However, one must be charitable. Perhaps I could find her employment. Yes, I do believe one of my parishioners needs a maid of all work.' He beamed a smile at her. 'I'll look into it. You must excuse me now. I have work to do on my sermon.'

'Your sermon can wait,' Evelyn said, in a voice Graine had never heard her use before. 'I have not finished. Please take a seat.'

Harriet gave an outraged gasp when John immediately did as he was told. 'How dare you tell my son—'

Evelyn turned on her. 'Sit down, Harriet, and kindly do not interrupt again. First, allow me to say that I *know* Graine is my sister. There's no doubt in my mind.'

Harriet opened her mouth then shut it again.

'John. I've been a guest in your house for several weeks, and have grown to respect you, for there's more depth to you than you care to show. However, what has taken place here today does you no justice. You knew how much I grieved for my sister. Instead of telling me earlier that God had spared her life, you gave the information of her survival to your mother. What I told you of Graine's background was a confidence between us. Somehow, your mother has learned of this, and has humiliated my sister in a public way, for something not her fault.'

John sent his mother a level look. 'I can only imagine she was listening to our conversation at the door, for I didn't break your confidence.'

'Nevertheless, you've allowed us both to be subjected to this shameful charade. In doing so, you've admitted that a seed of doubt existed in your mind as to my own truthfulness.'

John bowed his head and looked ashamed.

'As for you, Harriet. You are too opinionated and vulgar. You brow-beat your son, and because he is gentle and retiring by nature, you will not allow him to become his own man.'

Harriet gave a loud gasp.

'For the past few weeks I've listened to your endless discussions on how my money is to be spent after the wedding takes place. My wealth is not yours to spend. It will never be yours to spend.'

'Hah! May I remind you that when you are wed, your fortune will belong to my son.'

'You need not remind me, for I have heard it too often from your lips. Your greed is obvious. I have come to a decision. *If* I marry your son I will not share a house with you, for a home can have only one mistress, and that mistress will be me.'

John's eyes began to shine as he looked upon her with admiration.

Evelyn turned an unsmiling countenance his way and gave a slight shrug. 'For a man of the church I find you oddly lacking in charity, John. I can only imagine it's your mother's influence. I've decided that marrying for the sake of convenience is not a good idea at this time, and I intend to postpone the nuptials indefinitely. In the meantime, I will set up my own establishment with my sister, who will be endowed with half of my fortune – something I believe she's entitled to. It will help her to make a suitable match for herself.'

Saville's breath hissed between his teeth.

Harriet's hand flapped against her chest and she moaned, 'I knew no good would come of this.'

'You cannot,' Graine whispered, disbelievingly, 'I don't deserve it.'

'You do not have to deserve it.' Evelyn's smile was tender as she gazed at her. 'You're my sister and I love you. I'm so glad to find you're still alive, that my heart is full to bursting.' Tears in her eyes she turned towards Saville. 'I was wondering, my lord, do you know of a respectable establishment that will furnish my sister and myself with rooms?'

Saville gave her a little bow. 'There's one I can personally recommend, Miss Adams,' and Graine became the recipient of a stinging glance. 'I'll be happy to convey you and your *sister* there.'

'Don't forget, should you not honour the betrothal contract, there will be a penalty to pay,' Harriet warned, in as hectoring a voice, as she dared.

'I think not, Mama,' John Lamartine said, 'for Evelyn has not refused to wed me, she has merely postponed it.'

'You're a fool if you think that.'

'Which is not too bad a thing to be. If Miss Adams does dismiss my suit she will not be penalized, for I'm a sorry wretch who doesn't deserve to have her. Indeed, I consider myself a poor husband for any woman. I should have told her about her sister as soon as I heard.'

Saville's lips twitched when he gazed at his cousin, and a spark of amusement came into his eyes when John avowed, 'I must use the time to try and improve myself, so to change the opinion Evelyn has formed of me. In fact, once she is settled, I hope she'll grant me permission to call on her.'

There was a modicum of surprise in the glance Evelyn turned his way, and a spark of interest now. 'I will certainly consider the matter.'

'You would choose this woman over your own mother?' Harriet said, her chin thrusting forward belligerently.

'I only have one mother, for whom I shall always hold great affection and respect.' He smiled at Evelyn. 'And if I wed, I will only have one wife, who shall be honoured above all others, as the vows of matrimony dictate.'

'Perhaps you'd allow me to continue to handle the negotiations between you whilst I remain in London,' Saville murmured delicately, and Graine smiled at the thought he would still be connected to her in some small way.

'Hurrumph!' Harriet said and, rendered speechless at last, subsided on to a chair in a billow of purple skirts.

Beside her, Evelyn drew in a deep, satisfied breath. 'I'd be grateful for your help, my lord. And if you would oversee the division of our father's estate between my sister and myself, as well, I should be eternally grateful.'

Saville gave a slightly reluctant nod. 'I'll draw up the necessary papers.'

'No, you mustn't,' Graine said. 'I cannot allow Evelyn to do this for I do not deserve her consideration.'

'I request that you be quiet, Miss . . . *Seaton*, isn't it?' The barely concealed savagery in his voice bode her nothing but ill and the expression in his eyes was glacial. 'The least we hear from you at this moment, the better.'

Stung to the core, she whispered his name.

'From now on, if you're called upon to address me, it will be with the respect due to my position. I would prefer it though, if I was never again in proximity close enough to be addressed by you at all.'

'There,' Harriet snapped, rallying to the cause of righteousness. 'That will teach you to try and deceive your betters, girl.'

Saville's lips tightened a fraction. 'Do you understand, Miss Seaton?'

'Of course,' she whispered, then added, when he stared coldly down his nose at her, '*my lord.*'

Everything seemed to shrivel inside her. Her joy at Evelyn's survival had been earned by the loss of Saville's regard. Why had she embarked on such a web of dishonesty and deceit? The only one in this room who didn't condemn her for it was Evelyn, her beloved sister. *Her sister . . . dear God! Thank you for restoring her to me, and if I must exchange Saville's love for her life, than I'll rejoice in her survival and suffer the punishment of my presumption and pride.*

When she bit down on a sob, Evelyn took her hand in comfort. 'No doubt the earl wishes to discuss the situation with his family. We'll retire to my chamber and, whilst I pack, we will exchange our stories of how we escaped from the clutches of the sea.' She gazed at Saville. 'I do not have much, so it will not take me long. Perhaps you'd let us know when you're ready to depart.'

Saville nodded.

Passing him was the hardest thing Graine had ever done. The tension in him seemed to reach out and enfold her, so the sob she'd retained, swelled in her throat and cut off the air. She imagined he wanted to reach out his arms, wind his fingers around her throat and strangle her. Her head seemed to buzz with the pressure of it, her body trembled uncontrollably. She couldn't help but give him a glance. He hitched in a tiny breath when their eyes met. In the same instant, the spark of regret she saw there swiftly became cruel disdain.

I'll never love another, she thought, and hoped he could sense the burden of pain within her at deceiving him, and take comfort from it. Then they were past and the door behind them was firmly closed. She drew in a deep, quivering breath.

Evelyn took her in a hug when they reached her chamber, a plainly furnished, threadbare room of small proportions. 'My dearest Graine, we have much to talk about, and it must wait until we are settled. The disaster has taught me that life is precious. We must strive to make the most of it and be happy. From now on, you will want for nothing.'

Except Saville Lamartine, the Earl of Sedgley, Graine thought, and deep inside her she discovered a well of bitter tears for the love she'd lost.

Saville took the reins of the carriage as it conveyed them back to the hub of the city. He drove with his usual patience, his control of himself absolute, and with no indication of his mood betrayed.

They were good horses, well schooled. He smiled when he remembered his Eve coming into the grounds of Rushford at full pelt that day, driving the carriage and greys. Her eyes had been wide with alarm as she'd tried to slow the horses down.

But no, the girl was no longer his Eve, he told himself angrily. She was Graine Seaton, the bastard daughter of a womanizer and his doxy. She was a deceiver, a liar and an opportunist who'd turned out to be totally untrustworthy. How could he have allowed her to dupe him when the signs of her deception had been all to apparent? He hardened his heart against her.

As for the real Evelyn Adams, Saville had taken a liking to her immediately. Describing her as plain was unfair. He could see how her quiet demeanour would make her unobtrusive, but she had fine eyes and brows, and her warm smile when she'd set eyes on her sister, had been uplifting. The woman had a big heart, and had possessed the courage to stand up to Harriet in Graine's defence. Sister or not, he must caution Miss Adams about the girl's sly trickery and he intended to delay the division of her fortune as long as possible in case she came to her senses.

Surprisingly, John had stood up to his mother as well, on this occasion. In fact, his cousin had surprised him with his eloquence. Harriet had been beside herself with fury after the sisters had left the room, and uncomplimentary in her assessment of Miss Adams.

'My dear Mama,' John had said, seemingly unruffled by her tirade. 'Before you pass judgement on others, perhaps you should examine your own character traits. I will not hear another word said against Miss Adams. Furthermore, what has taken place here today will remain confidential, unless you want us to become a laughing-stock.'

Saville's attention became totally absorbed in negotiating the increasingly crowded road. When they reached the city he was thankful for such a steady team when a dog chased a squealing cat practically under their hoofs.

When they drew up outside his London home he smiled at Evelyn and helped her from the carriage. 'My home and staff is yours for as long as you wish. I will introduce you to my house-keeper.'

He turned to offer Graine his hand, because to slight her would be bad manners. Her hand was cold and trembling. He had an urge to warm it between his, but she snatched it away before he could succumb to the temptation.

The introduction didn't take long. Afterwards, he called for his manservant. 'I'll be living at the home of the Marquess of Falhampton for a while. Have my things sent around as soon as possible.' He kissed Evelyn's hand. 'I'll be in touch, Miss Adams.'

'Thank you, my lord. You've been most gracious under the circumstances. Truly, I'm grateful for your assistance.'

'The pleasure is mine.'

Graine was the object of only a cursory glance, for he couldn't bear to see the wounded expression in her eyes. She'd been badly bloodied in the skirmish, and mostly it was his doing. She'd deserved it, but he couldn't feel good about it, however justified it was.

'Goodbye, Miss Seaton,' he said and, turning on his heel, left her standing there – the girl he'd fallen in love with, almost a stranger to him now.

12

Evelyn was delighted to be parted from Harriet Lamartine, a woman she considered to be vexatious and overbearing. No wonder John retreated into his study every chance he got.

She was overjoyed by Graine's survival, and pleased the secret of their relationship was finally revealed. How silly of them both to wait for so long, each knowing, and neither able to confide in the other. There would be secrets between them no more, for Evelyn intended to publicly acknowledge their relationship.

Graine would also have everything money could buy her. In London society wealth bought invitations from the curious, and from those who were financially insecure enough to require a partner of means. In fact, they had hardly installed themselves in Saville's house when the first invitation put in an appearance.

'From Lady Salmsley. She's the wife of Bishop Salmsley, who is John Lamartine's superior,' Evelyn told her, looking pleased. 'She has invited us to take tea with her.'

'Considering my notoriety, that's kind of her,' Graine said absently, which caused Evelyn to gaze searchingly at her. Her sister was gazing at a portrait of the previous earl, which hung over the fireplace. There was a faraway look in her eyes.

Evelyn followed her glance. It was odd to think this man had been a friend of their father. He was handsome, with a devil-may-care twinkle in his eyes and a fleshy lower lip. His son was like him, except his chin possessed a firmer set, his mouth was broader and his eyes held a directness the father's lacked. 'The son resembles the father,' she murmured, which brought a smile to soften Graine's mouth.

156

'There is a likeness, of course, but Saville is more handsome, more honest, and much kinder than his father could ever have been.'

Concern growing in her eyes, Evelyn said to her, 'My dearest Graine, am I to understand from your expression that you've fallen in love with the Earl of Sedgley?'

Unhappiness racked the girl's expression as she murmured, 'The earl could have any woman he chose. Why would he be interested in a girl who's deceived him and proved herself to be a liar in his eyes? I have made it impossible for me to love him. I dare not love him, in fact, for to do so would cause me too much pain and suffering.'

Although a bright smile was forced to Graine's face, Evelyn could plainly see the pain behind the effort as Graine made an attempt to tease her. 'What about John Lamartine? I have the feeling you are not wholly averse to his company, despite your hard words to him.'

Evelyn was happy to talk about her growing feelings for John. 'I admire John greatly. He lacks greed or guile, and is of a gentle and compassionate nature. He is a man of habit who likes everything to be just so and has a great liking for his own company.'

'He is set in his ways then?' Graine said, and Evelyn looked at her in some surprise.

'Of course he is, for he's been a bachelor for too long. His study is an escape from his mother, who has always domineered him.'

'And you'll wed him, knowing this?'

'If he asks me, and I'm certain he will.' She laughed. 'When we are wed, John shall be coaxed out of his hiding place and become the man he should be.'

'And how will you achieve this miracle with his mother opposing you? The dreaded Harriet will not be parted from her authority easily.'

'John will be encouraged to stand up to his mama. She will be set up in her own establishment, at a distance to discourage visits on foot.'

'Can you change a man's attitude when it's been ingrained in him since birth?' Graine asked her. 'Can you make a man dispense with his pride?'

Evelyn gave a soft, exasperated sigh, for it was the pride John had already lost that she wanted him to regain. But her sister wasn't thinking of John, but of the earl. 'You know very well that you cannot. But what a man says or shows when he's angry or disappointed is not always what he feels inside. At such times, perhaps the softness of a woman can turn a man's pride towards the positive.'

Hope flared in Graine's eyes and Evelyn thought, however much she denies it, Graine is in love with Saville Lamartine. Although she doubted if the earl would ever forgive her sister for her deception, she was determined to throw them together as much as possible. She waved the invitation in the air and smiled. 'We shall buy ourselves a new wardrobe apiece. A dressmaking establishment has been recommended to me – owned by a Mrs Phillips.'

Graine's laugh contained a hint of her former merriment, her expression full of mock horror. 'Not by Harriet Lamartine, surely. She resembled a purple sofa when last we met. I was tempted to sit on her lap, except she was too formidable a dowager to approach without courting danger.'

Evelyn shouldn't have laughed, but she couldn't help herself. 'It was one of the maids. Millie, I think her name was. Or was it Mollie?'

'Millie, I expect. But whichever it was, we will go where they recommend, for they are both good with fashion and the latest hairstyles. Your hair is arranged quite beautifully.'

'I will instruct her to style yours too, for your present style is too severe for such a sweet face.'

Graine shrugged. She didn't really care how dowdy she looked. There was nobody to admire her now. She had to admit though, Evelyn had improved greatly in appearance. Without the constant sunshine, her skin had lightened, and Millie's skills had softened her appearance. Her eyes sparkled now she had a purpose in life and was free of the indolent living common to the West Indian plantations. Along with her improved appearance, Evelyn had also gained in confidence, something which came as a constant surprise to Graine, though her own was now sadly lacking.

Perhaps she should allow one of the Perkins sisters to dress her hair too. Whilst Jessie did her best, by trade she was not a ladies maid. But Graine couldn't order her to step aside for another, not when Saville had generously allowed her to remain in attendance on her. Reasonably, he could have been expected to withdraw all maid services completely. Also, it was obvious word had not filtered down to the staff for, as guests, they were treated with the utmost deference by the servants.

What became equally obvious was that Charlotte had been informed of her transgression and subsequent fall from grace before they'd left on that fateful visit to John Lamartine's house. Charlotte must have been affronted by the whole affair, for she'd departed without a word of farewell. Graine had penned her a note of apology, asking one of the footmen to deliver it personally into Charlotte's own hands.

It was several days before she received a reply, and that reply was delivered by Charlotte herself. Nervously, Graine presented herself when she was summoned to the drawing-room. She drooped like a limp cabbage leaf when she was impaled with a stare of utter disgust.

Charlotte said without preamble, 'How could you treat my brother so shabbily? He offered you his hearth and home, even risked his own life to save yours on occasion. He opened his very heart to you, only to have it spurned by a girl of low birth, one not fit to lick his boots clean. Why, I don't even know why I'm bothering to call on you. Have you no sense of shame?'

'I didn't—'

'Be quiet, girl. I have not had my say. How you must have laughed behind his back as you led him on to betray him. How you must have enjoyed having myself, a marchioness, dance attendance on you night and day, feel pity for you, and lend an ear to your confidences. Fie, girl! You took us both in.'

Tears filled Graine's eyes and she hung her head in shame.

Charlotte hissed at her. 'Ah . . . so you do have some remorse left inside you then.'

'Of course. I would never have hurt Saville willingly. I had no intention of hurting or deceiving him, believe me. As for your friendship, I was aware of the great honour, and grateful for your patronage, and I'm grieved by its loss. I'm truly penitent for the wrong I've done you both.'

'Penitent?' Leaning forward, Charlotte gazed intently into her eyes. Softening, she handed her a handkerchief on which to dry her eyes. 'An odd word to use. I cannot see you as the type to sacrifice her pride to anyone, Miss Seaton.'

Which reminded Graine of the sisters of the poor, who had raised her. She'd been trained to follow in their footsteps, and had learned to project a penitent expression despite the turmoil which always seemed to churn like rancid butter inside her. She could go back to Antigua if need be. She had the skills to teach children and the knowledge to tend to the sick and injured, or assist women in childbirth. All were worthy occupations and her life there would be fulfilling. She would not have time to think of Saville, or what life might have been for her if she hadn't been so foolish. Unlike Charlotte herself, who'd been raised in the lap of luxury, she was not too proud to scrub floors for her bread.

Taking a deep breath she straightened her shoulders. 'I am not as proud as you imagine, Charlotte. I bitterly regret my duplicity, but it was not aimed at the earl. In fact, my deceit was not aimed at anyone in particular. I thought my sister had perished and I had a moral right to her estate under the circumstances. I just had no means to prove we were related.'

'Hah! Then you admit you had no legal right to your sister's estate.'

'It was my father's wealth before it was my sister's. I truly thought she was dead.' But why was she explaining herself to this woman, who had always known privilege and wealth. Her chin tilted upwards. 'Tell me, Charlotte, have you ever had to go without a meal?'

'Certainly not.'

'Have you ever had to carry the sins of your parents on your shoulders, as I have mine? Have you ever been insulted over the circumstances of your birth, as you insulted me?'

Charlotte's head cocked to one side. 'My parents were not sinners. They were legally wed by a bishop in the house of the Lord.'

'Your father was in partnership with mine. The pair were adventurers and thieves. Your father's title will not change the fact that he was a criminal who was shot by Customs officers whilst smuggling contraband. Are you constantly being reminded of that, or did death absolve him of that sin? I didn't harm anyone, neither did I have an intent to steal what belonged to somebody else.'

Charlotte's eyes narrowed. 'You have an uncomfortable viewpoint of past events.'

'When you have experienced such undeserved scorn and destitution as I have, and when you are stranded in a strange land with no friends or family to turn to, then perhaps you will appreciate better the temptation to improve yourself. When you are given that choice, and when you turn that opportunity down, then, and only then, shall I allow you to preach to me of my shortcomings. Believe me, they are qualities of which I've been made well aware for most of my life.'

Silence stretched between them for several long moments. Charlotte's eyes gradually lost some of their hostility as her message was absorbed. Finally, she sighed. 'You are forthright, and the condemnation in your voice is unpleasant. However, I do believe you are sincere. The fact remains: you would have gone to the altar with my brother, in deceit.'

'I came here to wed John Lamartine,' Graine reminded her. 'Had Saville commanded it I would have honoured the betrothal agreement. I would have brought John Lamartine the means to better himself and provided him with children. I would even have tolerated your disagreeable Aunt Harriet. Nobody saw fit to properly forewarn me of her – a deceit in itself.'

Charlotte managed a slight smile at that. 'I believe Miss Adams intends to drive her from the house when she weds John.'

'*If* she weds John Lamartine.'

'If, then.' Charlotte seated herself. 'Now we have had our little chat perhaps you'd be good enough to send for your sister so we can be introduced. Saville has told me the family resemblance is too strong to be anything else but as close as you say.'

'How is the earl?' she said with some anxiety.

'He is well in himself, but reserved, as he always is when people disappoint him. He has a soft heart despite his size, and is talking of retiring to Rushford earlier than he first intended.'

'Oh.'

'I've persuaded him to stay, for he needs to wed and produce heirs for the estate.'

'Oh.' Graine's involuntary utterance was quieter this time, almost defeated.

'There are many candidates of suitable birth and means.' Charlotte's eyes sparked her way. 'I expect he has learned by now that it's better to put dreams of love aside and observe the customs of one's country and station in life. You understand?'

Straightening her skirts, Graine drew herself up. 'I understand. You are expressing your disapproval of me – and you put duty before your brother's happiness.'

'It's best for the estate.'

'I think your brother is intelligent enough to know what's best for the estate, which after all, is his. He has an heir in John Lamartine – or your expected infant if it proves to be a boy.' One of Charlotte's hands fluttered to her stomach. 'So, your concerns about the future of Rushford Estate are unfounded. Saville is a man who possesses a caring nature, so do not count on him picking the most strong and handsome mare in the stable. His attitude towards people of less fortunate circumstance than himself, is most laudable. . . .' Her voice faltered. 'But then, I must not discuss those activities which are private to him.'

Charlotte smiled at that. 'This has been an illuminating discussion, even though you have been overly forthright, Miss Seaton.'

'We have both been forthright, my lady. Does your position allow you more right to frankness than mine? Do you feel insult more keenly?'

'I believe that ground has been adequately covered, Miss Seaton, and I have no wish to listen to it again.'

'You must excuse me, then. I will fetch my sister. She will be more suited to your exacting tastes, for she's quiet, polite and good-natured, and possesses all the attributes which I seem to so suddenly lack now my past is made clear.'

Charlotte allowed herself a small grin when Graine swept from the room. She knew exactly what Saville got up to in the caves at Rushford. It did Graine credit that she hadn't blurted out the confidence he'd placed in her.

It was obvious Graine loved her brother. What was as indisputable, Saville loved her in equal measure. He lit up at the mention of her name, and even though Graine had made a fool of him, he would not hear a bad word said about her – though his injured pride would not allow him to be drawn into a conversation about her at less than a general level.

Because she wanted her brother to be happy, she intended to do her best to bring them together. She smiled when Evelyn entered the room and dipped her a curtsy. So this was the woman who was set to rout Aunt Harriet. She didn't look so fearsome.

'My lady,' Evelyn said, her eyes meeting hers directly. 'I'm honoured by this visit. I must tell you first, so we're fully aware of where we stand with each other, my sister means much to me. If you slander her name in my presence, I will leave the room immediately, and will never receive you again.'

Taken aback, Charlotte stared at her for a moment, then she smiled. It seemed that Evelyn Adams was just the ally she needed.

Saville was disinclined to linger in the capital.

He told himself he stayed for the sake of his cousin. John seemed greatly attracted to the genuine Evelyn Adams. Saville admitted that the woman had also greatly endeared herself to himself with her quiet strength. Although she was no great beauty, she was so right in temperament for John. In fact, on the occasions he spent talking with John, Evelyn Adams usually became the sole topic of conversation. This astounded Saville, for he'd never expected his academic cousin to become smitten with a woman so lacking in learning.

'For the first time in my life I feel that my studies have a useful purpose,' John enthused. 'Evelyn said I should write a series of sermons.'

'Good idea,' Saville said, trying not to grin as he gazed into his glass. 'Perhaps you could start with the evils of the slave trade.'

'I could not indulge in anything quite so controversial,' John murmured doubtfully, 'The church hierarchy would not like it and I depend on them for my living. Evelyn suggested that mother's sitting-room would make me a good library because there's more room for shelves. It also has bigger windows to catch the afternoon light so my eyes would not be subject to so much strain.'

'A good idea.'

'Mother would never agree to it, of course,' John murmured.

'She would have no choice if Miss Adams decides to wed you. She's stipulated that Aunt Harriet must move into her own apartments before she'll even consider marriage.'

John's face brightened at the thought, then he gazed at him in sudden consternation. 'Who will inform my mother of this?'

'Why, you must, John,' Saville said gently, 'And the sooner you do it, the better, for Miss Adams is becoming admired and it's possible you might lose her.'

'My mother will be greatly fussed.'

'Then you must make up your mind as to which of the two women you wish to spend the rest of your life with.'

John wasted only a moment of his scholarly thinking on the subject. 'As you know, I had not really considered marriage until Miss Adams was presented. She's competent, trustworthy and fair of face, much more than I expected or deserve. Although she's not learned on any subject she can manage the household accounts, which will save me the bother.'

'Save me the rest, John,' Saville said with a grin. 'I do believe you are in love.'

'I believe I am.' John cast an anxious glance around his dusty domain, to make sure they were not being overheard, 'Miss Adams is restful. She does not *prattle* as most women do. Given the choice I would choose her. I would not like to move to another house, though. Do you think Miss Adams will like living here? Is it grand enough for a women with her wealth?'

'She strikes me as a woman of simple taste. I had thought to dispose of this place once you were wed, though.'

John looked so anxious that Saville laughed. 'You would, of course, then be in the position to buy it. The schoolhouse will bring you in some rental income, and one day Chiswick will be a fashionable suburb. Would you like me to bring the matter to Miss Adams's attention?'

'Can you not bring yourself to talk to Mother, as well? She'll treat the idea of moving as a tragedy, and you know how melodramatic she can be.'

Saville had come prepared. 'Be firm with her, John, for purpose of mind is a quality Miss Adams will wish to see in you. There is an adequately sized house for lease a few miles from here. It's perfect for Aunt Harriet and I've taken an option on it. It's situated in a quiet street, and the immediate neighbours are both dowagers. I think it will be a suitable abode for Harriet. I will cover the expenses until you are wed. Once Aunt Harriet has settled in I'll buy her a lap dog and give her an allowance.' He consulted his pocket watch and gave John the push he needed. 'If you would like to inform your mother of this now, I will take you both to view it. Be firm, John, your future depends on it,' he said, as John headed reluctantly towards the door.

A few moment later there came a loud shriek from the direction of Harriet's sitting-room. This was followed by a flurry of shouting and a storm of dramatic sobs. John's voice was lost and ineffectual amongst it. Sighing, Saville unhurriedly rose to his feet and sauntered towards the sound.

'What on earth is going on?' he said. 'My dear Aunt Harriet, do dry your eyes. You don't want to make a bad impression on the countess, do you?'

Harriet was wearing brown today. Her eyes came up to his and there wasn't a trace of tears in them, only suppressed fury when she hissed, 'Countess?'

'She lives next door to the house we're viewing. I told her what a wonderful card player you are and she's quite looking forward to meeting you. They need another player for their set.'

'I suppose that Adams woman you're intent on marrying put you both up to this,' Harriet said, and sniffed as she bestowed on her son the darkest of glances. 'The very idea, being evicted from my own house without having a say in the matter. Not that I'd have stayed here once you were wed, of course. I'm not one to force myself on anyone, especially if I'm not wanted.' Her voice took on a whine that set his teeth on edge. 'However, I didn't expect my own son to be encouraged to conspire against his poor mother.'

Saville smiled pleasantly at her. 'Shall we discuss this in the carriage, Aunt Harriet? Good accommodation is hard to come by in the area and I was lucky to be given first option on it. We must make up our minds quickly though.'

Although Harriet found plenty to complain about, she was impressed by the small, well-furnished house. She was even more impressed by the countess, who by some quirk of fate, turned out to be as loud in dress and manner as she was herself.

The deal was done. Saville moved Harriet swiftly, before she could change her mind. She took her housekeeper and maid with her, and was presented with a pair of King Charles spaniels by Saville, which were immediately ensconced on a pair of silk cushions in the drawing-room.

Soon, Harriet was drawn into a small group of older women and joined in the round of incessant gossip, card playing and charitable works. Saville had never seen her so fully employed, despite the air of unresolved grievance and injured pride which lingered about her when they met.

Evelyn was pleased by the turn of events. She agreed to meet with John again to discuss a future together seriously. Soon, he became a regular visitor. The faltering marriage proposal which followed was accepted, the betrothal papers signed and witnessed.

Evelyn turned her full attention on Graine, who'd been looking down in the mouth of late. She knew her sister had been avoiding all social diversions in case she ran into Saville again. 'Now, my dear, you must attend the ball the earl is holding on behalf of John and myself.'

Graine said, 'I think I'll stay quietly at home.'

Evelyn fixed her with a firm eye. 'If you refuse to attend I shall regard it as a direct insult. It's about time you stopped behaving like a mouse and held your head up.'

'I cannot bear to have him look upon me with scorn,' she whispered.

'Come, come. The earl is more generous-hearted than you imagine. Not a whisper of your transgression has leaked out. The earl is too much the gentleman to go public with this.'

'You mean, he doesn't want to make a laughing stock of himself for being duped.'

'Stop being presumptuous. That's not what I meant, at all.' Evelyn crossed to where her sister sat and took her chin between her finger and thumb. She scrutinized her pale face. 'Isn't it about time you stopped wallowing in self-pity and found some courage?'

Graine gave a little gasp at the hard words served to her.

'You will have to meet him again one day, so now is as good a time as any. Once the initial exchange is over it will be easier the second time. You will attend the ball, yes?'

Graine managed a miserable nod.

'Good,' Evelyn purred. 'You shall wear that dark-red silk ball gown.'

'I don't like it much. It's too—'

'It's perfectly lovely, and in any case, is the only ball gown you possess. I know you have little interest in fashion, but it displays your shoulders to great advantage.'

Graine made a face. 'It's too sophisticated for my taste.'

'London society expects such fashions to be worn. I will instruct Millie to dress you for the occasion.'

'But Jessie—'

'Will do as she's told,' Evelyn said firmly, and that was that as far as she was concerned.

The day of the ball dawned bright and clear. As Graine couldn't summon up a credible headache to prevent her attendance, she duly subjected herself to the rigours of Millie's attention.

First the bath, scented with perfumed oils. As she lay back in the scented water with Millie's supple finger massaging perfumed soap over her skin, she began to contemplate the idleness of her life now.

The sumptuous chamber she occupied here was far removed from the sparsely furnished cell of her childhood, with its hard sleeping mat and the lizards chasing each other in and out of the cracks in the walls.

Her hands were soft and white now, the calluses long gone. Here, she was waited on hand and foot, served by a large number of servants, and in a manner far grander than the most wealthy of plantation owners could ever imagine. But here, the servants earned a wage, and for the most part were not treated as badly as the West Indian plantation servants, who were drawn directly from the labour force, then used or abused as the master willed.

It was easy to stand at a distance and criticize. How would

Saville react to seeing such misery on a daily basis, she wondered. Would he harden himself to their plight? Would he accept slavery as a necessary evil, for without the exploitation of slaves the plantation crops would fail. His motives were good, but would have little impact on the problem at large. Saville had never been without and had never been in the position she had, which was why he had difficulty accepting her deception.

The water streamed over her body when she stood to Millie's command.

'You'll be the most beautiful woman at the ball,' Millie promised, 'I shouldn't be surprised if all the men in London are queuing up at the door to propose marriage in the morning.'

Graine gave a little giggle at the thought, and Millie smiled at her. 'There, that's better, miss. You have a smile fit to break hearts.'

'I don't want to break hearts, it's a most uncomfortable experience. At least,' she amended, 'I should imagine so.'

'I had my heart broke once. I fell in love with a bread carter. One day he got drunk, toppled in the river and drowned.'

'Oh, Millie. I'm so sorry, that's tragic.'

'I'm not. I found out later that he had a missus and five children at home, so it serves him right for deceiving us all. Arms up.' Deftly, she slipped a filmy chemise over her head, then slipped on the corset and laced it tight. A skirt roll was tied around her waist and a robe slipped over. 'I'm going to apply some cosmetics, just a little almond paste and rouge and I'll pluck a few stray hairs from your eyebrows first.

'Do you think I should wear cosmetics?' Graine said doubtfully.

'Everyone does in London. Besides, the colour of that gown will make you look washed out otherwise. Just leave things to me, miss. I know what I'm doing. I learned my trade from Madame La Seine of Paris, who used to work for the French court.'

Graine tried not to grin. 'Madame La Seine was named after a river then?'

'Fancy,' Millie said cheerfully. 'Odd what people get named after, innit?'

A little while later a remote and glittering stranger stared back at her from the mirror.

'There,' Millie said with obvious pride. 'A pity you ain't got no rubies to wear with that gown.'

Pampered, powdered, plucked, patched and perfumed, Graine felt grand and remote, certainly a different person than the one residing inside her skin. She might as well have been playing a deception all over again.

Her gown was sleek satin with an embroidered and beaded bodice. Her breasts were pushed up and gleamed palely. The black lace edging the neckline just skimmed her nipples, to which, for some reason, Millie had applied a little rouge. A powdered wig framed her face. Her own hair was drawn back and concealed under it. She felt uneasy about herself, but Evelyn had chosen this gown for her, and she couldn't refuse to wear it without causing offence.

There was a posy of dark-red rosebuds, brought up by a maid. 'The earl would have sent these,' Millie said, deftly stitching a couple to a black velvet ribbon tied to her wrist. The remainder was pinned to her bodice.

Although Graine's heart had skipped a beat, she came back to earth when she went downstairs to discover that John Lamartine had arrived and Evelyn was carrying a similar posy of pink roses to match her gown.

The carriage bore them rapidly towards the venue. Evelyn looked elegantly regal in a gown of embroidered pale-pink taffeta, with a scalloped collar and tiered skirt.

On the opposite seat, Harriet Lamartine sat with her son. She resembled a squat toad in an oily dark green. The hostile look Graine received for her greeting boded her nothing but ill. Thankfully, Harriet said nothing to her for the whole journey. Instead, she fawned over Evelyn, ingratiating herself now the question of her son's marriage was finally settled.

When they arrived, John and Evelyn were swept away by a crowd of well-wishers. Harriet elbowed her aside and went to join a group of acquaintances.

Graine held back, hesitant, pretending to admire a painting of a country house. There were deer grazing on a lawn and she felt a sudden sharp pain at the thought of never seeing Rushford again. There was a curtained alcove set in a wall. Perhaps she could secrete herself there, hide behind the curtain.

A hand gripped her elbow and she turned to find Saville. Dressed in black brocade embossed with silver thread, this aristocratic gentleman was a far cry from the man she'd fallen in love with at Rushford. The smile he gave her was a fractional twist of the lips. 'Are you thinking you might avoid me, my fine lady?'

'No . . . yes.' Her heart began to do a strange dance in her breast. 'Saville . . . my lord.' She drew in a deep breath to steady herself, met his eyes and floundered in banality. 'It was good of you to hold this ball for John and Evelyn.'

'Not at all,' he murmured, and his eyes swept over her. Annoyance clouded them. 'What has become of my Eve? She was too young for such a gown.'

'I'm the same underneath.'

'You look like a courtesan. You appear to have lost your innocence.'

It was the cruellest thing he could have said to her, but when she would have pulled away from him he tightened his grip. 'No, my temptress. You've gained what you wanted, a fortune. Now you dress to attract a mate. We'll see how well you can handle it.'

All Graine wanted was him, but he was so far out of her reach now that she wanted to howl with frustration.

'Come, do not lurk here when you have dressed to be noticed,' he said, guiding her unwilling feet towards the music. 'Let's see if we can find you a suitor or two.'

When she would have pulled back he dragged her forward. 'The money should attract someone. If you can't hook a husband with that, then you might have to settle for becoming someone's mistress.' His eyes suddenly slanted her way. 'Mine perhaps.'

'The Earl of Sedgley and Miss Graine Seaton,' the usher announced.

Heads turned. There was a short period of silence, then a man whispered to his companion, 'So that's the bastard half-sister. She's exquisite. Who was her mother?'

'Some doxy who hung around the ports of Antigua. Her uncle owns the largest plantation in Antigua and is as rich as sin. The family has disowned her since birth, I hear. What's she doing with Sedgley?'

'I've heard she's his mistress and lives with him at Rushford.'

'Lucky dog,' the second man growled.

Harriet gave a braying, malicious laugh which disappeared into the music struck up by the orchestra. Saville took a couple of glasses of wine from the tray of a passing footman and handed her one.

Face flaming, Graine whispered, 'Was it you who told them?'

His face had turned to stone. 'It was Harriet, I expect. She dislikes you with a passion.' Turning to look down upon her, he said, 'I'm sorry, I didn't think it would be this bad for you. Would you like me to escort you home?'

'No, my lord. Be damned to Harriet Lamartine. I'm glad she's no relative of mine. As for you, my lord, you have the disposition and instinct of a dog. I will never settle for becoming anyone's mistress, especially yours.'

Shaking her arm free she lifted her chin and swept across the floor.

The insult took his breath away. She didn't mince words when roused to anger. His eyes narrowed. 'We'll see about that, my Eve,' he murmured, and lifted the glass to his lips.

When she reached the men who'd insulted her she stopped and stared at them, said coldly, 'I demand an apology. Bastard I may be, but I'm not and, never have been, mistress to the Earl of Sedgley. In future, couch your remarks with more care, sirs.'

Saville nearly choked on his wine. He started to chuckle when the men rose hastily to their feet, mouthing effusive apologies. It was going to be an interesting evening.

She nodded regally, then continued serenely on to disappear into the crowd without a backward glance.

13

The ball turned out to be the worst evening of Graine's life. Apart from the Lamartines and Evelyn, she knew nobody.

Now the news of her mother's infamy had spread – and she was left in no doubt it was Harriet who'd spread the word, for the woman obliquely reminded her of it at every opportunity. The women acknowledged her with icy courtesy before turning their backs on her, whilst the men subjected her to bold glances and innuendo. One went so far as to pinch her familiarly on the cheek.

Evelyn didn't seem to notice anything amiss, lost as she was in her own popularity and happiness. Since she'd been in London, her sister had blossomed into a confident and warm-hearted person, who was hard to dislike. She and John seemed genuinely fond of each other.

Apart from Saville, who watched her progress with a look of annoyance on his face, John was the only one who noticed her predicament. As he tucked her arm in his, he said, 'You seem to be finding it hard to cope, my dear. Let's take a turn around the room. Perhaps we can find a quiet place where you can tell me what's afoot; then I will see if something can be done about it.' He beckoned to a footman. 'Perhaps you would like some lemonade.'

A lump caught in her throat at his kindness, and when they were settled, she murmured, 'It seems I must be made to suffer for my parents' sins in public now. Will it never end?'

'You must not mind them. They have nothing better to do than gossip.'

'I shouldn't have come. I'm ruining the evening for you.' She pulled a determined smile to her face. 'I'm so pleased you and Evelyn are suited so perfectly, because I like you, John Lamartine. Evelyn is a wonderful sister to me and I know she'll be happy with you.'

He looked embarrassed. 'I care for her more than I can ever express.' He chuckled. 'I never expected to feel like this about someone at my age. It's quite strange.'

'You are not so old, touching forty at the most.' Then she remembered he was thirty-five and amended quickly, 'Less. At the least, thirty perhaps.'

'Quick thinking, Miss Seaton. That puts me somewhere nicely in between, doesn't it?' And he waggled his eyebrows and gave her an ironic glance.

She giggled, not in the least bit put out at being caught out by him. He was certainly no fool.

'And what of you, Miss Seaton. Do you have plans for the future?'

Saville must have overheard the query for he took up position the other side of her and said, 'No doubt she has, John. Miss Seaton's good at planning her future, especially if it's at the expense of another person.'

'Saville,' John remonstrated. 'Am I given to understand from that remark that you've appointed yourself the inquisitor of your guest? Such remarks are unworthy of you.'

Saville gazed at her for a moment, the expression in his eyes turbulent. 'My apologies, Miss Seaton. I withdraw them.'

'Perhaps you'd consider withdrawing yourself as well,' she told him, and he gave a stiff little bow and left.

John sighed. 'Insulting each other will cause irreparable damage between you.'

This cold, hard stranger was not the Saville who Graine had known and loved at Rushford. Gulping back her tears, she shrugged and gazed helplessly at John. 'It's my fault. I have disappointed him, I think.' Which, when all was said and done, was an understatement of the highest order.

John patted her hand. 'He has disappointed himself, for he has it within himself to forgive, and is too proud to do so at the moment. When he has rationalized what has happened he'll sort out what is important to him and swallow his pride. Then he will cease to be the tyrant.'

But to Graine, the gulf between them was now unbreachable. '*The tyrant is a child of pride, who drinks from his great sickening cup.*' she quoted bitterly.

John smiled. '*Recklessness and vanity, until from his high crest, headlong, he plummets to the dust of hope.* Sophocles, Miss Seaton?'

'Indeed it is,' She laughed at his surprise. 'You need not sound so amazed. Women are not entirely stupid, you know.'

'Most certainly, they are not, just unfortunate that they're not given the opportunity to enlarge on their intelligence. Saville has told me your education is advanced and I look forward to discussing literature with you. Are you familiar with the works of Plutarch?'

When she grimaced, he laughed. 'Ah . . . I see that you are. Perhaps Shakespeare might be more to your taste, then.'

Graine decided not to mention *Moll Flanders*.

John stood when a footman approached, and relieved him of their lemonade, deciding he liked this troubled girl.

Saville hadn't considered the effect that Graine's appearance might have on him. The fact that he hadn't seen her at any gatherings he'd attended served to heighten the impact of her appearance tonight. Her sophistication had not only taken his breath away, it drew the eyes of the men and the scandalized, but envious, glances of every woman there.

He closed his eyes for a moment, her shoulders had the patina of ivory satin. She was exquisite, her innocence a shining revelation in the wicked wrapping of her gown. She was being put on display.

How he'd burned for her when those remarks had been made, and was sure Harriet had instigated the gossip. He gazed at the woman now, noting the malice in her eyes as her glance first swept over Evelyn, then travelled on to where Graine stood talking to John.

Seated on gilt chairs in a secluded corner away from the dancing, the pair were sipping lemonade and engaging in an animated conversation. A smile touched his mouth. He hadn't thought his reclusive cousin to be so socially adept. His stomach tightened when she smiled. Then John leaned forward and briefly kissed her cheek.

From the corner of his eye, he saw Harriet rise from her chair and, with a determined look on her face, sail across the room to where the pair sat. It was obvious she'd been waiting an opportunity, for one elbow jogged under Graine's. The glass she was holding tipped and the lemonade was spilled into her lap.

'Such a clumsy creature,' Harriet hissed, bringing heads swivelling towards them.

But Harriet was not popular, and those who'd observed the mean act, disapproved. The opposite to that which Harriet had intended, happened. Soon, a half-dozen sympathetic women, who were led by his sister, Charlotte, surrounded Graine. Handkerchiefs feathered as they tried to mop the liquid from her skirts.

'It wasn't my fault, I tripped,' Harriet whined, when she realized the consequence of her action had not gone in her favour. 'The music is so loud and I have a headache.'

'I expect you've had one glass of wine too many,' Charlotte said loudly.

'I expect so. My poor head is buzzing. Will you take me home, John?'

'I cannot leave my guests, but will see you get away safely.' To John's credit he didn't lose his temper, but led Graine to Evelyn's side. 'Please look after your sister whilst I see Mama to the carriage. I'll be back shortly.'

'But—' Harriet began when he took her firmly by the elbow.

'Don't bother to argue, Mama. What you have just done is unforgivable.' John steered her towards the exit. By the time Saville reached them, Harriet had been bundled into a cloak and was being helped into the carriage.

Catching his eye when the carriage rolled away, John smiled with relief. 'Miss Seaton is soaked through. Evelyn and I cannot leave our guests, so would you be good enough to escort her home so she can change?'

Graine joined them then, her gown badly marked. She was

trembling, but more with suppressed anger than shock, for her eyes glinted and her body was tense as Evelyn eased her cloak around her shoulders.

'I must apologize for my mama,' John said.

Graine knew how to use situations to her advantage, Saville noticed. With a touch of a feminine artifice, she murmured prettily, 'It was an accident, nothing more.'

John's lips tightened. 'You are too kind and forgiving, my dear. We all know it was not an accident, but a petty and spiteful act. The night is still young and Saville will escort you home to change. I expect you back in time for supper and dancing. Look after her please, Saville.'

Saville's eyes narrowed, but he said nothing, just inclined his head.

When they were installed in the carriage she attempted to start a conversation. 'John Lamartine is a different man than the one you led me to expect.'

'Disconcerting, isn't it, Miss Seaton? Your sister seems to have wrought miracles, for John has always needed bringing out of himself.'

'So has Evelyn. She has changed much. The shipwreck seems to have changed her life. She is no longer meek, but has discovered a source of strength within herself.'

'She's lucky. Some only find weakness when put to the test.'

There, the conversation ended, mired in a slough of awkward uncertainty, so neither could express what was in their minds without meaningless talk. In the dark interior of the carriage they gazed at each other, regretting the consequences of the past, but unable to acknowledge the future.

When they reached the house in Hanover Square, she murmured, 'Please convey my apologies to your cousin. I have developed a headache of my own, and will not be returning to the ball with you.'

There was a sudden swirl of energy inside the carriage as he leaned forward and took her wrist. 'You lie too easily, Miss Seaton. You do not have a headache; you simply lack the courage to appear in public, especially with me.'

'No, I—' the words were strangled in her throat when he kissed her. It was a surprisingly gentle reminder of what they had once meant to each other – of the power he had to keep her hopes and needs alive.

He drew back when the coachman opened the carriage door. His voice was low and savage. 'You will change your gown and you will be escorted back to the ball by me. There, you will smile until your cheeks ache, and you will make meaningless talk until your breath dries up. You will flirt with me from behind your fan and dance until your feet are raw. In short, you will enjoy yourself whether you want to or not. I will not allow you to ruin this evening for John and Evelyn by indulging in brattish behaviour. Do you understand?'

'Yes, my lord,' she said bitterly, as he ushered her inside the house and up the stairs to her chamber.

'And, what's more, I shall choose a gown which doesn't make you resemble a London doxy on the prowl.'

Her blood came up at the insult. She gazed at him stony faced. 'One more insult and I'll slap you.'

'Will you, by God?' he growled. 'Pray be quiet or I'll throw you over my knee and beat your bare backside until it's black and blue.'

She opened her mouth, gasped at the threat, then hurriedly shut it again when he gave her a warning look. As soon as he looked away she said quietly, 'Evelyn bought me this gown and insisted I wear it. It's the latest fashion.'

'Evelyn should have known better. You are judged by your appearance and the neckline is immodest.' He turned and drew a fingertip across her bosom, then gently peeled a black heart-shaped patch from her skin. 'You are wearing rouge on your nipples, and pretty as it is, it's there for a reason – to invite the eyes of men and entice them to sample your wares.'

'It does not seem to entice you.'

'You're quite wrong. In fact, I can hardly keep my damned hands off you. If you think I don't want to drag that dress from your body and tumble you naked and willing on to the bed you are quite wrong.'

'I would not be willing, so such a violation would not occur.'

He chuckled. 'You would be unable to stop me, and if you think you don't want my attention, you are also quite wrong. Allow me

177

to demonstrate.' He reached out and grazed his thumbs gently over her breasts. As they pushed against the red satin bodice she closed her eyes for the short moment of ecstatic contact.

When he reached out and drew her close she crumbled against him, her mouth eager to receive the tender attention of his. His foot came around her ankle and she fell back on the bed with him half on top of her. He smiled gently down at her. 'It would not take much to take advantage of you, I think.'

When she resisted, he simply pressed her into the bed with his knee. Deftly, he unlaced her bodice.

'Stop it, Saville,' she protested, when he freed her breasts, to cup them warmly in his hands. 'I'll scream and bring the servants running.' She didn't struggle because it would only serve to inflame his senses more.

He covered her mouth with his and his tongue flirted with hers. Arousal was a swift and dangerous surge that filled her with desire and robbed her of will. She could only murmur with delight when he moved his mouth to her rouged nipples in a moist caress.

He gazed down at her, his eyes half-hooded, in full control of himself. Heat flooded her cheeks and she felt ashamed of her weakness. 'Let me up, I beg you.'

'I would rather you begged me to continue, my Eve. You have aroused me most powerfully.'

Despite her inexperience, she knew it. She could feel against her thigh the powerful drive of him, could feel in herself the need to accept that part of him eager to conquer. She wanted to spread her naked body to his will and have him make it his own. Was she shameless like her mother, who had been wanton with so many men, and had lost all respect in the process? Tears filled her eyes as she attempted to cover her nakedness. *Damn the woman to hell!* She whimpered. 'I am as you say. You have made me want you, and if that is your desire I will not be able to resist you.'

'I would never hurt you,' he said roughly, and his tongue gently curled the tears from her trembling lashes. 'You know, I still cannot stand to see you cry.' Then his weight was lifted from her body, allowing her to turn her nakedness to the pillow.

'I need to compose myself, and I daresay you need the same. I shall wait for you downstairs in the drawing-room. Shall I ring for Jessie?'

'No, she will be in her bed.'

But Jessie appeared anyway, to help her into the blue gown Saville had bought her. She was quiet, lacking her usual chatter. His gift of pearls was placed around her neck, a pearl ring on her finger. Jessie pinned the bouquet of rosebuds at her waist.

'The earl didn't like me wearing the red gown, so I'd best not wear the roses.'

'He sent you the posy, so you must wear it. Listen to Jessie, girl, for I've growed right fond of you. Yon earl is in a real twist over you,' Jessie said, letting her know she'd guessed what had taken place between them. 'His bark is worse than his bite. Sometimes he lets his temper off the leash, but if you stands up to him he soon comes to his senses. You won't come to any harm with him.'

Graine kissed the woman's worn cheek. 'Thank you, Jessie.' So, when Saville sent up a message to enquire if she'd be much longer, she plucked a rosebud from her waist and sent it down to him, deciding to make him wait a further ten minutes.

He was twirling the bloom impatiently between his fingers when she went down. He didn't avoid her eyes and, although Graine felt her cheeks warm, she didn't avoid his. He held the rose to his nose and contemplated her for a moment before nodding his approval. He placed the rosebud inside his waistcoat and growled, 'I was about to come up and fetch you.'

'Then your ears would have been soundly boxed, for I'm tired of your overbearing ways.'

Softly, menacingly, he said, 'Are you, now?'

'The fact that I'm a guest in your house does not give you the right to order me around.'

A servant handed him his hat with exaggerated politeness.

Saville's mouth twitched as he took it. 'You're being provocative, Graine.' A statement which made her stamp her foot and scream with frustration, but only in her mind, so he wasn't given an excuse to prove he was the master.

She changed tactics, her smile becoming as sweet as honey when she saw Jessie at the top of the stairs. The maid began to dust the banister with her apron. 'I'm sorry I kept you waiting, my lord.'

'Why did you?'

'I was taking revenge because your earlier behaviour was reprehensible.'

Mollie came wandering through a door to her left and began to polish a spot on a mirror.

The smile Saville gave was irresistible. 'You are behaving like a shrew. Into the carriage, Miss Seaton.'

She pushed her advantage a fraction when a burly manservant came in with a bucket of coal and began to place it, knob by knob, on the glowing embers. She hadn't noticed that the servants worked so late, before. 'I'd prefer it if the request was couched more politely.'

'Would you, by God!' he roared, making her jump from her skin. 'And I would prefer it if you stopped trying to make me look a fool in front of my household staff.' He stooped, and the next moment he had her dangling inelegantly over his shoulder.

The manservant rushed forward to open the door. His grin was a mile wide.

'Thank you, Mr Downey,' Saville said, and strode down the steps towards the carriage with her hanging like a sack of turnips over his shoulder. She heard the servants laughing when he nodded pleasantly to the couple of onlookers lingering in the vicinity.

Depositing her gently on the seat, Saville sat opposite, his face a study of amusement.

'Being manhandled is not funny,' she threw at him.

'No, I don't suppose it is. Now we've resolved who exactly is in charge, can we behave like the civilized people we are for the rest of the evening.'

'I certainly can. Can you?'

His eyes met hers. 'As long as you don't goad me into losing my temper, I can.'

'Good,' she said, and smiled pleasantly at him. 'Do you always lose it so easily, my lord?'

'No. Do you always have to have the last word?'

She sighed heavily. 'I'll allow you have it, if you insist. What is it?'

'I'm sorry for my behaviour,' he said, which not only robbed her of breath, but reminded her of what had nearly occurred between them and the pleasure she'd experienced. Spreading her fan across her face she fanned her blushing cheeks and wanted to kill him when he chuckled.

The rest of the evening was without unpleasant incident, though it was fraught with danger.

Saville partnered her in a dance only once, but he watched her constantly. Graine knew he was sitting in judgement on her behaviour, which made her edgy and stiff. Finally she approached him and, giving a sniff, said, 'Do you have to watch me so?'

To her surprise, he laughed. 'It's not you I'm watching, but those who would acquaint themselves with you. You have been approached by two of the wealthiest rakes in London. Take great care, Miss Seaton.'

'So far, the men who've approached me have been unmitigated bores. All they can talk about is themselves, and they credit me with no intelligence at all because I'm a woman.'

'Then perhaps I should tell them to watch out for you, because you are as tricky as a monkey.'

'And you're as grumpy as a pack of wolves suffering from toothache.' She rumbled a snarl at him. 'I am bored with your snapping, and would be greatly obliged if you'd hide your fangs and behave like a human being again, my lord.'

He chuckled. 'Take a turn around the room with me, my Eve. I promise not to maul you again tonight, if you promise not to do the same to me.' Their eyes met for a moment and the smile he offered her sent delicious shivers along her nerves. 'What will you do when your sister weds?'

'I have not given serious thought to my future. Perhaps I will use my skills to help the poor. I can teach children or tend to their complaints.'

Saville's thumb grazed across her wrist. 'No doubt, you are capable, but the poor cannot afford to pay for such services.'

'Have you forgotten that I shall have means?' she reminded him.

'But not to squander on others, for it will come in the form of an allowance so the capital can be preserved. From it, you will have to pay your servants and accommodation.'

'My needs are few, and I shall need no servants.'

He gave her a sideways glance. 'Did you know that Eve has resolved not to wed John until you are settled yourself?'

Dismayed, she gazed at him. 'But I've decided never to wed.'

His eyes hooded and his expression begged her to explain herself. 'Never?'

She couldn't tell him the reason why – that she loved him and would have no other. 'I have no wish to wed,' she mumbled. 'I will devote my life to good works.'

'You intend to martyr yourself? My dear Miss Seaton, how very touching and noble of you, when there are bound to be offers for your hand. Everyone is curious about you.'

'So I notice,' she snapped. 'Unfortunately, they seem to have gained a false impression of me if they think I'm your—'

'Mistress,' he suggested, and chuckled. 'Now, I wonder what gave them that idea, when a man's mistress is usually kept in separate accommodations.'

'Oh?' The question formed tantalizingly on her tongue and quivered there. Curiosity ate at her, so she tingled and throbbed with it. How hateful of him to fill her with such jealous angst, especially when his smile invited her comment.

Her teeth worried at her bottom lip for a moment, then she sighed, and returned his smile with a brilliant one of her own. She wouldn't oblige him because she didn't want to hear his answer.

'Tell me what Rushford is like in the autumn. I have heard the leaves on the trees turn turn red, yellow and brown, so it seems as if the foliage is aflame. Does that occur at Rushford?'

Rushford, he thought, and it filled his mind with a roar of longing. The place was his haven. There, he was away from the cut and thrust of London social life. Many of his associates were absent from their country estates for most of the year, but he loved to be there, and even a few short weeks away was too long.

He drew her into a seat in an alcove and told her about it, embroidering the soft warmth of autumn as Rushford fruited magically in his memory, for her.

She listened intently as he rambled on, his place in Rushford's future made clear as a custodian of the land for future generations. Finally, he ground to a halt, acutely aware that he may have bored her. He shrugged. 'You would like Rushford in autumn.'

'You make it sound so comfortable, as if it was part of your heart.'

'And my blood and my bone,' he said simply. But she was right, it was his heart too, the seasons turning as he aged, and would be turning long after he was gone – long after his children had gone, and his children's children.

'Perhaps we should find some refreshment,' he said, and with an effort, placed the getting of that future generation firmly from his mind.

Harriet Lamartine was nothing, if not determined. Now she was settled in her own establishment she could go about her mischief, unchecked. Seething with self-righteous indignation, and acting on the advice of her new acquaintances, she summoned a mystic to read her fortune. She intended to ask her for a charm, in case she needed to put a curse on her enemies.

The woman was a novelty in herself, a blackamoor called Eliza Jones, whose arms and ears jangled with gold ornaments. Under an all encompassing cloak and hood she wore a turban and gown of brightly exotic orange and turquoise silk.

The two spaniels leapt down from the cushions and scrabbled at the door to be let out. They took off up the hall, yelping, and with their tails between their legs when Harriet opened it.

Opening a drawstring bag, Eliza shook out the contents. The five bones clattered as they spun on the polished surface of the table. Harriet drew back when they stopped. Three of them were pointing at her, one to the side. They were lying over the remaining one.

'These three are the men in your life,' The woman said, her voice low and husky. She drew one forth. 'This is your son. Why does he hide from you? He's of scholarly disposition, but that's not the reason he conceals himself. He seeks the solace of his own thoughts, and needs peace. Soon he will wed, and where you have failed, his wife will succeed. She will draw him from his solitude and give him several fine children. Beware in your dealings, for the woman will usurp you in his affections. This has already started.'

Eliza smiled when Harriet gasped, and her finger slid another bone towards her. 'This man has great power and was once close

183

to you, but it was not by choice. I see a girl with him who is closely related. Your jealousy of this man's wealth and position over your son caused you to be cruel to him as a youth.'

Harriet remembered the times she'd locked Saville in a cupboard for days on end, of how she'd slapped and pinched him, or sent him to bed without his supper for the smallest transgression. He'd nearly died once. She'd left him outside in the rain in the middle of winter and he'd caught an infection in his lungs. If he'd died, her own son would now be the Earl of Sedgley. She shuddered. It had not been her intention to kill him, of course. She looked up to find the woman's eyes gazing slyly at her.

'I did not mean to be cruel.'

Eliza pushed the third bone forward. 'This is a man with no conscience. Beware, he will flatter and charm you, and then will use you for his own ends. Think carefully when he appears.'

'Mumbo jumbo,' Harriet snorted.

Eliza gazed into her eyes. 'Lady, you have the power to cause good, or great harm to those close to you.'

A smug smile settled on Harriet's lips and her eyes narrowed. 'I have always known that.'

Her finger slid the other one off of the bottom bone. 'This is your late husband, who turned away from you. He had a mistress named Catherine Prichard. They had a baby daughter. When he died the woman came to you for help. They were starving. You turned them from your door and the pair perished.'

Harriet's mouth suddenly went dry. 'Begone, I will hear no more,' she whispered.

'Yes you will, lady,' and the woman's eyes were liquid and penetrating as she touched the last bone. 'This is a young woman, a pivot around whom all the living others revolve. Her life has been hard, but what she has given to others she stands to receive twofold. She is beloved of the myla, so is protected by the forces of life.'

'Graine Seaton,' Harriet hissed, her anger bringing her out of her trance. 'I will hear no more, and don't think I'll pay you. You're a fake.'

The woman's dark finger stirred gently at the bones, 'What do you see?'

Harriet couldn't stop herself from glancing down at the bones: in their place was a mass of writhing snakes. She opened her mouth to scream but couldn't utter a sound.

'Heed that which I told you,' Eliza said, and held out her hand.

Delving into her pocket, Harriet hurriedly took out a gold piece and dropped it into her palm. The woman left a small linen pouch in its place.

A beam of sunlight came through the window and the snakes turned back into bones. Eliza slid them into the bag. 'Thank you, madam,' she said respectfully. 'I trust you will recommend me to your friends.'

There was an unpleasant sensation inside Harriet as she let the woman out, but she couldn't think why. 'Mumbo jumbo,' she muttered to herself. Then she remembered the charm and opened her palm. Holding it to her nose she recoiled. It stank. She dropped it on to a table.

14

Since the ball, it seemed as if Graine ran into Saville everywhere. If she went by carriage with Evelyn to take the air in Hyde Park, Saville would ride past and nod to them. When John Lamartine reluctantly took them to the Vauxhall pleasure gardens, Saville appeared, joining them in time to listen to the band and buy them refreshments. The place fascinated Graine. It was a whirl of colour and laughter. Music played, there was secluded arbours where lovers met, mummers and magicians to watch, and sweetmeats to try.

One of a party who had gone to watch the latest offering at the playhouse, she discovered Saville sitting behind her when she turned her head. After that, she could not concentrate on the play.

He attended the dinner held by Charlotte and her husband. Seated opposite one another, they couldn't ignore the other's existence. On that occasion, she had a gentleman seated at either side of her, both of whom proved to be charming companions.

Apart from being politely sociable, Saville paid her scant attention, but she noticed his eyes had a way of narrowing when she laughed at some witticism, or hid her blushing face behind her fan when paid a compliment.

'Were you looking for this?' he remarked, when she found herself accidentally alone with him after she returned to the table. He held the flimsy piece of silk and lace between his finger and thumb and regarded her blandly. 'Congratulations, Miss Seaton, you're fast becoming the toast of London.'

'To be quite honest, I find the place tedious.' It was true. The men were persistent in their pursuit of her, and already she'd turned down two offers for her hand. He held out his arm to her. 'You appear to be lapping up the attention, as would a cat a saucer of cream.'

How exasperating he was. 'I'm merely being polite. I have never experienced such varied entertainment as London offers. It seems to me that the inhabitants are hell bent on enjoying themselves come what may, for nobody seems to sleep. The novelty has long worn off for me, and I long for some peace and quiet.'

He slid her handkerchief into his pocket. 'Permit me to show you Charlotte's garden, then. It's a lovely warm evening, the moon is full and there are lanterns to light our way. We can pretend we're at Rushford.'

'I haven't seen lanterns there.'

'I'll make sure you do, if you visit me again.'

'Then it will remind me of here.'

There were other couples strolling the grounds, which were a fairyland of coloured lanterns. They hung from every tree. Their light was reflected in a pool fed by a cascade of water gushing from an urn, which was held under the arm of a curvaceous nymph clad in a filmy chemise.

They strolled in companionable silence, neither attempting to engage in conversation in case the wrong thing be said to spoil the magical rapport between them.

They stopped by the fountain and Saville's hand trailed through the water. 'I'm thinking of returning to Rushford, soon,' he said almost absently.

Although she heard her heart crack, Graine managed a smile. 'Autumn, when the trees are cloaked in fire. I will miss it.'

'But you've never seen Rushford in autumn.'

'Then I'll miss it all the more.'

'Yes . . . yes you will.' He turned towards her, his face half in shadow. 'You would enjoy it, Graine.'

How tenderly he said her name, as soft and as loving as a caress. She closed her eyes, capturing the moment, knowing she'd enjoy burning in hell if Saville was with her. But it was obvious that such a union was not to be.

He bore her hand to his mouth and kissed the palm. For a moment she savoured the sensation, then she remembered the insidious way he built on any liberty afforded him. She couldn't take the path her mother had taken, she couldn't! But that was what Saville would have her do. He was capable of taking her love, of using it for his own ends and making her his mistress. Any children from their union would be as tainted as she was by her lowly birth, and she wouldn't subject them to what she'd been through all her life. Stifling a sob, she wrenched her hand away and walked away from his danger as fast as her legs could carry her.

'Ah, there you are,' Charlotte said, grabbing her by the arm as she walked into the drawing-room. 'We're arranging some entertainment. John has told me you read well, so I've put you down to recite a sonnet by William Shakespeare.' She thrust a leather-bound volume into her hands. 'I have marked the place.'

So, a little while later, Graine found herself reading under the critical eye of the literati John counted amongst his friends.

'That time of year thou mayst in me behold
When yellow leaves, or none, or few, do hang. . . .'

She closed her eyes for a moment. It was the one she'd quoted to Rebel at Rushford in the library, and she knew it by heart. When she opened her eyes again it was to look straight into Saville's. He was on the far side of the room, smiling faintly.

She hesitated for a single heartbeat, a moment when he must have thought she'd forgotten the words, for he mouthed them to her as she finished the sonnet.

'This thou perciev'st, which makes thy love more strong.
To love that well which thou must leave ere long.'

People surged forward to congratulate her on the reading, cutting the contact between them. When Graine finally freed herself, Saville had moved to talk to a group of people.

She was cornered by a friend of John's, who expounded at length on her presentation of the sonnet. He was fond of his own voice and, when she was finally rescued by her hostess, she gazed around her to find Saville conversing with a woman.

They seemed to be old friends, for the woman was gazing up at him, flirting from behind her fan with sparkling eyes. They were laughing together in an intimate manner.

The woman said something to him from the corner of her mouth. A faint frown slid across his face, and was quickly masked as he lifted her hand to his mouth. He gazed into her eyes as a note was slipped from her hand to his. It took him but an instant to slip the note into his waistcoat pocket.

The woman seemed to be everything Saville had despised in her on the night of the ball. Her splendid figure was enhanced by a gown of shimmering ruby, trimmed with beads. It barely supported the swelling mounds of her breasts, and had the widest side panniers Graine had ever set eyes on. Her wig was high dressed, her face powdered and patched, her cheeks startlingly rouged. Rubies hung about her neck and graced her fingers.

Charlotte poked a finger in her back. 'That's Adrianna de Lisle, the famous actress. She is performing in *The Suspicious Husband*.'

'I did not see her at dinner.'

'She wasn't invited, but she likes to make an entrance.'

Graine glanced around the room. 'Which one is her husband?'

'She is unmarried, I believe.'

Goggle-eyed, Graine stared at Charlotte. 'You mean she's come here by herself?'

'Adrianna is known for her liaisons. She's probably looking for her latest lover.'

Jealousy seethed through her when the woman laid her hand possessively over Saville's. Graine's mouth dried up and she whispered, 'Who is her lover?'

'I've no idea. Would you like to meet her?'

But just then the pair were joined by another man. Saville smiled at him, kissed the woman's hand and drifted away Graine's sigh reflected her relief.

'Did you think that perhaps it was Saville who is her lover?' Charlotte whispered, with a small, mischievous laugh. 'Believe me, my brother wouldn't be easily attracted to a woman of her reputation. I believe his heart is engaged elsewhere.'

Graine gave Charlotte a sorrowful glance. 'If you're referring to me, perhaps I should tell you that Saville's affection is of a temporary nature only, for he offers me nothing I can accept with grace or pride.'

189

A frown sped across Charlotte's forehead. 'What are you saying, Graine? What type of offer has my brother put before you?'

Graine hung her head.

Lifting her chin with her fingers, Charlotte stared at her with concern in her eyes. 'You are surely not thinking of taking him up on such a suggestion?'

'No, for once I'd proved to him that I'd inherited the low morals of my mother, then he would scorn me and discard me.' She sighed. 'Yet, the thought of being with him in happiness, for even a short time, is tempting beyond measure.'

'Dearest Graine, you must not even consider such a thing.'

'I cannot help it, Charlotte, and I know Saville could persuade me to bend to his will, for he's already proved to me my vulnerability where he's concerned.'

'Proved to you?' Charlotte's voice dropped to a whisper and she shook her by the arm. 'What has happened between you.'

'Oh, nothing of any importance to him. He set out to frighten me, and succeeded, for if he hadn't been the stronger of us, I'd have succumbed to his advances. I have decided to return to Antigua, where I can use my skills to help the poor.'

'Surely you have no intention of joining the sisters?' Charlotte laughed out loud at the thought, 'Your disposition is not suited to such piety. Have you discussed this with your sister?'

'No; she would insist I stayed in London, and to stay would mean danger for me if Saville pursued me for any length of time. I'd rather die than be obliged to live the life my mother was forced into.' She placed her hands across her heated cheeks. 'We must talk of this no more, for the earl is coming towards us.'

Saville's eyes washed over her before he smiled at his sister. 'Your husband is about to propose a toast to the newly betrothed pair, and requests your presence by his side, Charlotte.'

When Charlotte left, Saville gazed at her through half-hooded lids. 'There's something I wish to say to you, Graine. I'll call on you tomorrow.'

He looked annoyed when one of her more persistent suitors came to join them and said, 'The marquess is about to make his speech, Miss Seaton. Allow me to share a moment of your time whilst he speaks.'

Saville bowed and moved away, his hand reaching inside his waistcoat pocket. She turned her head to see him reading the note. A frown creased his forehead, then he strode towards the door. From where she stood she saw the footman hand him his cloak and hat. A moment later the actress left her companion and joined him in the hall. The pair left together.

As Graine heard a carriage roll away a cold lump of misery settled in her chest.

Later that night, after Millie had been dismissed, she spoke of her suspicion to Evelyn. 'Do you think Adrianna de Lisle is Saville's mistress?'

Evelyn's hairbrush stopped in mid air and she raised an eyebrow. 'You should not be aware of such things.'

'If I shouldn't, neither should you.'

'I'm the elder by six years.'

'And I by life experiences. How can I not know, when my very own mother was reviled for being our father's kept woman?'

They had not spoken of this before and Evelyn gave a small frown. 'I am of the opinion that your mother was wronged by our mutual father. She was barely seventeen when she gave birth to you. Her own family cast her out when she needed support.'

Graine's eyes widened in astonishment. 'You blame our father for her plight?'

'And her family. Our father was a weak and immoral man; her family lacked compassion. It was rumoured that your uncle, Francis Seaton, had a hand in our father's death. He was stabbed in the back.'

Graine swooped in a breath. 'Why was he not arrested and charged with his murder?'

'There was no proof, and he had an alibi.' Evelyn shrugged. 'When your mother died, he swore he'd never acknowledge you as a Seaton.'

'She abandoned me in the first place.'

'Only because she was ill and desperate. It was lack of support which forced her into a life of degradation. You were left with the good sisters to raise, which was the best she could do for your future, so don't think too harshly of her. Seth Adams made provision for you in his will. It was used for your education.'

'That was good of him.'

'No it wasn't. It was conscience money. Under the circumstances he could have been a better father to both of us, Graine. He could have brought us up together.'

The condemnation in Evelyn's voice shocked her. 'How did you learn all this?'

'I had access to Theodore Chambers' desk when he died. Unfortunately, his papers are now at the bottom of the ocean.'

'Is any of my mother's family still living?'

'Francis Seaton. He inherited the family wealth. I received a letter from Emily Troughton just yesterday. Francis told her he was to set sail for London aboard the *Bristol Pride*.'

'Perhaps he's coming to find me.'

Her hopes were instantly dashed. 'The object of his journey was to purchase property for investment. He doesn't know you're alive, and you mustn't attempt to approach him under any circumstances. He is a most dangerous and powerful man, a man lacking in scruples or conscience.'

A chill ran up Graine's spine. Surely he could not be as bad as Evelyn made out. What was Francis Seaton doing in London? she wondered. If her uncle had heard that she was still alive, it could be that there had been a change of heart.

She kissed Evelyn's cheek. 'I don't know what I would have done without you.'

'You'd have coped, for you're a survivor.' Her eyes lit up with laughter. 'I expect you would have married John Lamartine and successfully become me.'

Graine hung her head.

'Do not take on so, Graine, I'm teasing. To tell the truth, I was flattered to know you were willing to live as dull a life as myself.'

'You're not in the least bit dull, and now I've grown to know Mr Lamartine, I find him very pleasant to deal with – not a bit like Saville described him.'

'But then, the earl is quite besotted with you, and he wanted you for himself.'

The joy went out of her mind. 'Had he ordered it, I would have wed John, as agreed.'

'Even though you are in love with Saville?'

Dully, she said, 'It seemed better to do so, than to follow my mother's fate at the time.' But now, it seemed that Saville wanted to bring about her downfall.

A warm hug enveloped her. 'I'm sure the earl will come around in time. If he does not, we will find someone else worthy to be your husband – and the earl must suffer the consequences. Already, there have been offers expressed by two worthy young men.'

Graine shrugged. 'Saville will not come around, for he despises everything about me. I shouldn't have pretended I was better than I am. Now I am nothing in his eyes, and will be glad when he returns to Rushford, so I do not have to see him again. As for the worthy young men, thank them for their interest but tell them to look elsewhere. I will neither see nor speak to them again.'

Evelyn shook her head in despair. 'What will you do if you do not marry?'

Graine didn't answer. She knew Evelyn would not willingly allow her to return to the West Indies and, if she didn't wed, then neither would Evelyn. To assure a happy outcome for her sister, Graine intended to remove the obstacle. Once she was accepted into the convent, Evelyn would no longer have to feel responsible for her.

Charlotte gazed upon her brother with displeasure. 'You would have me drop Graine from my guest list, but will not give me a reason? No Saville, I will not do that. I happen to like the girl. The minute I drop her she'll be ostracized by all of London society. Then the predators will move in. Is that what you want to happen? Are you out to ruin her because of one small deceit?'

'Miss Seaton is drawing attention to herself.'

'That's a lame reason. Since that first mistake she has not put a foot wrong. She is modest and doesn't venture an opinion, unless asked. Then her answer is intelligent and measured. She is always chaperoned by her sister. Why, our cousin John finds her delightful, and you know how hard he is to please.'

'John is in love, thus, he's easily pleased with everything around him,' Saville said, with a touch of sourness, 'He walks around with a smile on his face and hardly ever hears when you speak to him, like the village idiot.'

'He is well suited, so should be pleased. As for Graine, I should-n't be at all surprised if she doesn't make a brilliant match. Already, two proposals of marriage have been forthcoming. Gerald Phelps follows her around like a lost dog and Viscount Proctor cannot keep his eyes off her.'

'Young idiots,' Saville growled, looking decidedly put out by the news.

Charlotte grinned to herself when his expression assumed an ominous frown. 'Graine is most amused by his behaviour, I believe.'

'Amused!' Saville glowered at her. 'I suppose she leads them on then laughs behind the poor fellows' backs.'

'Nothing of the sort. She confides in her sister, who confides in me. Graine does nothing to encourage their attention, neither does she seek it.'

Subsiding into a chair, Saville muttered, 'They haven't got a brain in their heads, letting her torture them so. They'll not hold her interest for long.'

'They make her laugh with their nonsense. There's no harm in them, and Graine is too sensible to fall victim to the charms of either of them.'

'Then I hope she's aware of the effect an association with such a pair of rogues will have on her.'

'Oh, stop being such a bore, Saville. Pray, leave the preaching to John, who does it with more truth and conviction. They are young, and there is no harm in their flirting. At least they have offered her marriage, when it's plain your intention was to take her into your bed, and ruin her.'

Saville stared at her, shock written all over his face.

Laughter crept through her, then doubled her up for a few deli-cious moments. 'Oh Saville, why so shocked?' she mocked. 'I do believe you've been in the country for far too long. The girl is young, she is bound to confide her secrets in someone.'

Stiffly, he said. 'I'm thinking of going back to Rushford shortly.'

'Then go, for there's nothing to keep you in London. You can settle into your bachelorhood nicely there. John's wedding will not take place until Evelyn has settled her sister, which should not take long, for she's an engaging little piece who will soon forget her infatuation with you once you're not around to remind her.'

'She could live in John's house after he and her sister is wed.'

'So you could control her every move, whilst maintaining your disapproval. Graine's young. She deserves better than that. Either declare yourself and take her back to Rushford, or forget her. She will not wait for you for ever.'

'There's nothing to declare, for her breeding is too far beneath me for her to be socially acceptable.'

Nonsense! Charlotte thought, for she knew he was lying. Her brother had always been straightforward, but stubborn and proud. Graine's birth was being used as an excuse, and would not present an obstacle once he made up his mind. She gave him a bit of incentive. 'The girl tells me she's bored with the life we lead in London. She's thinking of returning to the West Indies to join the sisters of the poor, where her skills can be of use.'

'Not if I've got anything to do with it,' he said.

'My dear Saville, it seems to me that you're being very selfish about this girl. You profess not to want her yourself, but cannot bear the thought of her marrying another. Not satisfied with that, when I remit to you her intention to take up the religious life and serve the poor, you declare you will prevent her from carrying out such worthy pursuit. May I point out that, seeing you have no claim to her, you have no power to enforce your will with regards to her, *whatever that will may be.*'

For a moment Saville stared at her, an aggrieved expression twisting wryly at his mouth. Suddenly, his face cleared and he laughed. 'Damn you, Charlotte, you're as devious as she is.'

It had been a lucrative run. William Younger had picked up a shipload of slaves from the fever coast, the majority of whom were young and sound of wind and limb. No more than a dozen had died during the journey. They, and a further half-dozen who'd showed signs of the same infection, had been thrown overboard to save him the expense of doctoring them. He would claim the lot on insurance as spoiled cargo, and add to it the slaves Sedgley had helped to escape.

He'd sold the healthy slaves at an inflated price in Antigua, ensuring a quick return to England, loaded up with sugar. The weather had been fair, with a strong and constant following wind to fill the sails. The *Bristol Pride*, though fully laden, had made a fast run. He also picked up a passenger in Antigua, a sugar planter by the name of Francis Seaton. William couldn't believe his luck.

'My agent in London keeps his ear to the ground,' William said, over dinner the day before they were due to dock, and because his companion had sunk half a bottle of brandy, he seized the chance to broach the subject which had been on his mind since they'd left. 'I understand Graine Seaton is your niece.'

The sugar planter's silvery eyes came up to his. Fastidiously, he dabbed at his lips before answering, and William could see he was considering his reply. The planter was small in stature, and there was a cruelty about the delicately curved mouth when he said quietly, 'I rarely discuss family matters with strangers, and no doubt you've heard I do not acknowledge the girl. What is your point, Captain?'

'Miss Seaton is in London with her half-sister, and it seems she's to be given half of Seth Adams's fortune.'

'I see.' He gave a thin smile and his eyes narrowed, giving his face a cat-like alertness. 'Perhaps I will call on her whilst I'm in town, let bygones be bygones. It was remiss of me not to do so sooner. May I ask what your interest is in this matter, Captain?'

William leaned forward. 'I believe the sisters are guests of the Earl of Sedgley, who maintains a house in Hanover Square. Your niece's beauty is drawing attention, and there are rumours concerning her and the earl.'

The sharp eyes impaled him; the man's mouth twisted in disdain. 'To what extent is she involved with the man?'

William shrugged. 'She was his guest in Dorset over the winter, and tongues wag.'

'Unchaperoned?'

'His sister was in residence for a small part of the time involved, I believe.'

Francis leaned back in his chair and steepled his hands under his chin. 'I seem to recall the Sedgley name from the past. What type of man is the earl?'

'His father was an adventurer. Perhaps you know of him. He was a partner of Seth Adams.'

Air hissed from Francis Seaton's mouth and his eyes became venomous. 'So,' he spat, 'the affairs of my sister come back to haunt me once again. It was the Earl of Sedgley who introduced Blanche to Seth Adams. I vowed to destroy those who contributed to her downfall. I even arranged for the earl to be despatched. I had no idea he had a son to inherit. It seems as if he takes after the father.'

William leaned forward and smiled. 'He is not the adventurer his father was, but he is actively involved in the anti-slavery movement. He is a solitary man by all accounts, though none speak ill of him.'

The laugh Francis gave was thin and high-pitched. 'He might as well piss into the wind. The slave trade is too profitable and men are too greedy for it to be abolished. If it stopped there would be no sugar, no tobacco and no cotton thread. Pah! He's no threat there.'

'He's set up an escape route for runaways from my ships in Bristol, which costs me money.'

'You know of this route?'

'I will soon, for I'm in the process of sending a darkie through the system.'

'You cannot trust a slave.'

'Be that as it may. I've promised this one freedom and a passage back to Africa for his trouble.'

'Ah,' Francis said, and smiled. 'No doubt he will get his justly deserved reward in the end.'

'And once we know who our enemies are, we can deal with them together, yes? Mutual co-operation, my friend. If you will allow me to ship all your produce I will help you with your niece, who is in need of a protector now she has a large fortune at her disposal.'

'Ah yes . . . the fortune. I suppose the elder sister is her next of kin.'

'Unless she dies before she weds John Lamartine. Then your niece stands to inherit her sister's portion, as well. Under such circumstances, she would be an extremely wealthy woman. Let us hope she has not inherited weak traits from her parents.'

'My niece must be protected against her own nature. But someone might have discredited me in her eyes,' Francis murmured, his eyes gleaming.

'There is more than one way to circumnavigate a relationship. There is a woman of great stupidity and tediousness my agent has recently made the acquaintance of – the aunt of the Earl of Sedgley. The woman's nose has been greatly put out of joint by your niece, I believe. She would do anything to have the girl sent packing.'

The words quivered provocatively in the air between them.

15

Harriet Lamartine was introduced to Francis Seaton at a card assembly. He was most attentive, plying her with wine all evening. She found him to be charming, especially when he lost several gold pieces to her. She declined another game, knowing she couldn't afford to lose, and intent on keeping what she'd gained.

Really, it was too bad she was kept so impoverished,when her son was marrying a fortune, she thought. Evelyn kept a tight grip on her purse strings, and her allowance from Saville was just enough to cover her expenses. Things would change when John wed, she vowed, for she'd not allow that woman to keep the upper hand for long.

'Perhaps you'd keep me company on the terrace, Lady Harriet,' Francis murmured.

Harriet didn't correct his mistake in address, just took his arm in as grand a manner as she could manage. 'I believe you're from the West Indies, sir. Perhaps you're acquainted with my future daughter-in-law, Miss Evelyn Adams, and her half-sister, Graine, who are lately from Antigua.'

They took a seat in a corner, and Francis secured glasses of wine from a servant. 'I've heard of Miss Adams, but as I recall, we've never met.'

'Odd that the half-sister, Graine, bears the same family name as you,' Harriet mused, 'She has an . . . interesting, if unsavoury history, I understand.'

The man's eyes became as alert as those of a cat. 'Please do not continue if you are to revile her, I beg of you, my lady,' he said. 'I have been searching for my poor sister's child for several months and have, in fact, posted a reward for anyone who can help me find her.'

'A reward?' Harriet smiled. 'Why, I do think I can be of assistance to you, Mr Seaton. I know the dear child personally, and although I have tried to be of counsel to her, she is possessed of a determined streak, and has not responded to my motherly overtures. I must tell you, sir, your niece is very forward for her age, due, no doubt, to lack of parental control in her upbringing. Dearest Evelyn, she does her best to control her, but. . . ?' She shrugged. 'Such a shame your niece was raised without the firm guidance of a father's hand.'

'Unfortunately, I believed her to be dead, and didn't know of her existence until recently. Rest assured, when I gain proper guardianship, she will be obliged to learn some manners and bow to my dictates.'

A smile spread across Harriet's lips as she considered this. If this man proved to be Graine Seaton's guardian, she could be rid herself of the girl for good, preferably before the settlement took place. After all, why should Francis Seaton have it?

Her mind ticked over the possibilities. With Graine out of sight, the earl would soon forget his fancy for her, then she would pose no threat to the grandchildren John and Evelyn would produce, for John would remain heir to Rushford and the title. The earl had never displayed any inclination to wed. She'd heard him described as a man's man, so she wouldn't be surprised if he was one of those men who preferred—

Francis Seaton gently touched her arm, his face a study of concern. 'You are so wise, dear, Lady Harriet.'

'You have children yourself, Mr Seaton?'

He shook his head. 'Unfortunately, my wife has proved to be barren.'

'Then perhaps Graine will prove to be a comfort for you both. I know you didn't wish me to speak of this, but it's better you should know. Nothing definite, of course, but there are whispers about the Earl of Sedgley.'

'I'd heard he was a relative of yours.'

'My nephew by marriage, sir. He is a worthy fellow, but was duped by Graine's pert ways and pretty face. Strange, since to my knowledge he's not shown the slightest inclination towards the fairer sex before. She is too far beneath him to be considered seriously, of course. But sometimes men can be such fools where women are concerned, especially when they have estate and are expected to wed and produce heirs to inherit.' She lowered her voice. 'Saville is a man's man, by all account.'

'Indeed,' Francis murmured, looking not in the least bit shocked. 'I recall the Sedgley name was mentioned with regards to an escape route for slaves once. A worthy cause, if one doesn't rely on slaves for one's labour. I doubt if it's the same man though. An earl would consider himself above such a trivial pastime.'

Harriet slanted her eyes in as mysterious a manner as she was able. 'This must be kept as a confidence, of course. The earl disapproves so heartily of the slave trade, I wouldn't be at all surprised if he's arranged an escape route. I accidentally overheard he and my son talking about such a plan once or twice. They agreed that once a slave sets foot in English soil he becomes a free man.'

'That's true of course,' Francis murmured, 'But the slaves cannot handle freedom. They cannot think for themselves and must be directed in everything they do. To set them free in a strange, cold land is the cruellest thing one can do for them. Most of them die, for they're treated worse than dogs by the populace at large. At least on the plantations they are housed and fed, and they are kept gainfully employed.'

Harriet nodded. 'The earl said there is a sea captain who is particularly harsh, and he is determined to bring him to book one day. He invited Captain Younger to search the caves at Rushford Estate. Saville and my son were laughing about it. The caves were not the ones used to hide the runaways, but those used in the past for smuggling by his father and his partner, Seth Adams.'

Her hand pressed against her heart. 'Rogues, the pair of them were, but the old earl was so dashing a man I completely lost my heart to him. The son doesn't take after him though. Saville is much too clever for his own good. He is a dark horse and, although he is often reclusive, he can be ruthless when he sets out to be. That sea captain had better beware.'

Francis Seaton nodded. 'You're a very observant woman, Lady

201

Harriet. I imagine you know every little secret they try and keep from you.'

'Oh, they think I don't know what goes on,' she said bitterly. 'As if I could have ignored the comings and goings in my own back-yard for all that time. They bring the runaways there at night, using the river, then hide them upstairs in the sleeping chambers of the old schoolroom. The place is let as a warehouse, so it appears to be a legitimate business. They store goods in it, but the merchant concerned is known to be outspoken in his pursuit of ending the trade in slaves.'

Francis Seaton stood up and bowed. 'I've enjoyed our conversation. I do hope you will keep our discussion in confidence, especially about my niece. I wish to surprise her.'

Harriet was disappointed by his departure. She coughed as he turned to leave, saying delicately, 'You mentioned a reward, Mr Seaton.'

'Of course, Lady Harriet. Alas, you've won most of the cash I carried, and without giving me a chance to win it back. Also, I need to take a look at Graine Seaton and satisfy myself the girl is who you say she is. I will expect her to bear some resemblance to her poor, dead mother. Perhaps you could invite her to visit you—'

'Oh, no, I cannot! We've exchanged hard words and she would snub any invitation. However, I happen to know she will be shopping shortly with Miss Adams.' Her voice took on a sour note. 'They tend to squander money on themselves and patronize a dressmaking establishment in Charing Cross. They have an appointment at three o'clock for a fitting.'

When she imperiously held up her arm to have her hand kissed, the man pretended not to see it. She lowered it again, putting some chill in her voice. 'I'll expect you to call on me with the reward early tomorrow, Mr Seaton, before my son does. No doubt he'd be most interested in the conversation we've just engaged in.'

A pair of pale eyes flickered toward her, Francis Seaton's mouth stretched into a thin smile. 'My dear, Mrs Lamartine, women of your age and disposition should not indulge in threats, especially women who cheat at the card tables.' He palmed a knife from his sleeve. 'A couple of pricks from this little fellow could blind you;

202

a slash across the tongue could silence you; the tip embedded in the back of the neck could paralyse you. And who knows what the length of it could achieve when applied to the unsuspecting flesh of your son, who is an official of the church at Chiswick, I believe. You must keep your mouth shut, my dear, then no harm will come to anyone. Is that understood?'

Recoiling from him, she gasped, and nodded.

He leaned forward, picked up her hand and made every show of manners. 'Good. You must hide your avarice and learn not to push so hard, my dear. You'll get your reward, but unless you keep quiet the payment will not be as pleasant as you first expected.' He turned and walked away rapidly, leaving her shivering with dread.

Evelyn had developed an odd notion that they were being watched. She gazed around her, but saw nothing untoward. Still, the uneasy feeling persisted as they threaded their way through the bustling crowds, followed by Millie and Jessie.

Evelyn had taken to London with a vengeance. She loved the bustle, the rich variety of the population and the noisy street vendors with their colourful language. It was so unlike her former home it was like being in a different, and wildly exciting world.

Suddenly, there was shouting up ahead and a crush of people came surging towards them.

'Quick,' Millie shouted, trying to push her out of the way.

She wasn't fast enough. The crowd surrounded her and carried her forward under its momentum. Jostled here and there, her arm was grasped and she was pulled to one side and against the body of a man. Cold, grey, wolverine eyes touched briefly against hers, then she caught her breath as something punched her in the side.

A pickpocket, she thought, as hands wrenched the pocket from her gown and a brooch from her shoulder. Then she was down, saved from being trampled underfoot by a wall at her back. Struggling to her feet invited a cramping pain to attack her side. Overcome by dizziness, she sank to her knees.

A pair of strong arms came around her in support as the crush passed by, stampeded by God knew what, for there was no immediate cause for such rushing panic as had been displayed.

'Thank God you're here,' she whispered, when she saw Saville.

I think I have been injured.'

Millie arrived with Graine and Jessie at her heels. They were out of breath and frantic. Millie gazed in horror. 'Gawd almighty. Look at the blood on your gown.'

Already feeling faint, Evelyn took one glance at the seeping red liquid and passed out.

'The blood must be staunched before she is moved,' Graine observed, and Saville was glad she was not prone to hysterics at the sight of such calamity.

'Use my stock,' he said, and tried not to respond to the sensation of her fingers against his skin as she loosened his carefully arranged neckwear with which to bind Evelyn's wound.

There was not a sedan chair in sight. As soon as she was finished staunching the blood flow he set off for Hanover Square, his long stride carrying him rapidly over the ground. Evelyn was no lightweight when compared to Graine.

Graine followed after him, her heels tapping determinedly against the cobbles. Although the maids, laden down as they were with parcels, fell behind, she was practically running. After a while Graine began to pant, but she didn't complain. She put him in mind of a little terrier dog. Her breathing grew more laboured. He relaxed his pace a little. Getting Evelyn home quickly would be of no use if there was nobody there with the skill to look after her.

Barely fifteen minutes later, Evelyn was settled on her bed. Saville had been dismissed whilst Graine examined her sister, with Millie in attendance. Graine came out for a brief moment or two, to say, 'The wound is not deep enough to have caused serious damage, and it does not require stitching. However, I must probe it, for something seems to be lodged inside the cut. I will call you if help is needed.' She then bade him him arrange warm water, tweezers, salves, and strips of clean linen to serve as bandaging.

He passed the task over to Jessie whilst he sent a footman with a message for John. Taking a seat on the stair he winced when he heard Evelyn give a long drawn out groan, which was followed by soothing sounds from Graine. He refrained from rushing inside. His patience was rewarded when Graine joined him.

Pale-faced, she held out her palm, where a sharp piece of triangular metal nestled. Her eyes were troubled when he took it from her. In a trembling voice, she said, 'Somebody has stabbed my sister. She is badly shaken but should recover without ill effect after a few days' rest. Luckily, the knife tip broke off before it could penetrate deeper, otherwise the placement of the wound would have penetrated her vitals.'

'Who would do such a thing?'

'Evelyn has lost her purse and brooch, so I can only think that she was accidentally stabbed when the felon stole her pocket. She said the man had pale-grey eyes – but she's puzzled, for he appeared to be too well dressed to be a felon.'

'Dips come in all shapes and sizes. From now on you will not venture abroad without a manservant in attendance.'

'I'm sure there is no need—'

'Allow me to be the judge of that.'

She dipped him a curtsy, her face a tumult of rebellion. 'As you will, my lord.'

His eyes softened. 'You must not take offence, my Eve. There's good reason for me wanting you both guarded.'

'What good reason is that?'

After a momentary hesitation, he said, 'I believe the attack could have been deliberate.'

The remaining colour fled from Graine's cheeks. 'You mean, someone wanted to kill her? But why? Evelyn is well liked and has no enemies.' She searched her mind for the reason, but could find none, except. . . ? She stared at him, horror dawning in her eyes. 'There's only one person who would benefit from her death, isn't there?'

'Yes.'

'So, you think I'm capable of arranging such a despicable act?'

He chuckled. 'You are certainly capable, as you have displayed by your earlier conduct. The question is, would you?'

Crushed, she gazed at him, her stomach churning, the horror she felt clearly displayed in her eyes. 'I see nothing to laugh about. If it would help confirm what you suspect I'm capable of, I would gladly squeeze the very life from you at this moment. Go from my sight,' she whispered, 'for I cannot bear the suspicion with which you regard me. Send for a doctor to tend Evelyn. I will not go near her until she recovers, lest she be infected by some unworthy thought I may have.'

'Graine.' He extended a hand towards her. 'I did not mean—'

'Goodbye, my lord, you have wounded me beyond redemption, this time.' And in case he didn't understand how much she despised him at that moment, she struck him in the chest with her fist, then turned and fled upstairs to her chamber.

Locking the door, she threw herself on the bed and, ignoring Jessie's entreaties to be allowed in, sobbed herself to sleep.

Cursing his stupidity, Saville helped himself to a stiff brandy, then dropped the knife tip into his pocket. Hearing a rustle of paper, he drew out the letter Graine had written to him, always kept close to his heart.

My dearest love . . . one who loves you truly for all eternity . . . nothing can ever dislodge you from my heart.

He groaned. No wonder he'd thought she'd sounded young. She was young – and sensitive to her past. As a result of her parents' folly, she'd suffered. He could not tell her the reason for the precautions, that William Younger's ship had recently docked, and the message he'd received from him before they'd left Rushford had bode her no good at all. Younger had judged her guilty by association because the dog had sought to guard her.

And he had not been near them by chance today. He'd been following Graine, to ensure her safety. Only, his eyes had been on her dainty figure, not on Evelyn, who'd been targeted instead. Though for what reason, he hadn't yet figured out, for William Younger could have no grudge against her.

Who, but Graine, would benefit if Evelyn died? he wondered. Then his way of thinking shifted horrifyingly sideways, for she still had blood ties through her mother's family still residing in Antigua. Francis Seaton! Did his need for revenge extend to the innocent child of that ill-fated liaison between Seth and Blanche?

Poor Graine. How he'd wronged her. Since Charlotte had forcibly fed him her home truths, he knew that Graine could imagine no future for herself with the stigma of her parentage attached to her. No wonder she'd tried to conceal it from him. He'd have done the same under the circumstances, for, when all was said and done, his own father was little more than a common felon who'd brought disgrace upon the estate and title. He understood now, and although he still wished she'd confided in him, he was thoroughly ashamed of his treatment of her.

Graine was already up and quite composed when Jessie came to rouse her later in the afternoon.

'There's a gentleman waiting ter see you in the drawing-room.'

'If it's the earl, tell him I do not wish to see him.'

'It ain't the earl, but his lordship did leave a message. He said to tell you he has some urgent business to attend to. He begs you not to abandon Miss Evelyn, and to attend him in the drawing-room this very evening. He has something of the utmost importance he wishes to convey to you.' With an ear-to-ear grin, Jessie handed her a red rose. 'This here be his token. He picked it specially from the garden hisself. Now, don't that be real romantic?'

'The earl begs for nothing,' she said, and hurled the rose out of the open window. 'He knows I have nowhere else to take refuge, and turns it to his own advantage.'

'He sounded right sorry for hisself. "Jessie", says he, "whisper my words gently against Miss Seaton's ear".'

Graine recovered a little of her former self. 'If he's genuinely sorry, and if he isn't too proud, I'll allow him to tell me himself. Make sure he knows that when he arrives. And you'd better send someone to retrieve the rose. It would be a pity to let it wilt.'

Jessie picked up a brush. 'I'll tell him myself, miss. Now, let Jessie do your hair before you see the gentleman visitor. Perkins has showed me how to arrange a pretty hairstyle for you.'

Graine began to relax under the gentle touch of the slow brushstrokes against her scalp. 'Who is this gentleman? Not Gerald Phelps, I hope.'

'His name is Francis Seaton. He said he be your uncle.'

Graine's eyes shot open. Sitting bolt upright, she squeaked, 'My uncle?'

'That's what he said, miss. All the way from the West Indies, he came. He said you'd be surprised.'

Her eyes narrowed. That was an understatement if ever she'd heard one. Evelyn had told her that Francis Seaton had disowned her. It was rumoured that he'd murdered their father. So why was he here? A chill ran through her. Perhaps he's come to kill her too. She quickly squashed the chilling thought. He wouldn't give his name and kill her in broad daylight. Perhaps he'd had a change of heart, and was curious to what had become of her.

Her curiosity overcame her reluctance. He was her family, her mother's brother. She must see him. And make a favourable impression, if possible. Remembering Saville was calling on her later, and liked her in blue, she said casually to Jessie, 'I'll change into my blue taffeta gown with the laced bodice, and I'll wear my pearls.'

She didn't see the broad smile Jessie gave as the woman turned away.

Francis Seaton stood when she entered the drawing-room. His eyes swept over her and his voice was choked with emotion when he said, 'How like Blanche you are, my dear.'

'People who knew him say I look like my father.'

Francis Seaton pulled in a deep breath, but chose not to acknowledge the mention of her father. 'Blanche was about your age when she died.' He pulled a painted miniature from his pocket, dangling it on a chain from his finger; it twisted this way and that. 'This is her likeness. I thought you'd like it.'

Overcome by curiosity she stepped forward, her hand outstretched. The silver locket dropped into her palm. Painted on it was the face of a young woman. She was beautiful, but she had a spoiled and wilful look. Her hair was dark, her mouth was drawn into a fashionable pout.

The likeness disappointed Graine. Her mother was nothing like she'd imagined. 'Thank you, but you are mistaken. We do not look much alike.'

'My dearest Graine. I'm glad you are not, for it pains me to remember her. I have been looking for you a long time. At last I have found you.'

'You did not look very far, for I was left in the orphanage on Antigua and lived there for sixteen years.'

Her uncle frowned. 'I thought you'd died as a baby. I have business interests elsewhere, and spend very little time on the plantation in Antigua. However, I am not here to discuss your childhood. I have heard that your sister has died from injuries received in a street riot. As your nearest male relative, I'm here to assume guardianship of you. Will you not greet me, my own beautiful niece?'

Smiling, he took her into an embrace. The cloying perfume of him made her want to sneeze. The kiss he gave her was too long and too close to her mouth for comfort. She turned her head away in disgust, her skin crawling. Inside her head, she heard the song of the myla woman, warning her to beware.

'I need no guardian, sir.' She was about to mention her sister was still alive and well, when she saw his eyes, pale-grey and predatory. Evelyn had described her attacker as having such eyes. She began to tremble. 'I'm a guest in the house of the Earl of Sedgley. As he advises me on all business affairs to do with my estate, you will kindly wait whilst he's sent for. I'll order some refreshment for you.'

Her trembling must have alerted him, for her attempt to get to the bell pull was thwarted when he pinioned her wrists in his hands. The miniature flew from her hand and slid across the floor. A knife was held at her back. 'Unless you want to suffer the same fate as your sister, you will do as you're told and proceed without struggle to the carriage waiting outside. I will negotiate with this earl of yours, without your presence.'

She had no recourse but to obey. Jessie bobbed her a curtsy as they passed on the stairs. Graine sent her a glance of entreaty and she frowned. 'Is everything all right, Miss Seaton?'

'Get about your business, woman,' Francis snapped, a well-aimed foot sending the maid scurrying.

Terrified that Jessie would be hurt, Graine said sharply, 'Do as he says, Jessie. I'm just seeing my guest out.'

Jessie's eyes sharpened when she saw her mistress hustled out of the door. It closed noisily behind the pair. The next moment she heard the carriage horse clop off down the street. 'Where be all the fancy footmen when you need one,' she grumbled, heading for the back stairs.

Running into Mollie with an armful of linen, she told her what had happened, then was out of the door and running as fast as her legs could carry her towards Miss Charlotte's house.

It was not a great distance to travel, but they'd been conveyed to the docks at a fast pace. Wrapped in a voluminous cloak, a cowl drooping over her face, Graine could only see rough cobbles. There was a stretch of grey, stinking mud with a sodden, striped cat curled up on it. It was dead, but looked as if it slept comfortably on a cushion of mud. Seagulls screeched overhead and rough voices rang out.

Francis's grip tightened on her arm as her body tensed to run. Then came a narrow gangplank and a wooden deck under her feet. She was propelled down a narrow ladder, then down another and another, until finally she found herself in a small, airless space.

Francis Seaton had not said a word to her, which made him all the more terrifying. For a moment, he held up the lantern he carried. His eyes glittered in the flickering candlelight as he backed through the door, leaving her in darkness. There came the click of a lock.

She threw herself at it, pummelling at the rough surface with her fists. 'Let me out, you blood-sucking bat. Why are you doing this? My mother will curse you from heaven.'

A chilling laugh came from the other side of the panel. 'Your mother wouldn't spare you a passing thought, and far from being in heaven, she's probably supping with the Devil himself right at this very moment. The poor fool, Adams, thought he was in love with her – until he caught her trying to smother you with a pillow.'

Graine gasped.

'It was your father who put you in the orphanage, not me. I would have finished the job Blanche had started.'

'Did you kill Seth Adams?'

There was a moment of stretched out silence, then he said, 'He ruined her. He gave her opium and it drove her insane, set her on a life of licentiousness. She didn't know me in the end.' His voice dropped to a whisper. 'She offered me, her own brother, the use of her body for money. I was forced to put her out of her misery.'

Tears came to Graine's eyes. 'Why did you attack . . . kill my sister?'

'Now she's out of the way you'll inherit the Adams fortune. I intend to have control of it until you come of age.'

Graine bit down on her lip. This man had the madness in him.

She must be careful not to inflame him, or reveal that Evelyn was still alive. At least, he didn't intend to kill her. But an insane man said one thing and often did another. He would only keep her alive until he had control of her fortune.

She lowered her voice. 'What is it you intend to do with me, Uncle?'

'Look after you most carefully, until I obtain control of your fortune. You will write a letter, which will be witnessed by an attorney-at-law.'

'And if I refuse to write it?'

'I will whip you within an inch of your life,' he hissed. 'It's something I'm very good at, as any of my slaves will testify. I once flayed the skin from a slave inch by inch. It took me five days, and I enjoyed every moment.'

She sucked in a deep breath as the horror of such an act hit her. This ship was used for the transportation of slaves. Behind them, they had left the smell of their fear and sickness. With each movement of the ship she could hear the clank of chains. Suddenly, it pressed in on her, suffocatingly real. There came the cries of those in torment, and the voices singing of a homeland left behind them. She heard the crack of the whips of the slave masters as they drove them forward, and cries of anguish as they were penned up in this stifling darkness, like animals.

Nausea rose to her throat and she gagged. Clearly, she heard a voice incessant above the din. It was the myla woman. The song entered her heart and her mind, filled her with hope. Finally, her own voice rose in unison with it.

She was brought back to reason when someone grasped her hair and dragged her forth. A hand whipped back and forth across her face as Francis screamed, 'Shut that cursed din, you heathen bitch.'

In the darkness, she felt Sheba's presence. She smiled, despite the blood trickling from her mouth, knowing that she was protected. But she had to get out of this rat hole if she was to survive.

'I'll write the letter,' she said, for it didn't really matter. It wouldn't be worth the scrap of paper it was written on. Evelyn was alive and there was no fortune to inherit. Saville would know the note was a fake. And even though he despised her now, he would forgive her enough to rescue her.

When all was resolved, she would return to Antigua and join the order. She would work on behalf of the poor and the dispossessed. That would relieve her of the sins of her parents, and perhaps secure her a place in heaven.

She jumped when a pistol was shoved into her back. 'My dear Uncle Francis,' she pleaded, her holy thoughts fleeing in the face of this threat, for she didn't want her place in heaven quite so soon. 'Must you be so extreme? I'm only a girl. What harm can I possibly do to you?'

'I wouldn't put it past you to try and escape.'

She summoned up some sarcasm. 'You must be a crack shot from this distance.'

'From any distance,' he boasted and, taking aim, discharged the weapon at a shadow lurking in a corner. A rat exploded into bloody shreds. It didn't even have time to squeak.

Impulsively snatching at the opportunity, she dashed the lantern from his hand. He cursed when the candle fell out of the holder and rolled across the floor. It disappeared through a crack in the timber before he could reach it.

She headed for the ladder with Francis in hot pursuit. A faint, grey light above gave her hope. At the next deck Francis tripped up, giving her the opportunity to gain ground. The light grew stronger, the air cleaner. Just one deck to go. She scrambled upwards, and had just crawled through the hatch into the open air when a pair of boots came into her vision.

Gazing upwards, she saw William Younger staring down at her. 'Help me!' she gasped out.'

'Certainly, my dear.' He smiled and drew back his foot. It connected with her stomach and she sailed backwards through the hatch. For a moment she was flying though the air, then she crashed down on to something unforgivably hard.

Her breath left her body in one deflating swoop, and the square of light above dimmed into a sudden and painful darkness.

16

Dislodged from the lantern Francis Seaton had dropped, the candle had rolled a little way into the space between the double hull. The space, sometimes used for cargoes such as coal or slate, was empty now, except for an accumulation of dust, and nests made by enterprising rats, which had dragged torn pieces of sacking and papers into this place of relative safety.

The candle was still alight. As the tide ebbed the ship canted slightly. The candle rolled and its flame touched against a ball of fluff mixed with coal dust.

There was a series of tiny, sparking explosions as the gas trapped in the dust ignited. The ball of fluff began to burn, the blue flaming tongues licked delicately at the caulking between the wooden planks. The threads of oakum began to untwist. The tar holding them together began to soften and melt.

Graine felt sick and dizzy when she came round. She was lying on a bunk.

Her head was one big ache, and her face was swollen. The taste of stale blood filled her mouth. In a chair by the table, a man was seated. He turned when she groaned and tried to struggle to her feet. The man was Captain William Younger.

'Ah, you're awake, my dear,' he said. Picking up a decanter, he filled a tumbler with brandy and brought it over to her. 'Drink this. It will help speed your recovery.'

Suspicious, she shook her head.

He sat on the edge of the bunk and smiled. 'Come, Miss Seaton.

213

There is nothing in it to harm you, and it will save me holding your nose and pouring it down your throat.'

Believing his threat, she took the brandy and began to drink.

'Faster,' he said, when she would have slowed down. When it was swallowed, he brought her another. 'You may drink this one more slowly, my dear, but drink it you will.'

He was right, she did feel a bit better. After a while her headache left her and she positively glowed. Her ears were buzzing as she gazed around the small cabin. 'Where's my uncle?'

'He's gone to see Mrs Lamartine, who has been kindly assisting him in your downfall.'

Graine shuddered. How could Harriet be so evil. 'He's a bad man. The obeah have marked his soul,' she said. Her nose twitched. 'Can you smell smoke?'

'Of course I can. There's a vendor of smoked eels on the dock-side. Are you hungry? I could send for some, for you? They're oily, but would sit well in your stomach with the brandy.'

She shuddered at the thought and shook her head.

The captain smiled at her. 'Well, you only have to say the word. As for Francis Seaton, he's a fool to involve others in his schemes. I believe he wants you to write a letter to the Earl of Sedgley.'

She smiled at the thought of Saville. 'He's going to be nettled when he finds out about this.' She poked a finger through the air at him. 'He'll be after you, Captain, and Rebel will chew on your bones. You'll probably end up like your son. I believe the obeah caused his death, for when the nature of it was described to me, it sounded exactly like the yaws. Have you ever known anyone outside of a tropical climate suffering from that before?'

Younger scowled. 'Shut your mouth, girl. The earl doesn't scare me. Do you know why, my dear?'

'No.' There was a warm glow in her stomach now.

'Because he'll never find out what happened to you. When we sail, I'm going to take you with me and throw you overboard.'

'Hah!' she said, but uncertainly. 'The sea doesn't want me. It has thrown me back.'

'I'll make sure it takes you this time. I'll tie a length of chain around your ankles.'

Her face paled as she stared at him. 'You wouldn't do that.'

'I most certainly would, my dear. However, I might allow you to work your passage.'

Although she suspected that she suffered from intoxication already, because she was filled with a false bravado, she took a steadying gulp of the brandy. 'I don't know how to be a sailor.'

She cried out when he leaned forward and roughly pinched her breasts. 'I have all the crew I require. They're in need of entertainment, though, for a satisfied man is a happy man. I shall be the first to have you, then, when I'm finished, the crew can take a turn. You will make a nice change from the slave girls.'

She slapped his hands aside, her skin crawling. 'I can understand my uncle's motives, but why are you doing this to me? What have I ever done to you?'

'You helped to kill my son.'

'I had nothing to do with your son's death. He died from blood poisoning.'

'If it hadn't been for the interference of the earl in my legitimate business affairs, we would have not been on his land, and that dog of his would not have set about him.'

'What insane logic is this? The dog set about your son because he attacked me.'

'Nevertheless, I lost my only son. An eye for an eye, Miss Seaton. I'm taking you from the earl permanently, as my son was taken from me.'

She laughed. 'The earl will neither care, nor give me another thought. He despises me now he's aware of my poor birth. I cannot say I blame him. I hate myself sometimes.' She gave him a sly look. 'You must know what it's like to loath yourself most of the time.'

He smacked her across her swollen face. The brandy had made her reckless, though. Bunching her fingers into a fist she lashed out at him. He stopped her fist with his palm and squeezed, not releasing her until she screamed with pain.

'That was a stupid thing to do,' he ground out. Grabbing her by the hair he pulled her forcibly from the bunk to the desk, where he pushed her down on to the chair. There was a sharpened quill, a pot of ink and a clean sheet of parchment on the desk. He stood behind her, his hands digging into her neck where it joined her shoulders. 'Write to the earl telling him to sign your inheritance over to your uncle at the bank. I shall send it by messenger. And be careful, for I shall inspect every word.'

Knowing she was beaten, Graine picked up the pen.

> *My Lord*
> *Now that my dearest sister, Evelyn Adams is deceased. I will return to Antigua, to reside with my uncle, Mr Francis Seaton.*
>
> *As my nearest relative, Mr Seaton is now appointed my legal guardian and will hold my inheritance in trust until I'm of age. From now on, he will be accountable for any further dealings on my behalf. I trust you will assist him in this matter promptly by contacting the bank, forthwith. The matter is of some urgency.*
>
> *Because I sail on the morrow. I'm unable to attend Evelyn's funeral, but will mourn her in private. I beg you, sir, please respect my wishes in this matter.*
>
> *I have the honour to remain.*
> *Your Lordship's obedient servant,*
> *Graine Seaton*

Saville scanned the letter, smiling to himself when he saw the darker print emphasizing some of the words. *Francis Seaton – accountable – assist – promptly – beg you.* She had kept her wits about her. He should have known Graine would find some way of letting him know she was still alive, and informing him that those concerned in her abduction believed Evelyn had died in the attack.

'Who gave you the letter?' he said to the messenger.

'A sailor off one of the ships.'

'Did you see which ship?'

'No, but he smelt as though he came off a black-birder, and there's one in dock. You can't mistake the stench of slavery, poor devils.'

The *Bristol Pride*! Saville flicked the man a gold piece and asked him to alert the soldiers at the watch house. He then loaded a brace of pistols and strapped on his sword.

John, who'd never known his cousin to be aggressive, placed a hand on his arm to caution him. 'You must not go alone, Saville.'

Saville threw an arm around his shoulders in a brief hug. 'The soldiers will be alerted. Arm yourself then, John, for anyone who takes a woman from the safe haven of her own home and loved ones, has no scruples whatsoever. I'm not out to kill anyone, unless it is in self-defence.'

'I wouldn't know how to wield a sword, but I can shoot fairly straight, and have got a good punch on me when I'm pushed.'

'I'll be glad of somebody to watch my back. There's no love lost between myself and the captain of the *Bristol Pride*.' Saville called the manservants together and told them to detain Francis Seaton by any means they could, if the planter decided to pay him a visit.

Within minutes, the Lamartine men were heading rapidly towards the dock.

The first thing Graine did when she was left alone, was to try the door to William Younger's cabin. Not only was it locked, it was made of solid oak, so she couldn't break through it.

Rushing to the windows she threw them open and sighed with frustration. They were too small to wriggle through. How odd, she thought inconsequently, some half-a-dozen rats were running down the hawser tying the ship to the dock.

She could still smell the smoke. It was stronger now and it had a tary-like smell to it. Smoked eels, ugh! She resolved never to try them!

She needed something to pick the lock with. All the cupboards and drawers proved to be locked. Thwarted, she gazed around the small cabin. There were charts on the table. When she shuffled through them a gleam of metal caught her eye. She stared intently at the sharp points on a navigational aid. She had picked the door on her cell at the orphanage with a similar utensil, on occasion. They just might do. Smiling, she picked the instrument up and inserted the pointed end into the keyhole.

Wisps of smoke began to drift through the join in the window frame, to dissipate out into the open air.

Graine's concentration was absolute as she wriggled the instrument about, trying to get a purchase on the mechanism. The point caught on something and bent at an angle. There was resistance. Holding her breath she pushed, giving a satisfied grunt as a solid click reached her ears. She withdrew the dividers, keeping them in her hand to use as a weapon, if need be.

The smell of eels was much stronger now, tickling at her throat.

The darkness outside the cabin was thick with smoke. Good God. It wasn't eels. There seemed to be a fire on the ship somewhere. Surely they hadn't intended to burn her alive.

Placing her hand across her mouth she made her way to where the ladder was located and crept up. She was more careful this time. No noise and no haste, though it was hard not to cough with the irritation of the smoke. The higher she got, the thinner the smoke became. A thrill of fear ran through her and she began to cough. When she looked below she could neither see or hear any flames crackling, though the air around her had become extremely hot and she was perspiring.

When she reached the top of the ladder, she eased the hatch aside and sucked a deep breath into her labouring lungs. She was extra cautious, sliding over the top on her belly, to reach the deck without a sound.

Through the smoke she spied William Younger talking to a rough-looking man a little way off. A pistol was tucked in his belt. The pair had their backs to her, but they blocked her way to the gangplank.

'We'll take the girl with us, bosun. She'll provide us with a bit of sport, and can be disposed of easily enough when we're in open waters. I want the crew on board tonight, for we sail with the morning tide. If our passenger isn't back, we'll sail without him.'

'Fire!' Graine shouted at the top of her lungs. When the men turned and began to run towards the smoke, she headed frantically in the other direction. She could throw herself over the side if she had too.

But the bosun changed tack, turning and running back the other way, so he had her trapped between them. At he reached out for her she stuck him in the neck with her lock picker. Blood spurted and he screamed and staggered backwards. She headed hastily for the gangplank.

Standing on the dock, Saville watched Graine make her bid for freedom. Heart in his mouth he levelled his pistol at the man coming up behind her. Graine caught her foot in her skirt and sprawled face down on the gangplank. Saville pulled the trigger, but Younger bent and the shot whistled over his shoulder. He snatched Graine upright and pulled her in front of him to use as a shield.

'Don't shoot,' he yelled at the soldiers, who had just arrived and had lined up on the dock with their rifles pointed at the ship. They bristled with authority and menace.

William Younger dragged Graine back towards the hatch. She wasn't going willingly. She had made herself a dead weight and her heels dragged across the deck.

Suddenly, she dug those heels in and shot upwards, her head catching Younger under the chin and throwing him off balance. She picked up her skirt and ran pell-mell for the gangplank, and had just gained a foothold when Younger had himself under control.

Saville reached for his second pistol as Younger levelled his at Graine's back. A dark hole appeared in the centre of the man's forehead when Saville pulled the trigger. The ball must have whistled past her ear, for Graine threw herself sideways off the narrow planking. There was no splash, just a wet splat. Then came an explosion, as air rushed into the hatch to feed the flames. A ball of flame erupted upwards to consume the captain's fallen body.

A few moments later, something brown, slimy and slim crawled from the mud of the Thames and heaved itself upright.

The soldier's rifles trained on it and bolts clicked.

'Don't shoot,' Saville yelled frantically.

The apparition, decidedly female, was in a fine temper. Her hands went to her hips and slid off, so she stamped her feet and gave a series of small, angry screams. Stinking mud flew everywhere when she shook herself like a dog. Finally, a pair of irate tawny eyes were uncovered. She impaled him with one look, then yelled, 'Look at the state of me, you clumsy oaf! *My lord.*' The afterthought was uttered in such an uncivil manner that, behind him, both John and the soldiers burst into laughter.

As Graine stomped past him, Saville's hand circled her wrist and swung her against him. He smiled as she gazed up at him, her eyes seething with indignance in her mud-caked face. 'We must wash that mud off you.'

Alarm came into her voice. 'It must not be washed off, for my face is all battered and bruised and I am exceedingly ugly now. You will hate me.'

He had never loved her more than at that moment. 'I love you, Graine. Will you do me the honour of becoming my wife?'

'Hah, certainly not. At least . . . not until you explain to me about that actress,' she scolded. 'Why did you leave Charlotte's dinner with her, sir?'

He grinned. Of all the contrary women, this one had to be the worst. One minute she loved him, the next minute she didn't. She was a disaster! She was uncertain of temper, attracted trouble and was too clever than a woman ought to be for a man's comfort. However, he knew his life would be worth nothing without her.

'Adrianna de Lisle is part of the movement to abolish slavery. Sometimes she and her acting troop smuggle the runaways abroad. They'd discovered a spy in the troop, sent through by William Younger. He believed he'd be killed by Younger and confessed all to her. She wanted me to interview him.'

For a moment Graine stared at him, then she burst into tears. Small rivers of skin were uncovered, though her hair was hanging in slimy brown ropes and her aroma was growing more unattractive by the second.

'I thought she was your mistress, and I hated you for loving her and not me.'

'I have no mistress, and never will have. I love only you, Graine. I have done since the moment we met.' He quirked a wry grin at her and, gently wrapping his cloak around her, pulled her muddy head against his chest and held her close. He waited to hear the answer he intended to have from her.

Instead, she said in a tired voice, 'All is not over yet. Francis Seaton was responsible for the death of both my parents, and of the attack on Evelyn. I'm sorry to have to tell you that Harriet Lamartine is also involved with him in some way. He has gone to visit her, so it's possible she'll be in grave danger.'

Saville exchanged a glance with John over her head, who beckoned to the soldiers.

'Take me home, Saville,' Graine said to him, and he knew she meant Rushford House.

Harriet was pleased with life. She'd won a fortune the night before at the card table. The gold was piled up in tidy piles on her table so she could admire it. Such a pretty colour.

For some reason, she'd a craving for something sweet. She ate her way through a dish of bon-bons, carrying it back to her chair by the table and feeding tit-bits to the dogs.

Tomorrow she was hosting the card game. She made a tiny indentation with the tip of a knife at the corner of the last one in the pack of cards. The little tricks she'd learned of late were holding her in good stead, her winnings supplementing her income and buying her a few luxuries.

Absently, her hand reached for the last bon-bon. It smelled of almonds and chocolate. Her favourite flavour. Feeling the material rustle and something crunch between her fingers, she gazed at it. It wasn't a bon-bon, but the charm the fortune-teller had given her.

An insatiable curiosity filled her. She loosened the ribbons and tipped the contents into her palm. It was the bones her fortune had been told with.

As she stared at them they began to move. Her eyes widened with horror as they joined together to become one. Slowly, the snake lifted its head and gazed at her.

Paralysed with fear, now, she could only gaze at the loathsome thing as it began to slither upwards towards her chest. Then it struck. Clutching at her chest, Harriet fell sideways.

It was found that she'd succumbed to a severe attack of apoplexy.

Later that night, Francis Seaton walked into the trap that John and the soldiers set for him. He was caught in the act of sneaking into Harriet's house. Concealed in his sleeve was the knife with which he'd used to stab Evelyn, and a thin wire garrotte.

With the knife tip already in Saville's possession, there was not much doubt about Francis's guilt.

He was charged with Graine's abduction and with the attempted murder of Evelyn. Sentenced to death, he was still blaming obeah for the act when the final breath rattled from his body.

EPILOGUE

It had been a glorious day. As the carriage turned into the gates of Rushford, Graine had a sense of coming home.

Saville stopped the carriage and helped her out. The air was balmy and fragrant. The sun was molten gold. It poured over the tree tops, lit the windows of the house and burst in fiery ripples across the lake. Her eyes and heart overflowed with its beauty as he sent the carriage rolling on.

Their arms came around each other's waists, and they began to stroll towards the house.

'Rushford is wondrous fair in autumn,' Graine whispered.

Saville tipped up her face and kissed her mouth. 'You are wondrous fair all the time, my lady. Even when you're covered in Thames mud.'

She laughed, but shyly. They had been wed but a short time, celebrating a double wedding with her sister in the church in which John preached. The beautiful ceremony was conducted by John's superior, Bishop Salmesley.

It had been Graine's pleasure to become Saville's wife, but it was only in name, for they'd left for Rushford immediately after the ceremony.

'The estate workers will want to celebrate with us, and where better than at the harvest supper,' Saville had said. But Graine knew he was longing to return home, where his heart was.

Progress was slow, for Saville stopped to kiss her every five steps they took, and she felt obliged to return that kiss. She was filled with a strange and vibrant urgency to be alone with him.

A dog detached itself from the house. Its nose cast about in the air and it began to bark. Fixing its eyes on its prey, it hurtled down the garden, its legs a blur of movement. Graine laughed when Rebel overshot them in his haste. He did a somersault, then danced around them, twisting and turning.

'Damned dog,' Saville said, grinning fondly at the animal, who thrust his head into his master's hand to be fondled. 'I've missed you.'

When they reached the house they were obliged to run the gauntlet of servants, who tried not to grin when Jessie advised him, 'I've had the countess's things moved to the chamber adjoining yours, my lord.'

'Thank you, Jessie. We'll go and inspect them immediately then, for we need to rest after the journey. Your services will not be required at present, but you may serve dinner on the terrace.'

'Out,' Saville said to Rebel, as he tried to follow them into the chamber, and he smiled at her. 'My lady and I need some privacy.'

Heart beating fast, and overflowing with the love she felt for him, Graine moved into his arms.